ALSO BY HANNAH PITTARD

We Are Too Many

Visible Empire

Listen to Me

Reunion

The Fates Will Find Their Way

IF YOU LOVE IT, LET IT KILL YOU

IF YOU LOVE IT, LET IT KILL YOU

A Novel

HANNAH PITTARD

Henry Holt and Company
New York

Henry Holt and Company
Publishers since 1866
120 Broadway
New York, New York 10271
www.henryholt.com

Henry Holt® and Ⓗ® are registered trademarks of Macmillan Publishing Group, LLC.

Quote from THE SCHOOL by Donald Barthelme. Copyright ©
1974 by Donald Barthelme, currently collected in SIXTY STORIES,
used by permission of The Wylie Agency LLC.

Library of Congress Cataloging-in-Publication Data

Names: Pittard, Hannah, author.
Title: If you love it, let it kill you : a novel / Hannah Pittard.
Description: First edition. | New York : Henry Holt and Company, 2025.
Identifiers: LCCN 2024037716 | ISBN 9781250910271 (hardcover) |
    ISBN 9781250910264 (ebook)
Subjects: LCGFT: Humorous fiction. | Novels.
Classification: LCC PS3616.I8845 I39 2025 | DDC 813/.6—dc23/
    eng/20240819
LC record available at https://lccn.loc.gov/2024037716

Our books may be purchased in bulk for promotional, educational, or business
use. Please contact your local bookseller or the Macmillan Corporate and
Premium Sales Department at (800) 221-7945, extension 5442, or by email at
MacmillanSpecialMarkets@macmillan.com.

First Edition 2025

Cat illustration: @Viktoriia Ablohina / Shutterstock

Designed by Meryl Sussman Levavi

Printed in the United States of America

1   3   5   7   9   10   8   6   4   2

For Lucy C., Emily S., and MacDowell

And for Ann Beattie, belatedly

What void? she asks. What are you talking about? The void of the Universe, he says . . .

—Margaret Atwood, "The Female Body"

. . . And they said, is death that which gives meaning to life? And I said no, life is that which gives meaning to life. Then they said, but isn't death, considered as a fundamental datum, the means by which the taken-for-granted mundanity of the everyday may be transcended in the direction of—

I said, yes, maybe.

They said, we don't like it.

I said, that's sound.

They said, it's a bloody shame!

I said, it is.

—Donald Barthelme, "The School"

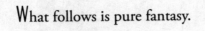

What follows is pure fantasy.

CONTENTS

ONE | Nice to Meet You, Please Take Care of Me   1

TWO | The Joys of Slow Dismemberment   77

THREE | #FPOP   171

FOUR | Easy, Darling   233

FIVE | Goat Show   265

IF YOU LOVE IT, LET IT KILL YOU

One
NICE TO MEET YOU, PLEASE TAKE CARE OF ME

Today I am restless, I text my friend Jane from the bathroom.

It's a Sunday, early fall, the day of my nephew's sixth birthday party. Yesterday was his actual birthday. I made three varieties of mac 'n' cheese from scratch. He informed me—a few hours before dinner and later made good on the threat—that he would be eating none of them. I let his littlest brother pick the pasta shape instead: wagon wheel.

That was last night. Now I'm in the bathroom, my bathroom, mine and the bald man's with whom I share my bed. It's on the second floor of our house. I'm watching my father, eighty this year, park his orange MINI in front of the neighbor's house across the street. My sister and her family live one house down from there. Her backyard is where the party is happening.

One week ago, Jane called to tell me my ex had written me into his debut novel.

"He means to keep it a secret," she said.

"From the world?" I asked.

"Only from you," she said.

"Is it bad?"

"I don't like it," she said.

"You don't like the book?"

"I don't like your portrayal."

"How am I?"

"Smug," she said. "Insecure."

"If I were an angry and unsatisfied man," I said, "that's exactly how I'd describe a woman with ambition, too."

Jane said, "You've got the hang of this already. You'll be fine."

I explained the situation to my boyfriend, the bald man. I told him that my ex had written me into his novel, one allegedly about our toddler of a marriage and his affair with my dear friend.

"Why a secret?" I asked. "Why from me?"

My boyfriend shrugged. "Maybe because you've written a memoir about the very same toddler."

I shook my head. "But that's not a secret."

He said, "Going into this relationship, I thought I was the only one with shared custody." He is referring to his daughter, the eleven-year-old, who lives half her life with her mother and half her life with us.

"I'm sorry," I said.

"Writers," he said, with not a little bit of disgust, before leaving the room.

There's a bounce house at my sister's and lots of booze. I haven't seen the booze yet—I'm still in a bathroom on the other side of the street—but I saw the bounce house earlier when my boyfriend helped my sister move a tiny desk from her garage attic to the six-year-old's bedroom. The desk is what? A gift maybe?

There wasn't supposed to be a bounce house, but my sister caved. Everyone knew she would cave, including the six-year-old, so there were never any tantrums. Earlier this week, my sister sent an announcement regarding the bounce house. When I showed my boyfriend, he said he'd never before seen an amended birthday invite for a little kid. I suggested anticipated attendance must be down, which was a joke, because my sister's boys have birthday parties that rival your best New Year's Eve.

I'm sitting atop a small white storage container, inside which are spare razors, spare toilet paper rolls, spare soap bars, spare bandages, spare liter bottles of shampoo, spare bags of cotton balls, and I'm waiting for

Jane to respond. *I'm lamenting life*, I text. Jane's a Shakespearean and lives one-point-two miles away in a house that gets great light.

Last week, after getting off the phone with her, I googled my ex-husband for the first time in seven years. I was hoping for more news of his clandestine novel. In doing so, I accidentally discovered a story he'd written in which I'd been knifed to death by a homeless man. For several years, I've been walking around with no idea! I liked my ending, which was dramatic but without fuss. The homeless man gets in several quick jabs, all of them meaningful. There's no chance of recovery.

I told my boyfriend that he and I had been turned into characters in a story by my ex. "We're married," I said.

"Only in our hearts," he said.

"Your name is Bruce."

He nodded. "I like that. Do I still have a daughter?"

"You do."

"Good," he said. "And I'm still bald?"

"It's unstated."

"I like being bald."

I did not tell him I'd been murdered, and he did not think to ask.

My boyfriend-husband—I'll borrow the name Bruce—has been part of my family for only five years. He is still learning our rope tricks. When my mother calls, for instance, I ask her immediately, "Have you fallen off a horse? Are you feeling sick? Have you gotten a diagnosis? Are you trapped in the attic again? Do you have intentions of climbing a tree while tied to a chain saw?" In this family, if you don't ask the right questions, you don't get all the information.

Jane texts, *Restless how? Lamenting what? Say more.* I send her a picture of the spider plant in the corner of my bathroom and several dozen of its babies, whose roots are soaking in jam jars I've crammed along the windowsill. Jane, who, like me, is childless by choice, writes, *Freudian*.

I'd be sitting on and texting from the lip of my clawfoot bathtub if I could, but it's fiberglass, and I'd dislodge the water supply lines were I ever to put any sort of weight on it. When Bruce and I bought three years ago, we assumed the bathtub was original to the house (1927), which means I assumed the tub was cast-iron and coated in porcelain.

You spend forty-five minutes in what will likely be the most outrageous purchase of your life; you have no idea what you're getting. I've spent more time looking at jeans online today than I spent in this house before deciding to buy it.

"Today I am lamenting life," I said to Bruce first thing this morning, when we woke up yet again before sunrise.

He said, "Is this an all-day activity?"

I said, "Intermittent, I think."

Then we had a quick fight about his early departure from the mac 'n' cheese dinner. Dishes had been cleared. Monologues had begun. He slapped his knees, popped up from the table, and said he was tired and therefore going home.

Bruce's daughter also popped up, declaring her own fatigue. She didn't clear her napkin or her water glass, and I didn't notice until after she and her father had already left. I didn't want to stay at my sister's house and hear any more monologues, but even less did I want to leave as some sort of family unit in which groupthink and joint decisions might appear the dominant mood.

My ex wants to keep secrets, and I want to confess:

I have never been pregnant.

I do not like children.

I am surrounded by family.

I often lie awake in bed at night and think, *When they are dead, I will . . .*

I have an oral fixation.

I dislike most people.

I am tired of men.

I am fascinated by the simplicity of erect penises.

I am haunted by my childhood.

I am living too much in the iterative tense, I text Jane.

The iterative what? she asks, playing dumb for my benefit.

The tense of routine, I write.

She responds with a picture of her entryway. The sun across the floor is disgusting.

Outside, my father is still in his MINI, the driver's-side door wide open. I consider taking a picture then decide against it. He's on a call. This—parked car, door open, speakerphone on—is his preferred mode of doing business. I send a text to my mother, saying that her first ex-husband is already here and that she should stop by my house for a quick glass of wine before heading to the party.

My sister and I (and our mother and our father)—we all live in Kentucky now. It's a long story, but I moved here first—years ago and with my ex. We never intended to stay. But now he is gone, and my family is here. "FOMO," my mother said when she heard of my father's decision to move to Lexington last year. "I divorced him forty years ago and moved out of state, only to have him show up in my backyard, not a mile from the place I'll likely die."

Bruce has spent the better part of the morning grumbling about my nephew's shindig. He'd rather stay home and reread *Beloved*, which he'll be teaching next week. Like me, Bruce is a professor of English (Americanist). Jane is also a professor of English, as is her husband, Teddy (another Shakespearean).

I zoom in on Jane's entryway. I text, *That's a gorgeous rug. Is it new?*

My immediate neighbor, a professor of mathematics, is walking down his driveway whistling. I'm watching him and am thrilled to witness the precise moment when his whistling stops, and he becomes aware of the giant man in a cowboy hat sitting in an orange MINI parked in the wrong direction on the opposite side of the street having a loud conversation. My neighbor is north of seventy himself. I see my father see my neighbor. If there is a standoff, my father will win. His entitlement isn't just willful, it's pathological. "Entitlement" is the wrong word anyway. Better to say that he is notably undeterred by the environment around him.

I've always been an inquisitive, even nosy, person. Eavesdropping on the conversations of strangers is among my favorite hobbies. But it wasn't until Bruce and I moved into this house—and I began paying very special attention to the math professor, his wife, and their four adult children, all of whom still live at home—that I purchased a pair of binoculars for outright spying. Actually, I purchased two pairs. Bruce sometimes joins me. The fact that he will occasionally turn off all the downstairs lights and call quietly up to me in my attic office and tell me to come down fast because the neighbors are acting curiously; the fact that he will crouch next to me as we skulk from window to window trying to get a better view of them . . . Well, that he tolerates, even encourages, this proclivity speaks volumes about our relationship and the reasons it persists.

Plus, there is the house. We are each separately in love with its brick walls and wraparound porch. We have more columns than anyone else on the street, including my sister. Last week, Bruce's students told him that he talks about me a lot. A student we share, Camille, told the class that I did the same. This delighted his students. He told them we talk about each other so much because we still like one another, which can't be said of all couples. I asked him if his assertion amused or terrified them. (There's a steep learning curve for students in Kentucky between the ages of eighteen and twenty-two. Some seem as though they've known since childhood that life is an unkind joke to be fretted over dusk until dawn, while others appear to believe their parents have never regretted a single decision.) By way of an answer, he said, "It's the Faulkner class."

I text Jane, *I'm desperately looking for small secrets to distract me from this brewing unhappiness. Yesterday it was a pair of Spanish leather boots that, when they arrive, I will tell Bruce I've owned since boarding school. Today it's indoor plants, which, when he notices them a week from now, I will say have been inside since June.*

She texts back immediately, *Boarding school strains credulity.*

I write, *grad school then.*

She writes, *You had money in grad school?*

I write, *credit cards and debt.* I send her a link to the Spanish boots.

Bruce and I have been married in our hearts since last year, about an hour and a half before his first colonoscopy. Because we aren't legally married, the kindly young man at check-in was resistant to my status as emergency contact. (The state of Kentucky takes its marriage laws and hospital forms quite seriously.) Things got heated, and Bruce—tall, broad shouldered, originally from Decatur, Illinois, and not a little un-scary when he's nervous or angry—declared loudly: "Sir, we are married in our hearts."

After a beat, the young man (he was wearing mascara) blushed and pushed the clipboard in my direction. "Just write *wife*," he whispered.

While Bruce stared coldly at the wall in front of him, I wrote *Wife* next to my name and tried for an air of contrition. It's my fault we're not married.

Several years ago—after my divorce, after my husband, then still a colleague, cheated on me with the woman, my dear friend, who'd originally introduced us—a graduate student of mine suggested that if things ever got serious again with another person, I ought to keep it weird. My student hadn't kept it weird: she was married with a daughter. But she seemed to have a firm and honest grasp on her situation as wife and mother, as well as on the incongruities of the world. (She once handed in a story to workshop in which a mermaid was roasted over an open fire and served to guests as a delicacy.) I was very much in the market for advice from interesting, clear-eyed, and absurd-minded women; I adopted hers with fervor.

About the time my ex was killing me in his fiction, I was explaining to Bruce that while I wanted to buy a house with him and was even willing to help raise his daughter, I did not want to be married to him, or anyone else, ever again. I wanted to keep it weird.

By keeping it weird, I assumed—naively—that I could skirt the official role of stepmother, a title I've despised ever since my father married a deeply sadistic architect when I was ten years old. My hope was that, despite living with Bruce's daughter half of every week, despite making extravagant dinners for her and cutting out giant hand-stenciled letters on her birthday and at the end of every school year, I'd somehow continue to exist merely as the eccentric childless girlfriend who happened to own fifty percent of a house with her father.

All semester I have been pestering my students about the perils of abstraction, but now I text Jane, *It's not a desire for infidelity or even something romantic outside the relationship, but it's parallel. When I'm not writing, I feel udderless. Instead, my brain is lustful for Otherness without feeling actual lust and honestly despising, even fearing, the actuality of Otherness.*

I reread my text. Then I add, *r*udderless.*

She writes, *my Freudian hackles are up, up, up!*

I write, *Basically I am aware of my domestication and would like one week as a wolf caterwauling at the moon, after which I'd likely be happy as a quokka for several more years.*

Before she can ask, I send her a screenshot of a smiling, pint-size marsupial with the hashtag "quokkaselfie." She sends me a picture of her guest bedroom/office. The sunlight is obscene. I search my archive, then send a photo of our new dining room table. She writes, *talk about strong rug game. Is THAT new?* Then she says, *Teddy likes it too*, and I wonder if she is signaling that we are not alone.

I know about signaling via text. Jane and I are not lovers. We just have a sympathetic view of life's illogicalities.

Jane knows that my lamentations have at least something to do with my ex and his book, but neither of us is tedious enough to say so. I send her a picture of my attic office, which I've recently rearranged. In a single photograph, there is a stuffed barracuda, a zebra rug, several skulls, a seventeenth-century rug, an art deco mirror, the skeleton of a piranha, and a ship captain's chair—all of it inheritance from my mother, who, about five years ago, decided to stop buying gifts and start giving away her possessions.

Jane writes, *you're a bohemian!*

I write, *In my heart I am a mid-century minimalist.*

She writes, *Can anyone with a child in her life be a minimalist?*

I write, *Can anyone with any kind of person?*

Early on, things with Bruce's daughter were fine. If I was, say, standing behind her when the UPS man knocked and she opened the door, she'd shove a thumb over her shoulder in my direction and say, "That's not my mother."

I'd say, without hesitation, "And that's not my daughter."

When her father wasn't in the room, she'd sometimes sidle up next to me and whisper, apropos of nothing, "I'll never kiss you. Never ever."

"That's good," I'd whisper back, "because I don't want to be kissed by you *ever ever*."

But now, three years later, she seeks me out while I am in the kitchen cooking dinner. She kisses my arm. She hugs my waist. She smiles whenever I make eye contact. She plays my favorite Guy Clark songs and sings along with me, especially during "L.A. Freeway." She beams when I go loud about the landlord: ". . . *sonaBITCH has AL-WAYS BORED ME!*"

Recently, as if to spook me, she said, out of nowhere, "You're basically my mom."

With fear in my heart and a knife in my hand, I said, "No. You have a mother, and it's not me."

She said, "Yeah, but basically."

Three kids tumble out of a giant SUV that's pulled momentarily into our driveway. A mother scuttles after them. The driver, presumably the father, backs up and pulls away. Is he looking for parking? Or going home? I tag the picture of Jane's spare bedroom and write, *Such a gift*, which is a joke between us, a nod to our students who traffic in canned language and hackneyed expressions.

My mother texts, *Can I park in your driveway?* I give it a thumbs-up. Then I snap a quick photo of the street below, crowded with my sister's guests' cars and my father's MINI, whose driver's-side door is shut now. How did I miss him shambling inside? He's had two hip replacements, but he still walks four miles every day. My mother still runs. I come from a family of akathisians, which is a fancy way of saying we can't sit still.

A few days ago, my father called me, weeping. He wanted to talk about my mother and their divorce, now four decades in the past.

"I'm sorry for everything," he said.

"No more talk of the divorce," I said. "No more childhood, no more apologies. You promised."

"I feel things," he said. "I feel things more than most people."

"I'm busy," I said.

"I hate days like this," he said. "I didn't sleep worth a turd last night. I'm an emotional guy, you know?"

"I've got class," I told him. "I can't do this right now."

"Do you think I could hurt myself? Your sister thinks I could hurt myself. I left my guns with her this morning."

"I'm hanging up now. Is that all right?"

"Criminal," he moans. "This is criminal."

In the background I heard the slosh of water. "Are you in the tub right now?" I asked. "Are you taking a bath? Are you calling me from the bathtub again? We talked about this."

"I can't get the water hot enough. I'm creaky all over, and I can't get it hot enough. My regular masseuse isn't answering."

"I have to go," I said. "I'm sorry."

Before I could disconnect, my father hung up on me, which is how he ends every phone call with anyone ever, and he texted my brother: *Your sister is a heartless woman.* My brother sent me a screenshot of the text with a thumbs-up emoji followed by a winking smiley face. I sent him the middle finger. My brother lives in Denver and runs hundred-milers and says things like, "My body is my temple." He is universally adored. He'll never move east.

I open the door to my bathroom slowly, as though I am an intruder, as though I am up to no good and desperate not to be discovered. The sensation of sneaking—of pretending to sneak—is infinitesimal and divine. The bedroom lights are off. There's a mountain of laundry needing to be sorted and folded that's strewn across the bed, my bed, our bed, the bed I share with the bald man. The laundry makes me want to throw myself onto the rug and bang my fists against the floor until there are bruises. Instead, I burrow facedown into the pile of clean clothes and throw a quiet make-believe tantrum. This, too, offers a sliver of ecstasy. I am not alone in this house, but there is no one in the world who has any inkling about my immediate whereabouts and activities.

"Don't let the cat out of the bag," I say to myself in a gravelly voice.

"Joke's on you," myself says back. "There is no cat."

Last night, when I finally came home from my sister's, Bruce and his daughter were in the basement watching a show, and I embarked on a one-sided cold war in the kitchen. I ground the morning coffee beans, finished the dishes, put away a few of the heavier pots and pans, then started the dishwasher, which sometimes produces a loud whooshing sound through the pipes closest to the television's speaker.

Later still, in bed, Bruce asked me how mad I was. "On a scale of one to five," he said.

"Mad at you?" I asked.

"Yeah, how mad at me are you?"

I said, "Not mad at you. Mad at life." I had to look away so he wouldn't see me smile.

Even later, I pushed him onto his side and curled up behind him. In the morning, I informed him of my restlessness.

My mother texts, *Can you please unlock your side door and let me in? Glass of wine?*

I'm still upstairs, still buried in clean laundry, so Bruce beats me to the door. But I'm in the kitchen by the time he says to her, "One good fact: What insect produces milk more nutritious than a cow's?"

She hands me a bottle of white wine. "Open that?" To Bruce, she says, "An *insect*?"

Bruce pulls out her regular chair—she lives a half mile from us—and says, "A roach!"

She says, "That's vile. Your street looks like a parking lot for the Keeneland racetrack." As of this morning, more than seventy people had RSVP'd for this kid's party.

I hand the unopened bottle of wine to Bruce. He swaps it for one from our Sub-Zero. For the next thirty minutes I clean and chop vegetables while Bruce and my mother argue politics and Shakespeare. (My mother was once a high school English teacher.) We finish the bottle.

Last night, after pushing Bruce onto his side, I didn't sleep. I concentrated on my pillow, which is foam and has two cutouts for either ear depending on which side I'm sleeping. It resembles the head of a hammerhead shark. Without the pillow, I get earaches. At first, we tried a mouth guard. By "we," I mean my dentist and me. But this was also in the era of my ex. He and I had just moved to Kentucky. In Chicago, where we used to live and teach, the earaches had gotten so bad that there were tests, then X-rays, then MRIs. The Kentucky dentist was amused that no one in Chicago had considered a solution so simple as a mouth guard.

For the first few months, the months when my ex and I were our happiest, which preceded the months and then the years when we were our unhappiest, I'd wake up, having slept like a kid koala, only to realize I'd dislodged the bite guard sometime during the night. Mornings, I'd search the bedroom to find it. Sometimes it was under the bed, sometimes it was on the bathroom counter, sometimes it was between the mattress and the box spring, often it was under my pillow.

One night, I didn't dislodge the mouth guard and that was the last time I've ever been able to sleep without wearing it. The earaches didn't go away. Eventually my husband did.

About the time Bruce and I bought this jewel of a house, I discovered the online world of TMJ pillows.

My mother says, "You know how when you're surfing the Web, you sometimes get a pop-up and the doctor in the ad asks if you want to cure your toe fungus?"

I sputter, and wine escapes my nose.

Bruce says, "What are you talking about?"

My mother says, "I'm going to have all my toenails removed."

I leave the room, and Bruce, as I am making a note of my mother's exchange on a legal pad, says, "You know she's writing this down, right?"

My mother calls out, with real panic, "If you give me toe fungus, I will never forgive you. I will leave the Rolex to your sister."

I walk back into the kitchen and give my mother a look to indicate that I have no idea what she's talking about. My sister, with the sixth sense of a platypus, texts, *I can see Mom's car. Where are you guys???*

Here are three things I am envious of—Jane's sunlit entryway, her box beam ceilings, and the fact that there is no child in her life.

Bruce says, as I moodily clean up vegetable debris, "You're milking your life's lament."

My mother says, "Oh, is she depressed?"

I say, "*I guess I think I'm sad,*" which is something one of Bruce's students said, an expression that floored us both for its vulnerability.

Now, a year later, we say it to each other as an inside joke. There are lots of inside jokes between us, sayings whose origins sometimes predate our status as a couple. Last week, what did I say as we accidentally ran the red light? I said, "We don't have time to obey the law!" Bruce echoed me, laughing, then said, "What's that from?" And I told him about my first boyfriend who once ran a stop sign on his way back to our apartment, and I said, out of nowhere, my voice a high-pitched cartoon, "We don't have time to obey the law!" The phrase stuck. We used it together for six years. Maybe he and I share its custody.

My mother tells us she is looking for her soulmate. Or someone to take her for a glass of wine.

"We'll drink with you anytime," Bruce assures her. "Have wine with us."

"Yes," my mother says mildly. "But you drink in sweatpants. I'd like someone to get fancy for." Currently, she has three boyfriends, but they are all online, and they are all in different states.

The ski instructor is pushy, she says, and I encourage her to cut him off. To the retired army man she texts a photo of the bottle of Haut-Médoc Bruce opened. His reply is instant: *I don't like Medoc.* I encourage her to cut him off, too. There is also a Canadian, but my mother says little about him, and I haven't yet asked.

My father is also looking for his soulmate. He placed his ad in the newspaper, print edition, old-school style: *Adventurous Tall Dapper Gentleman Seeks a female companion.* My father was proud of the ad and shared it with me eagerly. I shared it with my brother, who was intrigued by his approach to capitalization. I noted that "female companion"—the ostensible purpose behind the ad—hadn't measured up.

My mother remarried first. When she finally introduced us to the man—dinner at a restaurant—he opened his mouth to reveal a chunk of bright orange cheese he'd pressed against his tongue. The second time we met him—lunch at the same restaurant—my mother told us they were getting married. I was eight. He had thinning blond hair and was overweight. His younger sister had been the first Jewish debutante in Atlanta. I was skeptical that this doughy man with a penchant for soft cheese could have anything to do with a debutante, much less with my mother.

The man who would become my stepfather hated two things: people who hated Jews and the fact that he was Jewish. "Jewish by birth," he'd say to me when I was older, "atheist by the grace of god." He'd been married once before. They'd had no children. He didn't drink. I met his father on a handful of occasions. He'd been an extra in *Driving Miss Daisy* and before that, in real life, an important and prominent lawyer. He'd had several wives. He was a man who didn't especially like children. By the time I met my stepfather's father, he was already dying of cancer. From my stepfather I learned to be observant and dismissive, cynical and dishonest.

I am not looking for my soulmate, in part because I have Bruce and in part because I disagree with the category, akin as it is to vampires or talking kittens, both of which are favorite subjects of my undergrads every fall. I regularly assure Bruce that I am like neither of my parents. When he is gone (as in dead), I will not be looking for someone to replace him. "You're it," I like to say. "Never again after you."

"Please stop imagining your life when I'm dead," he says to me, and so I do not tell him of all the improvements I make each night as I lie awake in bed next to him and fantasize about my life in our house alone. I do not tell him about the plunge pool or the mudroom or the tile roof or the slate-floored entryway. I certainly do not tell him about the Saarinen table in Verde Alpi or the Wishbone chairs he'd find so uncomfortable.

Also, there is Theo, the mailman, on whom I've developed a crush in the three years since Bruce and I have lived together. I could say it is a platonic crush, but that would be wrong and serve only the purpose of protecting Bruce's feelings, and he is perfectly aware of my own toward the mailman.

Theo is somewhere between six and a half and seven feet tall. He is Black and has a beautiful bald head. There is another mailman, Oscar, who is also Black, also bald, and classically more beautiful than Theo. But Oscar is not my crush. It is not Oscar who honks the horn of the

U.S. mail van and waves at me when he sees me running and far from home. It is not Oscar who compliments the smell of my cooking as he wedges the day's catalogues into the mail slot. It is Theo.

Last month, while I was replacing a hinge on the front door, Theo stopped to admire my handiwork. "Damn, girl," he said, shaking his head. "Is there anything you can't do?"

It is hard not to consider Theo.

Bruce and I didn't have sex last night. I was tired. Also, I was mad.

Now I show my sister's plea for our company to my mother and Bruce.

He says, "When my daughter was little, there weren't random family members hanging around at the birthday parties."

My mother says, "Speak it, Othello."

I go upstairs to tell the eleven-year-old, who's reading a book while sitting up in bed, that we're heading to my sister's. "You look like Alice James," I say.

She primly tucks an edge of blanket under her thigh. "I resemble that remark," she says.

Sometimes, offhandedly when talking to her friends, the eleven-year-old will refer to me as one of her parents. Sometimes, to my face, she'll flat-out call me her stepmother, and I will remember all over again how wrong I was to imagine that marriage has anything to do with the love a child feels toward a grown-up. At the same time, I will look at her with absolute dread, worrying at her large and open heart, wondering at her capacity for and willingness to be vulnerable. When I was her age, I locked myself in the bathroom because I didn't want to go to the court-mandated psychiatrist. I tore lines in my skin with a ballpoint pen to distract myself from the headaches I got from crying so hard. I kept a packed bag of my favorite stuffed animals shoved under my bed—one at my mother's house and one at my father's—ready to be grabbed in case of a fire or a pop-up kidnapping or the eventual and unavoidable arrival of the evil thing I knew with unreserved certainty was lurking, at all times, just around the corner.

Attendance for the eleven-year-old is optional, so we leave her to her voluntary bed rest, and my mother, Bruce, and I walk across the street. My father spots us immediately and pulls me in for a hug. Now my face smells like Polo.

He says, "Your sister reinvented motherhood. You look terrific, kid."

Next he grabs my mother by her upper arm. He says her name. He says, "How are you, girl? You're a sight. You working out?"

If she wasn't already intending to wash that sweater tonight, she is now. Not because she thinks my father has cooties or anything. It's the Polo. My father buys the stuff by the gallon. That isn't a joke. Just like it isn't a joke that my father installed a full-size fiberglass bathtub *inside* the shower stall at his apartment, which is a rental. It's an exact replica of my bathtub. If I'd known he was going to buy one and put it in his bathroom, I would have offered him mine for free. Except for watering the upstairs and attic plants, we never use it.

My father also lives a half mile from us, but in the direction opposite my mother.

Nodding at Bruce, he says, "How's your roommate?" My father has called every man I've ever lived with, including my ex-husband, my roommate.

I would like not to be bothered by the news of my ex's debut. I would like for Bruce not to have looked over my shoulder this morning only to find me reading an early review. I would like for him not to have said, "You're obsessed," and I would like for the obsession not to be true.

In my ex's book, the ex-wife character is a commercial hack of whom he and his more intellectual friends make much fun. In his book, I am wildly successful and dull.

Someone has put a glass of cider in my hand. (Cider is the family business; as in, my brother-in-law makes cider for a living.) My nephew sideswipes me. The cider sloshes but recovers. He runs the length of the yard, then hurls himself against the bounce house. There are squeals. He's dressed as a police officer—baton and hat and everything. My nephew is beautiful and blond. I have thoughts about his costume. His little brothers are dressed up the same way.

I whisper to Bruce, "Am I high or are a bunch of the kids dressed as cops, not just my nephews?"

He says, "You might be high. That might be one of your little secrets. But there are, separately, at least a dozen officers."

I say, "Is that weird?"

He says, "It isn't Halloween."

I say, "Am I high or are my nephews' costumes really well-made while the other kids' costumes look like they'll ignite in direct sunlight?"

Bruce says, "I'm beginning to think you actually are high, but if you're trying to figure out whether or not your sister shelled out extra money—"

My mother interrupts: "Does anyone want my cider?"

There was a time, just after Bruce and I bought our house and began living together for the first time, when I wouldn't have sex with him if his daughter was home. Not even if she was fast asleep in her bedroom with its door closed and we were in our bedroom with its door closed and it was three in the morning. I would not have sex. Her proximity inhibited my ability to move outside myself, which is something I need to do to enjoy sex, and I enjoy enjoying sex.

By "move outside myself," I mean to not be aware of or in contact with the version of me who chops vegetables or folds clothes or bakes bread or pays bills. I do not like to be "Woman making love with Man because he is the Man she loves and on whom she can depend." I prefer to be "Body having sex with Body that happens to fit well and please well and anticipate well and tease well, this wellness having been established over years of satisfying practice." Hearing myself think these things, I am dumbfounded by the fact that I was ever married.

When we fight—which isn't often—if I cry, I always tell Bruce to ignore the tears. "That's not me," I say. "That's just society's conditioning."

And he says, "It's okay to have emotions."

And I say, "Please don't use that word with me."

I am like this—willful, stubborn, withholding—until there is a morning like *this* morning. Suddenly, I announce my lament. I am deadpan and dry-eyed. It's astonishing there are two sets of binoculars.

A chintzily dressed officer rushes past and shouts to another kid, not dressed as anything, "I told you there was no piñata!"

It's true: I am a little high. I wanted to tell Jane, but I didn't want her to judge me. In general, I don't get high, but I recently ordered some gummies advertised on *Bon Appétit*'s website. I thought the gummies sounded useful—tiny sugary pathways with expensive flavor profiles that might lead me out of myself for a few hours here and there.

The gummies, just as Bruce suspected, are in fact one of my petite private confidences, though I won't ever admit it and he'll never know, since I have a credit card set aside for just these trifling purposes. He does know about the credit card. Our finances are combined. My one request was that we never get married. His one request was that we join our accounts. All this to say, we're knotted together as good as the next couple. But I like it that I can say to the eleven-year-old's Kentucky-raised friends that her father and I aren't married. So far, not one of them has cared. One day, I comfort myself, someone will surely be bothered, and it will be as spectacular as the sunlight across Jane's entryway rug.

Wag the dog, I tell my freshmen, is an image that houses an idea. *Irrelevant circumstances are dictating our actions* is an idea without an image. Give me images, I tell them. They give me images by way of clichés—as in, *My mother's love was a gift*. I say, yes, an image, readers love images, but can you make the image your own? They describe the gift's wrapping paper. Better, I say. Still wrong, but better.

One book review goes into some detail about a plot point in which my ex lets an undergrad teach his class so he can have sex with his mistress. Knowing my ex, this likely happened. I bet he wrote the scene well. I wish I could read it without reading the book. I wish I could move it outside itself. I wish I could divorce it. I'm not trying to be punny. This is my brain on drugs.

I know a poet who wrote a beautiful book about her divorce. In the book, she asks herself something along the lines of, "What if I'd been *watching* the relationship instead of living in it?" I read that question and gasped. I said aloud to no one, "What if I had been *in my marriage* instead of watching it?" Then I clasped a hand over my mouth and felt very scared.

The bounce house is shaped like a castle. Because Bruce and I are fundamentally flawed people with big hearts, we have both done quick Google searches on how much my sister and her husband are paying for this party. We don't yet know about the mutual googling, but later, lying in bed, the lights out, each of us separately wondering about sex—me: *too tired? not too tired? interested? penis?* him: *sex sex sex sex sex boob boob boob boob*—we will admit to having earlier in the day stepped away from the party to find the number. Maybe I go first, maybe he does. But our research renders matching results: in the state of Kentucky, four hours costs ninety dollars; for 20 percent more, you get the whole day; or, tack on 60 percent and you can make a night of it. I love the use of percentages in lieu of hard-and-fast prices.

There's something going on at this party with all these cop uniforms that isn't right.

"Old lady, push me," says a neighbor boy to someone's grandmother. I scan the crowd for the kid's father. It takes me a few minutes to locate him because I've been looking in the wrong place. I've been looking for him anywhere *not* within hearing distance of his kid. Instead, he's leaning against the swing set. He's right there. The kid says it again: "Old lady." The father hears. I can see that he hears even if his face registers nothing. (I know a thing or two about faces registering nothing.) I am seconds away from diving onto the lawn, pulling up grass by the fistful, shouting, *I know you can hear him. I know you can hear him. Why won't you do something?* when Bruce edges near me and says, "There's a lid for every pot." He gestures with his chin in the direction of the alcohol tubs, where my father has cornered my mother.

My father, a tall man, is wearing his large-brim, custom-made cowboy hat, a white turtleneck, and a yellow bandana.

"That," I say to Bruce, "is an image that contains a thought."

He says, "I want to strangle that kid on the swing."

This conversation must have happened earlier or later, because here is where my mother, smelling distinctly of Polo cologne, breaks in with her unwanted cider and says to Bruce, "I looked it up. Only one type of roach gives live birth and nurses her offspring." To me, she says, "You look green."

It must be the gummies. I say, "Roach milk makes me want to barf."

She says, "Doesn't everything make you want to barf?"

"Ouch," I say. She is referring to my decades-long eating disorder. Think of it as an inside joke between two women who know and love each other to excess.

"Oh, is she feeling ill?" my mother sings in a halting falsetto. *"Her face is eau de Nil!"*

"What's that from?" I ask.

"Word of the day," she says. "Bruce turned me on to it."

Bruce, pointing at my sister's neighbor's chimney, says, "That's an adverse possession."

I ask him what he's talking about and if he'd know such a term if his ex-wife weren't a tax attorney. He explains that the chimney is on my sister's property but obviously belongs to her neighbor.

"So, whose adverse possession is it? My sister's or the neighbor's?"

He says, "The neighbor's."

I say, "Huh." Then I add, "There's a metaphor there."

We drink more cider and watch the officers attack one another with plastic batons, which are leaving visible welts.

Toward midnight, while Bruce and I are in bed, possibly having had sex, possibly not, my phone lights up.

Bruce says, "Must be your boyfriend."

I unlock the screen. My sister has written, *R u ok?*

I write, *What kind of question is that?*

She writes, *Yr face looks sad.*

I write, *YOU CAN SEE ME?*

Our blinds are pulled; our lights are off.

She writes, *At the party, your face looked sad . . .*

I write, *Not sad, just high!*

She writes, *Fun!*

Then she writes, *Cocktails soon?*

I thumbs-up the invite, then screenshot the exchange and send it to Jane.

In the middle of the night, Bruce jostles me awake.

"Who are you?" he asks.

I tell him I am me. But my mouth is still asleep, and so I hand him the thought with my mind. He does not hear me.

"Who are you?" he asks again.

There is a ten-year age difference between us, but it is too early for early onset.

"If I'm Bruce," he says into my ear, "who are you? What's your name?"

A motorcycle thumps down our street, its single cylinder pulsing into the late-night air. We listen as it passes.

"I'm Angela," I murmur. "He named me Angela."

"Angela," he repeats quietly. His daughter is asleep in a bedroom down the hall. "My wife, Angela." In his voice, there is a funny suggestion of relief.

Bruce squeezes my thigh once, then turns away from me and onto his side, pulling most of the blankets with him. Within minutes, his breathing relaxes. His shoulder rises and falls in rhythm with his breath. He leaves me awake and alone with my thoughts. I slip out of bed and tiptoe down the stairs.

I creep along the walls of our home, moving back and forth between rooms. I avoid the windows, stay in the shadows. I am terrified by my own silence, by the distance I can travel in this dark house without making a single sound. I imagine myself sleeping in the room above me. I imagine my boyfriend beside me. At the end of the hall is his daughter. We are so vulnerable up there—our sound machines purring, our fans whirring—all of us unknowing. I creep and pretend to be someone else, someone sinister, someone out to invade a home for no purpose at all except that I can.

Who am I?

I am a reluctant stepmother.

I am a selfish sister.

I am a very private person.

I am addicted to transparency.

I am frightened by infants.

I live the majority of my life in my head.

I want to confess.

I am trying to confess, but there are so many secrets.

Here is a secret. Before I knew my husband had cheated, I cheated, too. He'd been gone all summer, jumping from one writers' retreat to another. I didn't know how to feed myself properly—a holdover from the eating disorder—so, while he was gone, I ate out several nights a week.

I met the Irishman in late May at a bar known for its tofu burgers. By early June, he had my number. By late June, though we'd never seen each other any place other than the burger joint, he was texting me nightly. His nickname for me was Hot Stuff.

And then it was July.

And then it was July sixth.

And then it was late afternoon on July sixth.

And then my husband was calling me. He was calling me from a residency in Upstate New York.

Here is what I remember from that day, that night. I remember taking the call from my husband and being instantly annoyed by his tone. He sounded whingy, a little tipsy. He expressed a desire to come home early, then pouted about Labor Day and how we hadn't nailed down plans with our dear friends in New York. Would they come to us or would we go to them? he wondered aloud. I reminded him we'd both be back in the classroom by then. The only option would be for them to come to us. He wanted me to call them. He said they'd need to book tickets soon because of the prices. I remember being amused about his concern for their finances and wishing he'd show more concern for ours. Two weeks later, when I found out about him and my dear friend—with whom he was already having an affair—I'd think back to that phone call and wonder at my husband's desperate desire to arrange for her visit. Had he imagined they might sneak time together in our fifteen-hundred-square-foot home with its flimsy plywood walls?

I remember saying goodbye and then sitting down at my kitchen table—not yet knowing he'd been unfaithful—but sensing something was off about him, about us. He'd sounded like a stranger.

I pushed my phone away. I tapped my fingers. I looked out the window.

Time passed. The light outside turned from turquoise to sunless amber; inside from lavender to ash. An hour came and went, and I found myself sitting in a gloomy kitchen all alone. My stomach growled.

I had the unsettling sensation of having driven a hundred miles without remembering any element of the scenery, without observing a single highway sign, without once recalling accelerating or changing lanes or applying the brakes or signaling to exit. Yet there I was, inarguably one hundred miles away from where I'd begun.

I checked my watch. It was 4:15 p.m., which meant the burger place would be opening soon.

What happened after this—the events that followed, during the course of the next twelve hours—remains muddled. There are extended flashes of clarity, crisp as daybreak, indisputably factual occurrences. There are spans of blackness that register as the gaps between transparencies on a cardboard disk inserted into a stereoscope; there even exists a plasticized clicking sound that accompanies the darkness, as when a View-Master's lever is engaged and the reel advances slowly forward. But after each segment of darkness, there is lightness again, and there are more colorful three-dimensional episodes. But these later reveries, their mosaics blurry, are questionable, otherworldly, mere possibilities of what may or may not have transpired.

Here is what I do know. After coming to from my trance at the kitchen table, I turned off the location provider on my cell phone. Next, I went for a run. When I got home, I ate a handful of pistachios, a significant detail only in proportion to the amount of alcohol I would later consume. By the time I'd showered and shaved—legs, underarms, bikini line—I had a text from my husband: *Did you stop sharing your location with me?* I wrote back: *My phone's been funny all day. Tracking not working on my watch either.* He wrote: *Did you call them about Labor Day?* I didn't respond.

After this, I styled my hair, something I hadn't done in months. I spritzed myself with perfume. I applied eyeliner and mascara, more things I hadn't done since late spring.

By 7:00 p.m., I was out the door. On my way to the bar, my phone buzzed: *Hot Stuff—Will I see you tonight?* All summer, I'd known there'd come a day—my husband's return—when I'd have to give up this texting nonsense. All summer, I'd also imagined there might come a night—before that day—when I might deliberately slip, just the once.

Save me a seat, I wrote.

No seats at the bar. But you can sit at the table with my friends and me.

You have friends?

I have colleagues, he wrote.

No foolin'?

I felt giddy, listless, incongruously in control of myself and the direction of the evening.

But several minutes later, when I walked into the packed bar, I stumbled. The Irishman was sitting at a large table with seven or eight other men. I'd assumed he was joking about the colleagues.

I looked away before we could make eye contact. There was one empty seat at the bar, and I took it. The confidence I'd been enjoying moments earlier had vanished. I ordered a glass of wine. The Irishman and his men were behind me. He could watch me, but I couldn't watch him. At most, we were ten feet apart.

Sit with us, he wrote.

Not in a million years.

The man next to me asked if I'd pass him the drink menu. I did. After a minute or two, he asked which wine I was drinking. I told him.

He ordered a glass of the same. After another minute he asked what I was doing in town. I said I was visiting family. My phone vibrated.

Wine is too slow, the Irishman wrote.

Too slow for what?

Too slow to get drunk.

Maybe I don't want to get drunk.

Too bad.

How drunk are you?

Drunk enough to be taken advantage of, he wrote.

Barking up the wrong tree.

Am I?

I didn't write back.

Get a drool cup, he wrote.

Because you're getting sloppy?

That man is drooling all over you.

What man? I haven't noticed.

You've noticed.

His name is Virgil, I wrote. *He loves red wine and kitten memes. He's a dear drinking companion.*

He's a deer.

How's your wife?

How's your husband?

The bartender put a bourbon in front of me.

"I didn't order that," I said.

"I'm buying," said the man next to me. "You turned me on to a good wine. Let me turn you on to the best bourbon you'll ever have."

Turn me on, turn you on. I imagined the Irishman taking us in.

The bartender waited.

"Sure," I said, holding the glass aloft, letting the edge of mine glance the edge of his. I imagined all those men behind me watching. "As long as you don't mind that I'm married."

The man held up his hand and displayed a ring. "Same here."

We drank.

Time passed.

Someone at the table behind me asked for the check.

Have a good night, wrote the Irishman.

You too, I texted, devastated.

Join us, he wrote.

Where?

Strip club.

No.

You sure?

Born sure.

I was angry. I felt pathetic, let down, hurt.

I won't stay long.

I didn't respond. I drank my bourbon. The man beside me offered to buy me another. I accepted.

While the Irishman's party settled up, I excused myself.

The hallway to the single-stall bathrooms was narrow and dark. I expected the Irishman to follow me. Perhaps we would begin there, in a restroom, my back against the door. Affairs had started in less sexy venues. I listened for his footsteps. For the thousandth time, I read the framed signs across from the toilet—I ONLY DRINK ON DAYS THAT END WITH Y; IF YOU NEED A SIGN TO HAVE A GLASS OF WINE, THIS IS IT; THE BEST BEER IS AN OPEN ONE; FORGET THE DOG BEWARE THE WIFE. I waited for a knock. There was nothing.

By the time I returned to the bar, the men were gone. My phone had two messages. The first said: *Meet me in an hour.* The next was an address.

I finished the bourbon. The man who bought it left and was replaced by a loud-talking woman. She showed me pictures of strangers on her phone. They were pictures of other pictures, as though she'd gone around her house or another's and taken photos of framed photographs she wished belonged to her. "I went through all my memories," she said. She told me her dealer was coming. It's possible she offered to sell me drugs. The blackness hadn't yet descended, but the images had begun to swirl into themselves like watercolors on a page.

Time passed. I settled my tab. The woman next to me pleaded for me to stay: "Don't leave me with all these lousy men."

I walked. My footsteps were troubled, my footing unstable. A few times I stopped, admonished myself, then continued. The sidewalk was too close or too far, but never where the sole of my shoe thought it should be. The sky was dark. I felt anonymous, safe, that no one who might look could see what was hidden inside.

The first click of blackness came then, as I was walking: the slow plastic lever moved down and the transparency shifted right and before the next picture fell into place, there was only the flatness and blackness of the cardboard reel.

When I came to, I was standing in front of what looked like a residential building. It was tall, brick, plain. There was a metal gate beyond which I couldn't get without access from within. I looked at my phone.

When you're here, he'd written, *ring 4. They'll let you in.*

In the morning, I would study this line—*They'll let you in.*

I pressed the number. I waited. I heard a long, loud buzz. The gate disconnected from itself; I pushed through.

All this happened before my family moved to town.

Things I remember: a stairwell, vintage lights high above me as I stepped down, a large door that was difficult to push, the smell of cigarettes, the green vest of a bartender.

I don't remember finding the Irishman, but I do remember being with him at a small booth. I remember the word he used—he used it repeatedly, perhaps every time I regained consciousness, and he registered my confusion: "speakeasy." I remember laughing at the word, at its ridiculousness. A tea candle was in front of us. The table was small. We huddled close. A bar was somewhere beyond us. There was the green vest again. The lights were low. His hand was on my knee, on my thigh. He ran his fingers along the inner-thigh seam of my jeans. I remember, later, our hands under the table, my fingernails carving an arc in his palm, his shin tucked urgently behind my calf. Then blackness. Another hallway. Talk of a car. Talk of privacy. Laughter. Shoes. Socks. His chin. My hand in his hair. His chin again. "You smell so good." I remember him saying this. He said it often. I can hear it, even through the darkness.

"I just want to kiss you," I said.

"I just want to fuck you," he said.

And then it went dark.

Before sunrise, I wake up, having slept only a few hours. I take out my mouth guard quietly and check my phone.

There's a text from Jane: *YR FACE LOOKS SAD!*

There's also a text from my mother: *Thoughts on Bumble?*

There's also a text from my father: *Family meeting. I'm weak as a kitten.* Family meetings aren't a thing in my family.

When I roll back over, there's Bruce, also awake, watching me. "Creep," I say. "How long have you been spying on me?"

"How's my little sad sack today?" he asks.

"What's the opposite of 'restless'?"

He pauses.

Let's say a garbage truck lumbers down the street outside. Let's say the first crow squawks. Let's say the tree frogs aren't too cold to holler back.

He says, "You're grounded," and my brain whirrs: *lights out by 9pm! no TV! no cell phone! do the dishes! empty the dishwasher! scrub the pots! fold the laundry! no dessert for you tonight!* Someday, this will be an inside joke between us, one whose origin we will long ago have forgotten.

"I'm grounded," I agree. "Now bite my shoulder so we can get out of bed." He bites my shoulder; we get out of bed.

My 11:00 a.m. class asks me to tell them a story, a classic delay tactic.

"What kind of story?" I ask. "Happy or sad?"

"Funny," says someone. "About your brother and sister."

I shrug. "Can't really think of anything off the top of my head today." In fact, the first thing I think of is the time my brother and sister and I were in a hot tub together. Because they were older, they had friends over, who were also in the hot tub. I might have been five years old, maybe four. The grown-ups—our parents—were inside. Maybe there was a dinner party. Maybe the other kids in the tub weren't my siblings' friends but the children of my parents' friends.

At some point, my brother scooted close to me and asked if I wanted some lemonade. My answer was yes, obviously, and he hopped merrily out of the hot tub and ran inside, not bothering with a towel.

Do I remember the giggling of my sister and the other kids? I do, whether or not it actually happened. Do I remember the darkness of the night sky and the way the top of the water frothed and bubbled in the muted purple light from the bottom of the hot tub? I do, I do, I remember these details, as well as the black-and-white-checked linoleum just inside the kitchen, which I could see from the edge of the hot tub, a trail of water from my brother's feet pooled and glistening from where he'd moments earlier skittered across the floor.

In my memory, it's a red plastic cup he brings back to me. In my memory, the cup is warm, the liquid steaming, and I know something is wrong without knowing what the wrong thing is. The giggling is louder. All the children are staring at me. I know I shouldn't drink it, but I do. Because it's from my brother. Because my sister is there. Because everyone wants me to drink and expects me to drink and without me drinking, the others will be deprived of a punch line. And so I do, I drink it. And I know immediately what it is, and my face contorts into an involuntary frown, which triggers a muscle memory, which morphs into quiet weeping. The other kids squeal and shriek with laughter, and that's where the memory ends.

I look at my students, all of them in their late teens, early twenties, with two exceptions, a nontraditional scholar with graying hair and a guy called Mateo, a university employee who's been following me from course to course for a couple semesters now. (I tell my students, "Never name a character who isn't pivotal to the plot." I also tell them, "Name everyone. It doesn't matter. Good writing will out the vital players.")

Before me, Mateo followed around a different colleague, a man. That he is gender neutral in his stalking is a relief. I get the impression he gloms on then gets bored, nothing truly sinister. If there's room in the class after all the typical students have registered, he's allowed to enroll. A perk of employment. My point here with ages is that I'm not about to tell these kids or the gray-haired lady or Mateo about the one time I was tricked into drinking my brother's urine.

"Tell us about your book," someone says.

"My book?"

"Yeah. Your book."

It happens a couple times a year that one of my students will finally look me up online and realize that the reason I teach creative writing is because I am a published author. Their astonishment astonishes me. What do they think my background is? Pottery?

"Mateo told us you wrote a book."

I look at Mateo; he gives me a thumbs-up and a big possum-eating grin. The problem with Mateo is that he is good-looking in a way that appeals not only to my particular tastes, but also to the tastes of most women, including his more age-appropriate classmates. I don't like that Mateo usually takes the other end of the seminar table in my workshops, but I also don't like it when he doesn't.

"I've written four books. Not one." A kid whistles when I say this. My end-of-semester course evaluations routinely indicate that I'm an overcorrector. "And I've got a fifth one about to be published." Also that I'm defensive.

"What's it about?"

"Enough procrastination," I say. "We've got stories to discuss."

"It's about her ex-husband," says Mateo. "He used to teach here. Until he had an affair with her best friend."

The class oohs and ahs. I sigh. "It's about my divorce, yes, and when it comes out you can all read it. For now, we have class."

"I had him," says Mateo, "as a teacher." The wisp of a girl seated next to him—Willow, who's got a tattoo of an anatomically correct heart across her sternum—gets out her phone and asks my ex's name.

"No," I say. I make eye contact with Mateo. "Do not say his name, not while I'm in the room anyway." Now I'm looking at Willow. "And my policy is no phones—that's right, put it away, off the desk—and right now, no names."

"No fun," says Willow, but she does as she's told and pockets the phone.

After class, I give in and attend my father's family meeting, which is happening on my front porch. For the sake of my relationship with Bruce—who, like my brother-in-law, is sitting this meeting out—my father isn't allowed in our house.

"I suppose everyone wants to know about the elephant in the room," our father says.

In preparation for his monologue, my sister and I have mixed ourselves generous gin and tonics.

"Are you the elephant?" my sister says. Our father is six-foot-four.

He cuts his eyes at her but does not deign to answer. He clears his throat. "It's responsible for me to tell you that I have begun a course of psilocybin treatments with my doctor."

"'Have begun'?" I repeat. "As in, already *began*? What doctor?"

"He's dropping acid," my sister says to me. "Are eighty-year-olds allowed to drop acid?"

"It's not dropping acid," he says. "It's microdosing. My colors move from right to left," he explains, "low to high, batik to paisley."

"That's not microdosing," I say. "That's tripping. You're hallucinating. I know about hallucinating."

"I really wish you'd ask our permission before you do this sort of stuff," my sister says. "It puts an unfair burden on us."

My father's announcement regarding this new life phase is both typical and unexpected. He is a man who communicates by way of announcements. Six months ago, he announced he was leaving the house of his fifth wife and sixth child and getting an apartment of his own. Six months before that, he announced that he was leaving Huntsville and moving to

Kentucky to be closer to me and to my sister, who'd moved here herself the year before, and also closer to his first wife, our mother, who'd moved here the year before my sister. He didn't ask our permission then either.

After our father leaves—several gin and tonics later—I tell my sister that I've been murdered by my ex, and also that he's publishing a book in which a questionable version of me is prominently featured.

"How are you feeling?" she asks.

"Gutted," I say.

She nods, solemnly. "How did Bruce take the news?"

"I didn't tell him about the murder."

"He'd be livid about the estate taxes."

"Twenty-five percent just because we're not married and live in Kentucky."

"You should marry him and not tell anyone."

I nod, too. "Not a chance."

A man and a dog walk by. The dog, his muzzle white with age, pulls in my direction. The man pulls back. The dog whines and pulls harder. I smile at the man and then, with my mind, tell the dog that he is a very good boy and has lived a very good life. The dog lets up his strain on the leash and finally trots off. It has always been this way for me with dogs.

"What's your favorite part of this homeless man story?" my sister asks.

"There's a throwaway line," I say. "It's as he's narrating the news of my death, which arrives via an unexpected email from a former colleague, which includes the details of the accident. From the setup—I'm driving home alone; I've had a few glasses of wine—you think the news is: DUI. You think I've crashed and burned, et cetera. But the narrator—that's my ex—jumps in *exactly* as the reader is making this assumption and says something like, *This didn't go where I thought it might.*"

"Huh," she says, making a face to show me she is unimpressed. "Sounds *writerly*." In a different life, I sometimes think she might have made Bruce a very happy man. "Why a homeless man?"

"Some sort of dig at me, I guess."

"Meaning?"

"In the story, I pull over and offer the guy help. I'm not minding my own business or I'm being unnecessarily solicitous or I'm proving to no one that I'm a good person. As a result, I get the knife."

"Didn't you write a book about a woman who gets beaten up and left for dead by a homeless man? A woman that's basically you?"

"All my women are basically me."

"Unless they're me."

"Unless they're you."

In my third novel, I imbued a struggling couple with idiosyncrasies that belonged almost entirely to my then-husband and me. He's a Luddite obsessed with the past and himself. She's a control freak who's afraid of the dark but addicted to the news cycle. Before the book begins, the me of the story is attacked. She's not robbed, not messed with, just knocked out cold by the butt of a gun. It's a commentary on the senselessness and randomness of violence. And maybe it's also a quiet indictment of the ways in which women—motivated by a desire to be perceived as polite or chill or cool with the world—will sometimes drop their guards at just the wrong time. Maybe it's also a tacit dig at privilege: you can buy, buy, buy, but no matter how comfortable you make yourself, there's always the unknown, the unexpected, the outside world with its own designs.

"Dad called me crying last week," I say.

"He called me crying this morning."

"How worried should we be?"

"He's up; he's down; he's up again. He's a cat. He lands on all fours."

"Weak as a kitten."

"How's the memoir?" my sister asks.

"Fine."

"When can I read it?"

"Soon. When it's published. Soon."

"You're so mysterious," she says.

"You won't say that once you've read it."

"See? You can't help yourself."

"It's not like it's some tawdry tell-all," I say. "Don't get excited."

In fact, it is a tawdry tell-all, complete with sex, booze, Botox, and dildos. My mother, because I know my mother like the inside of my elbow—and, also, because I have access to the future—will say, first thing, very first thing, when she finishes reading it: "Wow. You've really opened your kimono," and all I'll be able to imagine after she's said this is a man opening his bathrobe, displaying a large erection for the world to see, or for whatever unlucky woman happens to be in his hotel room at the time.

To be fair to my mother, it's me who's got the obsession with erect penises. But to be unfair: for the rest of my life, when I hear the word "kimono," I'll think first of my memoir and then, within less than a nanosecond, of a man with his arms spread wide, hips thrust forward with vigor and determination, the hem of his robe bunched in either fist, and an erection.

When I was a little girl, I used to draw unartful pictures of stick figures having sex. The stick man was always lying down, several large dark lines protruding straight up from his waist. The stick woman was always sitting astride the stick penis.

Once, during a session with a court-appointed therapist, I was shown a series of black-and-white line drawings of men and women in various troubling situations. I was old enough to be familiar with the idea of the Rorschach, and I was disappointed when the therapist didn't show me abstract ink blots about which I might have invented farcical responses: a dog in a hot-air balloon, a shark on a diving board, the outline of an amusement park with a kitty cat just visible beneath the Ferris wheel.

Midway through the line drawings, the therapist—a man—showed me the image of a woman lying on a single bed, her breasts exposed and her eyes closed. A blanket covered the area between her belly and her feet. A man was sitting in a chair at her side. He was fully clothed and looking in my direction. The therapist wanted to know what I saw. He wanted me to describe the scenario. I was sure the woman was dead, sure the man had killed her, sure she had been messed with in some unspeakable way before she died.

I shook my head.

"What do you see?" the therapist asked again, pushing the picture farther across his desk in my direction. He tapped the woman's chest, and I began to cry.

Sometimes, I worry about the origin of my impetus to draw erect penises. Sometimes, when I think about my parents and all the rooms they allowed me to be alone in with strange men—in the name of my well-being and in the hopes of a satisfactory custody settlement—I can become agitated.

My nephews emerge from their house across the street, their father behind them. They see their mother and me and wave; then the six-year-old lowers his pants and pees off the front of their porch in our general direction. "That's my cue," my sister says. She leaves me with the wreckage of our cocktails, and just like that I am alone.

Before my parents divorced, when I was still a little girl, there were tennis lessons, swimming lessons, ballet lessons, music lessons, riding lessons, and monthly shopping sprees at Lenox Square and Phipps Plaza in uptown Atlanta. We spent entire summers on Sea Island in a rented blue cottage with a swimming pool and a diving board. The house was half a block from the ocean. In the morning, early, you could hear the waves from the kitchen. We had a spending account at the Cloister, and every Sunday we walked to the end of the island for lobsters and a bonfire.

During the school year, we lived in a farmhouse with a horse barn and a dozen imported dressage horses. There were chickens and pure-bred dogs and more barn kittens than we could keep track of. There were imported German cars and two all-terrain vehicles. There was a trampoline, a mud pit, a swimming hole, a barn manager, and a nanny. There was a pony and a lamb for each of the children. My pony was a Shetland, barely taller than I was. Her name was Martha. Once a year, for show-and-tell, my mother trailered Martha into the city, and my classmates walked single file to the parking lot, where my mother and Martha would be waiting for us. One Christmas, in a bathtub, there were two baby geese as gifts. The geese became our pets. Later, there were airplanes.

There was the night someone left a gate open, and the horses got out and walked along the highway. There was the night the barn kittens mysteriously died, and the morning after when we buried them in pickle jars. There was the afternoon my brother and sister played a game of chicken on their ATVs and ran headlong into each other, both of them breaking an arm, my sister shouting and laughing, "I'm no chicken, I'm no chicken." There was the day my brother ran over a hornet's nest and was stung by a thousand hornets. There was the day I climbed a tree for the first time and fell headfirst onto the ground when a dead branch gave way beneath my weight, and we all piled into the Mercedes and drove an hour to the emergency room. There was the week we had chicken pox. There was the hour the Orkin man came when no parents were home and, afterward, pretending he was still in the house, my sister found a revolver in our parents' bedroom and we roamed from floor to floor, room to room, taking turns with the loaded gun, pretending to search for a burglar. There were cookouts and dinner parties and lazy nights when we huddled together on a couch in the living room, listening to my mother reading aloud James Herriot or to my father playing Motown records. There were afternoons when we churned butter or made ice cream or played hours and hours of what felt like the most dangerous games of hide-and-seek. Sometimes our parents dressed up—my mother, six feet tall before she put on heels, looking like a runway model, and my father looking like Alan Alda in a suit he'd had tailored in Italy. Those nights—when my parents were gone—we watched movies and ate popcorn and stayed up with the nanny, who sometimes showed us her *Playgirl* magazines and once showed us where my father kept a stash of *Playboys* and *Hustlers*.

And then there was the day the adventures ended; the day the barn manager's daughter told me my parents were divorcing. I called her a liar and told my sister, who punched the girl in her face and then ran to tell our mother. I followed, understanding nothing. We found my mother in her bedroom. We were scolded, me for calling the girl a liar when she wasn't and my sister for the punch. That was the day everything changed—no more shopping sprees, no more summers on Sea Island, no more ponies as show-and-tell.

Decades would pass—in which I learned to bifurcate my personality, conceal my true identity, conform to others' narratives, contort my own desires, invent stories on command, placate anything and everything—before I understood the extent of the lie we'd all been living.

Tonight, as I lie awake in bed watching the light in the upstairs window of the house across the street, the window of my sister's bedroom, I think about permission. My ex didn't ask permission to marry me off to my boyfriend in a piece of his fiction. He didn't ask permission to write a novel about me. For that matter, I did not—while we were still married—ask his permission to write a novel about him, and certainly after our divorce, I didn't ask his permission to write the story of our separation in my memoir. But the trespass feels different now that we are no longer together. This joint custody of our past has sneaked up on me, and I find I am unprepared. My ex didn't ask permission, but neither did my sister when she bought the house across the street. She simply texted Bruce and me one afternoon to say that she and her husband and their Realtor—also *our* Realtor—were sitting on our front porch writing a contract.

There's a Barthelme story called "Some of Us Had Been Threatening Our Friend Colby" that I teach most semesters. In the story, Colby—a dear friend of the collective narrators—has gone too far and must be put to death. The story is absurd. There is no explanation except that he's gone too far. Too far with what? We'll never know, but now his friends must kill him, and they are all very sad.

Sometimes, of my family—especially recently, especially when I think of my mother and her men or of my father and his batik hallucinations or of my sister's little boys watching me on my porch from their porch across the street, all of them now within a half-mile radius—I think, they have gone too far. This time, they have certainly gone too far.

Somehow, I am in the middle of telling my seniors (*and* the gray-haired lady *and* Mateo) about the time I sent my husband an email pretending to be one of his students. This is their favorite kind of story—one that paints me not only as human but also as slightly deranged.

"Wait wait wait," says one of them. "How long did you keep it up? How many emails? He actually wrote back?"

"Oh geez," I say, "the better part of an afternoon."

I tell my workshop how we'd been sitting across from each other at the kitchen table. This was a decade ago now, maybe longer, back when we were newlyweds in Chicago. Classes had only just started, and we were both going over our attendance sheets and putting last-minute touches on our course syllabi. My ex, not yet my ex, had finally been given an advanced workshop, and he was eager about the intimacy of the class size. He'd bragged about his first day and the way his students had regarded him with a near palpable reverence. I had an itch to be bad.

Sitting across from him, I logged out of my own email and created a brand-new account. It took fewer than five minutes. Then I enjoyed crafting a lengthy letter from a person claiming to be registered in his advanced workshop. *Hey, Professor!* I wrote. *Awesome first day. Looks like*

I've already misplaced the syllabus and workshop schedule. Mind sending me both? I gave the kid a milquetoast name (something like Jared) and congratulated myself on his lightly entitled voice, a kind of modern-day Wally from *Leave It to Beaver*. I pushed send and then took our dog for a walk.

When I came home, my husband was standing at the table, a bunch of rosters spread out in front of him. He was mumbling angrily to himself, which delighted me. Typically, I'd have asked what was wrong, but somehow I knew not asking would make him even angrier, which delighted me even more. I unleashed our dog, gave him a treat, then reclaimed my seat at the table. My husband, now my ex, gave me a look, as if to say, *You're just going to sit there and pretend not to notice I'm in extremis?* In return, I gave him a bright smile, as if to say, *Love you, honey!* Sometimes, for me, playing obtuse can be as pleasurable as a self-induced orgasm or a perfectly cooked steak with a beautifully rendered cognac sauce.

I opened my new email and bit down on the insides of my cheeks. He'd already responded: *I'm sorry, Jared. I don't see your name on the class roster, and I certainly don't remember signing you in during attendance. I'm afraid you've got the wrong course. Best of luck sorting things out.* "Professor" was his sign-off.

I thought for a moment, then hit reply, and wrote: *Hi. Me again! I'm definitely writing to the right guy about the right class. I was a little late coming in—I got lost on the way. I must have missed attendance. Would love to get that syllabus and workshop schedule.* I pushed send on this, too, then busied myself with a little light paperwork. By then, my husband had reopened his computer.

"What the—?"

I looked up. "Everything okay?"

"This kid," he said, staring at his screen. "What the fuck is with this kid?"

"What kid?"

"There's some kid saying he's in the advanced class. But he's not."

"Maybe he registered late."

"I'm looking at the roster. His name's not here. I'm looking right at it. See?" He punched at his computer screen with an index finger. I couldn't see, because I was still on my side of the table.

"Weird," I said.

"Weird?" he said. "*Weird?*"

"Write him back. Tell him he's wrong."

"I did write him back. I did tell him he's wrong."

"Like I said, weird." I pretended to resume my work.

My husband muttered something and then began typing furiously. His response landed within minutes:

Dear Jared. I'm certain that you are not enrolled in this course. I am look-ing at an updated attendance sheet. Your name is not here. No one came in late to my class. I will not send you the syllabus, nor will I share the workshop schedule, as you are not a member of this workshop.

I hit reply immediately:

Prof, I, too, am looking at an updated course schedule. I assure you I <u>am</u> registered. You were wearing a plaid shirt and a skinny pink tie. You talked for 45 minutes without asking any student a single question or doing any kind of get-to-know-you game like every other teacher. Instead of sitting at your desk, you stood in front of it and leaned back. A little cock-forward if I'm being honest! I think some of the girls were uncomfortable. You might check that behavior in the future.

I pushed send, closed my computer, then went to the bathroom, a balloon's worth of giddiness in my chest. In the mirror, I made faces at myself and stifled my laughter by imagining our dog running away and being hit by a car and left for dead. I considered masturbating but didn't.

I emerged just in time to hear my husband say, "Are you joking? Are you fucking joking? This is unbelievable. This is un-fucking-believable." He was standing again. "Look," he said, pointing at the computer and making eye contact with me for the first time. "Look at th—" He must have seen it in my face, because then he said, "You? *You?* 'Cock-forward'? 'Check that behavior'?"

I shrugged. "I took a guess," I said. "I've seen you teach."

My students eat the story up. I leave out certain details—being alone in the bathroom doing facial exercises I learned in middle school drama, imagining my lost dog, the possibility of masturbation, "cock-forward"—but I give them almost everything else.

They want to know what happened next.

"Don't remember," I say, though of course I do: What happened next was sex, which was what always happened after I'd done something outrageous, or he'd been in a bad mood that I'd helped alleviate, until it wasn't what always happened . . . Until we got to that moment in our marriage when I'd be outlandish and he'd be sour, after which I'd feel alone in my mind with a vision of the world that, for a little while at least, I'd tricked myself into believing was his vision, too.

About the Irishman—

I told my husband, while we waited for the divorce to be finalized, "Of course there's no one else. Everyone's getting fucked but me."

I told my sister, "There's this guy. It's nothing. He's got a crush on me. It's flattering. He's tall."

I told my mother, "It'll be a year before I even think about dating."

I told my doctor, "To be safe, let's go ahead and do Plan B."

I told Jane, "It was just the once. I think it was okay. He got a little rough. What did I like about him? He called me Hot Stuff. Anyway, he left town."

I told my shrink, "I can't say for sure. I blacked out."

When I get home from school, my father is on our front porch. He's alone.

"I didn't realize we had plans," I say.

"We don't." He's got a blanket across his lap and a mug of something cupped between his palms.

"Hm," I say, dropping my bag and taking the seat beside him.

"I just got here. Your roommate brought me this tea."

"You can't stay for dinner."

"I don't want to stay for dinner," he says. "I just want thirty minutes, forty minutes. You can give me fifty minutes, can't you?"

Bruce emerges with a glass of wine, which he hands to me. "We have a pop-up," he says, nodding toward my father.

I smile demurely and take a sip. Pop-ups are something Bruce and I have talked about—as in, Bruce has requested that my father and my sister stop doing them; my mother has immunity. Bruce has said to me, "When we got together, your family didn't live here." I've said to Bruce, "I never wanted a child in my life." He's said to me, "When we met, I didn't hide her. You knew she existed." I've said to Bruce, "I feel like a kid in my house is roughly the equivalent of several local in-laws not in the house." He's said to me, "They're not my in-laws. We're not married, remember?" I've said to Bruce, "I'm giving your daughter a family." He's said to me, "You're a family of navel gazers." I've said to Bruce, "This isn't what my life was supposed to look like." He's said to me, "So leave already." I've said to him, "Not over your dead body." He's said to me, "That's not how the saying goes." I've said to him, "Yeah, well, who cares?"

Now my father says, "I don't know. I don't know. Should I have given the guns to you?"

"Guns," says Bruce. "What guns?"

"No guns," I say. "More tea?"

My father shrugs, then begins a lengthy explanation for why it's imperative he travel to Amsterdam at the end of the month to partake in a truffle experience he believes will course correct his life. Bruce, meanwhile, is locked on me with his death-stare eyes. I shake my head and mouth the words, *No guns, I promise, no guns.* He considers this. Then he slowly turns his glower in the direction of the house across the street.

I learned to shoot skeet before I learned to drive. I learned to aim a rifle when I was six years old, during my first summer at a month-long evangelical camp in the hills of North Carolina. I've driven cross-country with a double-action revolver tucked beneath the driver's seat and slept with a loaded pistol under my pillow. A few years after my father's father shot himself in the head, my mother's brother drove out of state and did the very same thing in a rented motel room. Right now, there is a shotgun—disassembled, locked, combination long forgotten—in my office in the attic. It was a birthday present from my father the year I left for boarding school, the year I turned thirteen. Bruce didn't grow up with guns and is opposed to them and everything they stand for. Bruce—who sometimes refers to the antique inheritances in my office as used furniture—claims the shotgun in our attic is just another example of my family's fascination with the past, which sometimes amuses him, sometimes confounds him, but mostly just infuriates him.

When my father finally leaves—two drinks and forty-five minutes from now—Bruce will turn to me and say, "No guns, heirloom or otherwise," to which I'll readily agree, nodding vigorously even as all I can suddenly think about is my father's father, from whom, by the time he died, I was estranged.

About my father's father—

His funeral was open casket. I touched his face. I couldn't stop myself. I will never forget his skull—the pale color of the material stretched across it, the feel of it, the out-of-body image of my fingers on it, near it . . .

About my father's father—

He wasn't suicidal until he was.

About my father's father—

Everything is there: divorce, infidelity, secrecy, madness, guns . . .

My students would accuse me of having too many through lines. My students would say, if they could interject, "Where's the plot? Where's the causality?" My students would say, "Good art is in conversation with art that's come before. Isn't that what you're always telling us? Why don't you ever let *us* experiment?"

"Experiment with what?"

"Vampires!" they'd shout. "Talking kittens. Fan fiction!"

"Fine," I'd say. "Fine. You win! Write whatever you want. Just no school shootings. No sexual violence."

"What does it even mean, that line you're always repeating, *Tell the truth but make it up?*"

Maybe Mateo would cut in here, nearly in my defense: "At least she isn't writing about dreams. At least there's that."

But his seatmate Willow would counter: "That's only because she doesn't sleep. I bet the minute she gets one good night, we're going to have a dream sequence on our hands, and dreams are the kiss of death. An inorganic trick whereby a half-rate novelist attempts to sneak in meaning and ostensible depth. Also, side note: What's with all these old people who can't sleep through the night?"

"Enough," I'd cry. "Enough! Once you've learned the rules, you've earned the right to break them. I've told you this a million times."

And here a universal groan might go up from the room. They'd scoff, turn away from me, nudge one another with their shoulders in that knowing way, and whisper giddily among themselves: "Said every aging writer ever . . ."

Jane texts, *How's your restlessness?*

I text, *Maybe restless is the wrong word.*

She texts, *ennui? Acedia? Malingering?*

maybe boredom?

My mother says—you're bored? I have some chores for you!

I text, *what if this isn't my life?*

She texts, *You can never leave: your sister, your house*

Are you poking me?

Do you mean provoking?

Distinction without a difference?

Maybe, she writes, *you have a creeping feeling your troubles are frivolous*

maybe I'm feeling selfish. Also: ouch!

homeless people have problems

Sure sure, I write. *Literary people on the other hand . . .*

Professors . . .

What if contentment inhibits my writing? I ask.

your boredom is From a Place of Privilege

I text, *#FPOP*

She texts, *I stole three organic avocados from the store #FPOP*

I text, *talk about privilege . . .* Then, my thumbs hovering, I type and send the words, *I saw the Irishman today.*

She writes, *?*

I write, *Hot Stuff*

She writes, *Oh.* Then she writes, *OHHH!* Then she writes, *Did he see you?*

I was running. We were both at stop signs. I can't be certain. But yes? We both stayed at our stop signs longer than we should have.

She writes, *As a runner, you stop at stop signs?*

LOL

I wish I knew what he looked like.

I do a quick google and take a screenshot of him in a blue suit standing next to his wife and another couple at a charity event. I send Jane the photo, making sure his name isn't visible.

She writes, *He looks like McNulty.*

I write, *McDreamy?*

She writes, *Guy from* The Wire. *Dominic something.*

I write, *Only he's got Very Intense Eyes.*

She writes, *I see.*

I write, *But maybe it wasn't him.*

She writes, *GTG. Will brainstorm on your ennui. xx*

I am lying facedown on Bruce's side of the bed, wearing only my under-pants and a tank top. It's bedtime. His daughter is at her mom's. Bruce is in the bathroom brushing his teeth. This isn't a sex thing.

For some reason, he closed the door tonight while brushing his teeth, which freckled me with suspicion, which activated a yearning to lie facedown on his side of the bed and play dead.

I close my eyes. I wait. I reposition myself so that one arm is hanging off the edge. I bend a knee and try to become one with the mattress. I take short, controlled mouth breaths and imagine I am an actress playing her dead self. I lie very, very still. (I get my stamina for lying still from my mother, who was once told, by a professor who was likely trying to get into her pants, that she was the stillest student he'd ever had. I wonder now, as I melt into the mattress, becoming one with our Tempur-Pedic, if maybe he *did* get into my mother's pants.)

I lick my lips. The bathroom door opens.

"What the—?" Bruce asks.

I don't move and, obviously, I say nothing.

"Okay, weirdo, move over."

I think of kittens being run over, of baby mice freezing to death, of my long dead dog breathing his last breath, his muzzle heavy on my thigh.

"Come on," he says. He runs a finger along the sole of my foot. I do not move a muscle, not even an involuntary spasm.

He says my name playfully once. Then he says it again, a slight worry, maybe annoyance creeping in. He sits on the very edge of the bed—I haven't left him a lot of room—and the side of his ass cheek presses against mine. I let my body Jell-O toward him as he sits down, as it might if I were dead and had no control, no ability to keep it in place, which nearly knocks him off the bed. He puts a hand on my lower back and jiggles me. He says my name again. I let myself be jiggled.

He says, "I can see that you're breathing."

Without moving anything but my lips, I whisper flatly, "I'm dead."

"You're what?"

"I'm a dead body," I mutter.

He picks up the arm that's hanging over the edge of the bed and then lets go. My arm drops down heavily, my fingertips thwacking against the wood of the bed frame. I do not let myself wince, though the pain is not insignificant.

"What's the plan here?" Bruce asks.

"Try to move me." My voice is shallow because my lungs are deflated, and my face is smushed into the mattress.

"I can move you," he says.

"Then do it."

"I don't want to hurt you," he says.

"I'm dead. You can't hurt me."

He lets out a deep sigh as though he's exasperated, but I think he might finally be getting into it.

He puts his hand on my shoulder, cups me, then lifts up the right side of my torso. I don't offer any help at all.

"You're heavy," he says. I don't respond. He lifts my shoulder higher, and I let my body do what it would naturally do if I didn't have a say. He pushes me, right to left, so that my torso rolls onto its back awkwardly. My left arm, the one that wasn't hanging off the edge, is now pinned uncomfortably beneath me. I let my jaw go slack for effect. In another minute, I'll probably be able to produce a line of drool.

"Ta-da," he says. "I moved you. Now can you go back to your side of the bed?"

I slit open an eye. Bruce is blurry, but I can see he's smiling. I mumble, "You've killed me and I'm dead and now you have to get rid of me. How do you do it?"

"Is your arm okay? That looks like it hurts. You look like a doll with a limp limb."

I close my eye and let out the drool that's been pooling in the floor of my mouth. I am the Marie Kondo of playing dead, and everything about it brings me joy, including the searing pain in my left triceps. My tolerance for discomfort must be exceptional.

"Have it your way," Bruce says. He stands up, my body jostling from the movement of the mattress. He grabs my right foot and pulls my leg straight alongside the left one. Then, his hands around my ankles, he pulls me toward him. This frees my left arm, which will surely be sore in the morning. He pulls me toward him again. I make my body a marionette, and my arms spread naturally up and away as my legs and torso are yanked down. My feet are on the floor now. My left ass cheek is fully off the bed, my right ass cheek barely hanging on. "Whoa there," he says. "Don't topple over on me." He puts a hand on my right hip bone to pin me in place. "Wait a minute while I get situated." He's talking to me, but he's also kind of talking to himself, like I might not be here anymore, like I really might just be a body without a brain. I like it. "If I put that arm here and shift that arm there, I think I can heave you off the bed and over my shoulder." The idea of this thrills me, but as he's trying to figure things out, he accidentally lets up on my hip bone, and my right ass cheek slips off the bed and I go down hard, my left knee and thigh taking the brunt of the fall. I leave my body where it lands, which is on its side, my left arm high above my head and flat against the floor and my right deltoid pressed against my face.

"Shit," says Bruce. "Are you okay? Let me see."

I do not move. It is all I can do not to detonate with pleasure.

"How far are you going with this?" he asks. "I'm not taking you down the stairs."

Into the skin of my arm, I instruct him: "Out of the bedroom and into the hallway. Get me to the top of the stairs and I'll give up."

Without saying anything, Bruce picks up my feet, shifts me so I'm on my back, and pulls me across the rug, out of the bedroom, and into the hallway. By the time we're at the stairs my shirt is bunched up under my shoulder blades and I'm laughing so hard my sides hurt and it's difficult to breathe.

"Are you satisfied?" he says, letting go of my ankles so that my heels hit the floor with a thud.

I open my eyes. My body feels like a living bruise, alive and sprightly and coursing with endorphins. I hop quickly to my feet. "Your turn," I say.

Later, Bruce says, "This story your ex wrote. How do you know it's about us?"

It's five in the morning. I stretch and turn away from him and clench down on my mouth guard. For all he knows, I'm still asleep.

"I know you're awake," he says, "because you're never asleep."

I lie very still, and he pushes his very erect penis against me. I respond by pushing my ass in his direction. He pulls at the elastic of my underpants. I assist.

Afterward, I roll in his direction. He says, "Tell me how you know."

"You could read it yourself. Draw your own conclusions."

"Not gonna happen."

"The ex-wife is smug and insincere."

"So?"

"Her new husband has a daughter."

"So?"

"They're both professors."

"Anything else?"

"Bruce is chair of the department. The narrator has quit academia and is now living a bohemian life with a woman who used to be my friend."

"Ah," says Bruce, rolling onto his back and sliding his arms under his pillow.

"Also, we're bourgeois."

"Good," he says.

I run my hand over his bald head.

"Are we liberal?" he asks.

"It's unstated."

"Wealthy?"

"Quite comfortable, I'd say."

"What's the story about?"

"A costume party."

"That's the plot? A costume party? Writers get away with murder."

"No," I say, and then I tell him it's Halloween, and the narrator is calling to tell me, his ex-wife, that they're pregnant at long last, which is something I never wanted to be—in the story or in real life. But my ex doesn't get the chance to tell me because my stepdaughter needs my help with her costume and we're running late already, and I have to get off the phone, and . . .

Bruce says, alarmed, half sitting up in bed, "Did that happen? Has he called since we moved in together?" I regard him with annoyance that morphs almost immediately into fondness. His vulnerability is surprising and sincere.

The real plot of the story—details I don't tell Bruce—is that I'm dead, and my ex has just found out and his new wife is in the hospital almost—but not—losing her baby while her husband enjoys a final bout of nostalgia and self-indulgence as he recalls our last phone call, when he tried but never got the chance to tell me about the pregnancy.

The story reminds me of all the promises my ex and I made just after our divorce, especially the ones we didn't keep. He swore he'd tell me if they ever got married so I wouldn't have to hear it secondhand. I swore we'd always be friends.

As Bruce slumbers beside me, I indulge in my own bout of nostalgia. I wonder now if my ex ever tried, in real life, to pick up the phone. I wonder if his wife, my one-time friend, walked in while he was thinking of me, and he put the receiver down and never thought of me again.

Maybe, I think but do not say aloud, the story is an admission, a regret, a quiet apology dedicated to me for our various broken vows. Then I remember the homeless man and the knife.

"Nope," I say.

And Bruce, half-asleep, says, "Did you say something?"

And I say, "Nope."

Picture me seven years ago, one week away from finding out my marriage is over: It's three in the morning. There is a woman, *this* woman, lying on top of her covers. She is fast asleep, a flattened shadow in the darkness of a bedroom. Off camera, there is a noise. In her brain, a flash of light. Later she will wonder at both: auditory hallucinations, retinal explosions, or something more visceral, something external and more undeniable?

Regardless, her body jolts awake. The night and its events do not immediately return, not yet, not fully, not ever. For now it is a slow reassessment only of self and body. This is her bed. This is her room. These are her arms. These are her sheets. She is in her own home. She is alive. These are her very first thoughts. She is dying of thirst, but before she can drink, she runs to the toilet and vomits. She's on her knees, her hands on either side of the porcelain. Her knees are cold. Her legs are bare. She isn't wearing any underpants. She's wearing a bra and, on top of that, the same shirt she'd gone out in the night before. She's also wearing one sock. She vomits again.

After, the woman, again *this* woman, rinses out her mouth and washes her face. For the first time, she thinks of the Irishman. He'd been here, too, in her home. She's sure of it. She can smell him, his cologne, sandalwood and cedar. She remembers his chin. She remembers considering it, biting it. She remembers his hair, too. Thick, curly, coarse hair, different than her husband's. It's possible she'd made this observation aloud and to him. It's possible she'd made other observations aloud. She can't be sure. She puts a hand between her legs. She can't be sure of this either. There is no pain, no sting. Her fingers smell sour. Her shoulders ache just standing at the sink. Her wrists, too.

Using the wall as her only support, the woman staggers downstairs. In the air is something unexpected. Not cologne, not sex, but the intense smell of a fresh and recent rain. The woman shivers from an inexplicable breeze. At the landing, the skin on her arms and legs breaks into gooseflesh. In the living room, she discovers the reason for the chill. The front door, the door to her home, is wide open—open to the world, to the dead of night, to anyone who might care to come in.

She throws herself against it, closing and locking it with the panic of a child in the deep end, convinced suddenly of a shark at her heels. The dread is that real, that profound. She can feel her heartbeat in her teeth. The door closed, she wheels around, surveying her home in its darkest, blackest state. It's empty. She senses this instantly. Even so, she pulls down the bottom hem of her shirt, still naked where it matters, then crawls back up the stairs and into bed.

When I came to the second time, it was late morning and there was one text: *We cool?*

I wrote, *Of course.*

He wrote, *Brown bag flu?*

No.

You feel OK then?

Perfectly fine.

About us?

I wrote, *Perfectly. Fine.* I thought, *Say more, say extra, say anything good.*

I'm sorry, he wrote.

Sorry?

For introducing you to that guy.

Virgil?

Me.

I'm home alone, watching my neighbor, the mathematician, haul his Christmas tree to the front yard. It's still got the colored lights wrapped around it.

Last year, from inside our house, the blinds divided, I watched as the mathematician dropped his tree at the curb, bent down, then proceeded to dig through its branches like a man checking for lice. It was drizzling. After several minutes—he'd gone all the way down to his knees—he stood up, turned toward his house, and raised one hand high. He was holding an ornament. I told myself his wife was inside watching, then set down my binoculars and took a picture. He wasn't smiling.

Today, I am sitting on our front steps, and I am brazenly observing him. It's sixty-five degrees and sunny. The clouds are caricatures of themselves. I take a picture when his back is turned and send it to Bruce. I am losing my decency.

Bruce hearts the photo. I write: *Anything from grocery?*

He writes: *Bananas.*

I don't add them to the list. This year alone, we've already thrown away seventeen bananas. I know this because I started keeping track immediately. I started keeping track immediately because I realized on

New Year's morning, first thing when I woke up, that the banana situation in this house wasn't magically going to fix itself just because it was a new year.

When the eleven-year-old asked for my resolution, I said, "To track your father's banana waste."

Bruce, who was in the kitchen with us at the time, said, "That's funny."

I got out my phone, lifted the trash can's lid, and counted the bananas. I wrote down: *Bananas IIII*. Then I shared the note with him.

It's possible he's joking about the bananas today; but it's also possible he wants them and will be mildly annoyed when he gets home from teaching and finds I've ignored his request. Tone is so difficult via text.

At the grocery store—a place I love provided I park at street level and not in the garage, which is a place I'll never park and therefore I can't say for sure that I'd still love the grocery were I forced to park there—I watch as the man entering just in front of me grabs a cart and steers *away* from produce, in the direction of dairy. I shiver, then text Jane: *would you ever date a man who didn't start with produce first?* She texts back immediately: *I will never date another man.* I text: *Because you're married.* She texts: *because I hate men.* I send her a smiling turd.

At the wet wall, which is what grocery employees call the wall of produce, which is a term I know because the nontraditional scholar called the local Kroger to get the right lingo for a story she handed in to workshop, I swipe from my grocery list over to Instagram. Margaret Atwood has posted a humorously ruined birthday cake. It's not her birthday.

In the comments section, under hundreds of hearts and best wishes, I write: *What am I doing in this old man's body?—from "Soul," David Ferry*. I am desperate for Margaret to notice me.

I switch back to my list, check off carrots and kale and green onions. All that's left is celery, which is how I got in trouble the last time I was here alone. All I needed was two stalks for a mirepoix. I snapped two off, threw them in a bag, and kept on shopping. An employee, some kid, was apparently spying on me when I did it. He ratted me out to his manager, who caught up with me in the sparkling water aisle. He pointed at my cart. "Is that yours?" he asked.

Because I didn't yet know why or how I was in trouble, and *not* because I was playing deliberately obtuse, I said, "The cart?" He said, "The celery." I said, "The celery is mine in that I intend to buy it. Is this an existential question?" He said, "That's not allowed." I said, still not being willfully obtuse, "I'm not allowed to buy celery?" He said, "You're not allowed to break off stalks." I said, "I'm *not*?" He said, "No." I said, "But it's by the pound." He said, "There's a rubber band around it for a reason." I said, "There *is*?" He said, "Yes." I said, "Maybe you should have a sign." The manager regarded me mutely. I said, "I do it all the time with the bananas. Everybody does it with the bananas." He said, "Bananas are different." I said, now developing a feel for my obtuseness, "They *are*?" He said, "Obviously." I said, "Bananas are by the pound." He said, "Please hand me that celery." I said, "But you're joking?" He said, "If you want celery, you can buy the whole bunch."

Just when I was about to start laughing at the absurdity of the situation whereby this manager figure was apparently intent on taking my two stalks of celery, I suddenly became very sad. I thought, *Oh my god.* And then, *This is real. This is my real life. This is really happening in my real life in which I am a person who spends too much time at a grocery store looking at Instagram and gets in trouble for not following the rules and oh my god this is not what my life was supposed to be, is it?*

I handed the manager my celery, abandoned my cart, walked out of the store and then all the way home.

When I opened the front door, Bruce looked at me for a very long time. Then he went to the side entrance of our house, opened that door, and looked in our driveway. He said, "Where's your car?" I said, "At the grocery store." He said, "Where are the groceries?" I said, "Same place." Then I started crying.

Now, a week later, Bruce texts again: *I'm serious about the bananas FYI.*

In the pasta aisle, where I will buy nothing because I make my own pasta but which is an aisle that gets excellent cell service, I check Instagram again. No message from Atwood.

When I get home from the store, my neighbor is standing next to his car, which is parked now on the street, near the Christmas tree, and he's attempting to inflate a rear tire with a bicycle pump. I pull only partway into my driveway, roll down the window, and take a picture.

My father texts: *keep it between your ears ; don't let it get out . you've always been my favorite*

The text is for my sister. It is addressed to her by name. This isn't unusual. He often texts the two of us, addressing his comments only to one of us, as in—

> *Hana if you think about it sometime give me a call*
> *Sissy I will drag some grub over to Your house Im craving barbecue*
> *Hello Hana baby there's some extra barbecue over at Sissy's I'm coming*
>   *circa six-ish you're welcome to come and get it or eat it*
> *Sissy you are a perfect mother you make beautiful babies*

While it isn't surprising to read his words, this is the first time he's ever openly declared a preference.

I ignore the text, and, within minutes, he invites himself over for a porch sit. When he arrives, I ask him if he wants anything. He says, "I'm not picky," then he asks for a fizzy water, one cube of ice, and a squeeze of fresh lime. I bring him his drink, which I've already prepared, because he is always not picky, and he always wants a fizzy with a cube and a squeeze. He also always eventually wants vodka, and today will be no different. In thirty minutes, he will say, "How about some vodka?" And I'll say, "Are you still good with soda water?" And he'll say, "Whatever. Sure. I'm not picky. Or tonic if you've got it and more lime." But that conversation won't happen for another half hour; first I must undo his rearrangement of my porch chairs. He's turned the Adirondacks toward each other, attempting to force a tête-à-tête. I return them to their proper places and sit down so that we are both facing the street and the house that is now my sister's.

He says, "How I am? Here's how I am."

My father wants to be a charming character in one of my books. He's keeping notes, he tells me, of all the zany antics he gets up to. "Shenanigans," he says. I do not tell him there's no need to keep notes; I am keeping them myself. I do not tell him that in the state of Kentucky, a person does not need permission to record a conversation.

He says, "I guess you want an update." For the last week, he's been in New Orleans with a woman thirty years his junior. I assure him I do not want an update.

Sometime during my senior year of college, I went back to Atlanta for a visit. The year before, my father had declared bankruptcy. Not long after, the sadist divorced him. By the time I visited, he'd moved out of the mid-century masterpiece on Tuxedo Road he'd bought in 1986, after divorcing my mother, and into a modest but tidy bungalow just off Lenox Road in Pine Hills.

He picked me up at the airport and drove us to a nondescript office building downtown, where he left the car running—me in it—while he went inside. He returned with an envelope, which he asked me to open. It was an unemployment check for several thousand dollars. While he drove, he took the check from me and signed the back of it, using the steering wheel as his desk.

From there, we went to a liquor store where I'd been with him more times than I could remember. Again he left the car running, and again I waited in the car. He emerged with a brown paper bag, the kind my mother might have used for packing lunches when we were little.

I knew what was in the bag because I'd run this particular errand for him countless times, back before the bankruptcy, usually on a Friday afternoon, usually when we were headed out of town—to Cancún or Callaway Gardens or to try unsuccessfully to recreate those lost summers at Sea Island but now without my mother.

My father took a couple hundred-dollar bills from the bag and shoved them into his wallet. Then he stuffed the paper bag, still very full, under the driver's seat.

"I'm thinking oysters," he said. "And champagne."

The last time he'd taken me for oysters and champagne was the year before, in the midst of the bankruptcy. He was still living on Tuxedo Road, but there were boxes everywhere. My stepmother was still living there, too, but sleeping in a different bedroom. I knew there was no money, though I didn't understand why, and I'd suggested we do something cheaper—chips and dip or a slice of pizza—but my father wanted oysters. He was happy to see me. It was an occasion, he said. So I agreed.

It was midday when he pulled into the parking lot of a little French place in Buckhead—too late for lunch, too early for dinner. I had the impression the place wasn't actually open for business. But my father parked, and we were seated at a small table in a corner.

Can I say for sure when I noticed the pillowcase he'd brought inside with us? Can I remember with undeniable accuracy that it was white with scalloped edging? Or that he'd tucked it under his chair where it remained largely forgotten until it was time to pay?

I can't.

But I do remember the bill—more than a hundred dollars—and I do remember the moment he placed the pillowcase on the table between us and began counting out coins. And I remember the panic and shame and sadness as we sat there, the bartender watching us, as we counted out the full amount of the tab together.

In the car that day, my father cried as he drove. I cried, too. He held my hand and thanked me. He congratulated me for understanding, for having a heart, for being filled with such a great amount of empathy. He told me he was proud to have a daughter like me, proud to have played any part in the way I'd turned out. I let him hold my hand. I let him think my tears had anything at all to do with his.

Today, now, my father kicks my bare foot with the toe of his loafer. "Isn't that something?" he asks.

I nod, having heard nothing. "Really something," I say. A baby bunny drops from the sky onto the sidewalk in front of us. Before I can stand, a kestrel swoops down, snatches the kit, and is gone. "Sure is something," I say, my heartbeat racing.

And my father says, "How about some vodka?"

The next day, my father sends another barrage of texts—

I'm a lonely dude.
My second ketamine experience is today
Should I have given the guns to you question mark
*Am after an oceanic view with a new perspective just need to lessen the
    load on the pack mule of life*
*&head downhill toward a beach and a beautiful woman I can buy a
    cerveza*
Wish me.

I silence my phone and sit down at the head of the workshop table.
Fifteen faces regard me with expectation, excitement even. I do not
linger on Mateo's. I have the sense recently that Willow is aware of
the *zing* that sometimes occurs between us. I have the sense she would
prefer to be zinging with him herself.

According to the surveys my students fill out every semester, in
addition to my defensiveness and relentless correction, it's often also
said that this is their *easy* class, their *fun* class, the place where they can
express themselves and *be vulnerable*. In this moment, I find that I am

utterly unprepared for either their company or their edification, and certainly not their vulnerability.

"In-class writing assignment," I announce.

They grumble.

"Get your pens out."

"Tell us a story!" they beg, but I am in no mood for this today.

"Write about the moment when you stopped being a child," I say. "Is it the day your best friend lied to you? The day your parents said they were splitting up? The day your dog died? The day you saw your first boyfriend kissing someone else? Write about the event that taught you to look at the world differently, that introduced cynicism and distrust and awareness into your life."

They stare at me, wide-eyed and panicked.

"Or, you know, make something up and write about that." Tension leaves the room.

They write. I daydream.

I'm trying to make sense of my childhood, of the disparity between my memories and what I've been told. My parents split us up by gender—my brother, twelve, the oldest, went with my father; my sister and I went with my mother. "That's fairy-tale cruelty," Bruce said when we were first getting to know each other. He didn't believe me. But that was before he'd met either of my parents, before either of them had moved to town.

When did I stop being a child? It might have been the day my stepfather started shouting and then my mother slammed into my bedroom and grabbed me by the arm and dragged me out the back door and down into the woods and then pressed me into a dirt patch behind a giant magnolia. My father had arrived with the sheriff; he was demanding to take me home. We stayed in the woods, weeping, cheeks and stomachs pressed into the ground, for more than an hour. I didn't know why we were hiding.

Or it might have been the day my mother cornered me in the laundry room. I was ironing my uniform. I was in sixth grade. "Has your father ever touched you?" she asked. My cheeks went scarlet. "Has he ever put his hands on you in a way that made you feel uncomfortable?"

I was mute. I shook my head. "I had to ask," she said. "The lawyers said I had to ask."

Did the lawyers say she had to ask? I wonder. That was the day I started feeling differently about my father, the day I started feeling ashamed. I put a distance between us. I stopped holding his hand. Never once had he touched me inappropriately. But after that day, I guarded myself against him and every other man. I wouldn't kiss a boy until I was seventeen. And after that one kiss, I wouldn't kiss another until I was twenty.

Toward the end of class, my students ask me to share my own coming-of-age story. Instead, I tell them about the day I watched our German shepherd kill our border collie. I'd been alone outside with them and hadn't realized when their playing morphed into something else. At some point, the shepherd got the collie's neck between her jaws, and she shook him to death. I stood there, alone on a trampoline, not bouncing, just watching.

When I finish, several students suck in air.

"Dark," says Willow.

"I would have guessed yours would be about a dog," says Mateo. I do not dare meet his gaze.

I end class early, but instead of going home, I walk across the street to a taco place and order a margarita. The bartender tells me it's two-for-one Tuesday. I pay and tell her I'll take both now.

In Kentucky, there is no law barring a person from having two alcoholic beverages in front of them at the same time.

My father texts again—

2nd ketamine experience now over

I order another double round and then—

I'm OK it was quite a ride

And then—

Yeah I'm OK it's anytime you wanna talk I'll tell you about it

And—

Just wonder if there's any time in the forecast we could get together and
have a glass of wine
I'm thinking eight of these rides in three weeks is likely to move an
elephant
Impossible to describe but it is having an effect on my processing I
think
Some call it opening up
I'm gonna run ; turning in here shortly to see if I can sleep
Not in a great place as you know
Was hoping to catch up for a quick glass of wine sorry I missed you
Just not in a great place right now

Later still, the eleven-year-old is watching me put groceries away—a task that's made more difficult by the margaritas—and her lurking is irking me. I try to get rid of her by asking if she has anything productive to do—homework, piano, Duolingo—but all she has to say is "Nope. Nope. Nope."

Bruce comes in while I'm cramming a bag of lemons onto a bottom shelf and asks where the cotton balls are.

Before I can answer, a lemon falls from the ledge onto the floor, and the eleven-year-old says, "It's because the fridge is small."

I pick up the lemon and slam it into the fruit drawer.

Bruce says, "No, it's a standard-size fridge."

She says, "Mom's is bigger." Her mother has a double-wide Viking.

He says, "That might be true. But our refrigerator isn't small. It's perfect for a family of three."

A family of three? I can't look at either of them. Who even says a thing like that?

She says, "Whatever you say," and leaves the room.

"Family of three?" I ask Bruce when she's out of hearing distance. "Who even says a thing like that? Standard-size fridge?"

"What about it?"

"You have an answer for everything."

"I'm a father."

"What's that supposed to mean?"

"I have answers."

"I wanted to snap her in half."

"I could tell."

"Why do you need cotton balls?" I pull a bag of soggy radishes from the back of the drawer and lob them onto the counter.

"I've got poison ivy on my ankle."

"And?"

"You're supposed to apply the calamine with a cotton ball."

"You can't just use your hands?" Because I grew up feral on a farm in rural Georgia, I can be dismissive, even judgmental, about Bruce's attachment to clean hands and proper procedures.

"I want to follow the directions."

"Can I show you after I finish with the groceries?" I ask.

He says, "You can't just tell me?"

I say, "No," then wipe my hands on my jeans and start walking upstairs to our bathroom.

He says, following me, "I can find them myself if you'll just tell me."

I say, "I can't tell you. It's not that simple."

He says, "It's not simple for you to tell me where the cotton balls are? Shouldn't they be in an easily accessible, common area?"

By now we are in our bathroom, and I am on my knees, rooting around in the storage bench beside the shower.

He says, "You couldn't have told me to look in that cabinet?"

"No. I couldn't have told you which crappy plastic box inside this horrible little container houses the cotton balls. Maybe," I say, now on my feet, now holding the bag of cotton balls, which I know I am about to throw at him even as I am telling myself not to throw them, "if we had a functional storage area instead of this dead space above this fiberglass bathtub that we've never once used, then I would have been able to tell you to look on the second shelf to the left."

"You want functional storage?" he says. "That's great. I love functional storage. Let's buy you some functional storage."

"*Common area?*" I say, walking quickly out of the bathroom and back down the stairs to the kitchen and the groceries. My breathing is strained. "*Easily accessible*? Why should cotton balls—that only I have used in the three years we've lived together—be in a common area that's easily accessible? Maybe you should get your own cotton balls."

"What?" calls Bruce, following after me. "What are you saying? We're not supposed to talk to each other from other rooms. That's one of your rules. No shouting. Right? *Right?*"

"I hate that we have cotton balls," I hiss so that his daughter can't hear. I'm shoving boneless skinless chicken thighs behind the mountain of spinach Bruce insists upon, since his New Year's resolution to eat more salad. "I hate that we have a fully stocked first-aid kit. I hate that we have a storage bin with spare toothbrushes and spare bandages. I hate that we are prepared. I hate hate hate that we are prepared *for everything.*"

"So go be a kid again," he says. "Go over to your sister's and whine about your fortunate childhood. Go play drunk crybaby with your mommy and daddy."

"You bore me," I say, having no idea what's coming out of my mouth or why. "You and your family of three."

My left eyelid spasms, then my rib cage, then both knees. I want to tell him that I think I might faint. I want to tell him we should probably get me on the floor, onto my back, in case I start convulsing for real.

"Do I?" he says. "Do I bore you?"

Instead of backtracking, instead of saying, *Never mind,* instead of saying, *It's my sister, my mother, my sister, my father, my ex, my father, your daughter* . . . Instead of saying, *What I mean is that I am overwhelmed by it all, by life, this family, by work and my ex and the not knowing and because writing was so much easier when I had less, when I hurt more, when rent was tight and bananas were a luxury, when there wasn't so much to lose and there were fewer people to mind and to be mindful of and oh god there was so much more to say when the future was uncertain and I was scared—always so scared—that I couldn't pay my bills and wouldn't find an audience and* . . . Instead of saying any of this, which might have been the truth or at least closer to it, I close my eyes and lower my whole face into the refrigerator.

I gasp for air, and then I whisper, "Just not in a great place right now, you know?"

My arms fall to my sides. The fridge doors close onto my shoulders. My nose and forehead are pressed into a giant head of cauliflower.

I am trembling, and now Bruce is holding me, and I am ice and slime and sulfur, and I am gone.

On the other side of the planet, glacial tides beneath icebergs have inexplicably slowed. Orcas have begun attacking tourist boats. Monkeys in captivity are escaping. In Kentucky, an unexpected cold front moves east to west across the Appalachian Mountains. It's negative five degrees. Classes all over the state are canceled. It's unsafe to be outside.

My father shows up at my front door, on foot and unannounced. He is wearing a sports coat and a button-down. He isn't wearing gloves.

"How did you get here?" I ask.

"I feel worse than a knot on a dog's dick."

"How did you get here?"

"I walked."

We're standing on my front porch, which is slicked with ice. I'm shivering.

"You can't do this," I say. He is crying. Tears are crystallizing on his cheekbones. "I can't help you."

"I needed you to have this." He shoves a manila folder into my hands.

Behind me, from somewhere inside the house, Bruce is shouting at me to let my father inside.

"Do you need gloves?" I ask. "I can get you socks. You can wear them on your hands. You can't be outside in weather like this."

"I'm fine." He is already turned away from me; he is already leaving.

"The steps are slippery," I call to him. "Use the railing."

At the bottom stair, he pauses, turns, shouts up at me with open arms, "*I FUCKING LOVE YOU, YOU KNOW?*"

I nod, speechless.

Bruce pulls me inside, lets the storm door close, and takes the folder from my hands. "Offer him a ride," he says.

I look at him coolly.

"It's freezing out there," he says.

"I offered him gloves. He wouldn't take them."

"Offer him a ride," he says again.

I jerk the folder away from him and open it. Inside are my report cards from eighth grade, scribbled with handwritten feedback from my teachers. I flip quickly through the first few pages. *Hana is this Hana is that Hana is liked Hana needs to concentrate Hana is quiet Hana is withdrawn Hana is struggling Hana sits alone Hana is gaunt Hana is crying Hana is Hana is Hana is Hana is Hana.*

"*You* offer him a ride," I say. And Bruce does. And my father doesn't take it. And within the hour, the manic texting continues. He is home. He is safe. It is always the same. But somehow now it is the same and it is worse.

By morning, the ice will already be melting.

But tonight, before the sudden thaw, I will wake up crying, and Bruce will also wake up. He will hold me and tell me again that it's okay. He will ask me about my nightmare. I will tell him it wasn't a nightmare. It was a dream. It was my dead dog again, sleek and handsome and by my side. I will sob and sob, and Bruce will tighten his hold—a veritable ThunderShirt of a man—and if he knows I am lying, he doesn't say so, and I will be both relieved and let down when he doesn't say so.

The narrator of my second novel—her name is Kate—makes a partial list of the secrets she keeps track of each night as she lies awake in bed, unable to sleep. Is it plagiarism if I present the list again now for what it really is? The truth?

I wish more people liked me.

I wish people liked me more.

Sometimes I steal gum at the grocery store.

Sometimes at Starbucks I take someone else's order, even though I've paid for my own.

Sometimes in the middle of the day I go to the bathroom and undress completely and just stare at myself in the mirror. I always look different from the way I think I should. I am always 10 percent too tall, 10 percent too large, 10 percent not as good-looking as I want to be.

When I was fifteen, I taught myself to vomit after meals.

Sometimes, when I was married and after my husband had fallen asleep, I'd masturbate in bed next to him. I did it quietly. Sometimes I wanted him to catch me. He never did.

In the middle of the night now, I sometimes wake up and can't breathe just thinking of all the things I've accumulated. Several moving trucks' worth of junk. And I feel so empty and sad and weighed down by the emptiness. A house. A home. The idea of a home. Of a household. Of a family inside. A family of three. And another family just across the street.

Two

THE JOYS OF SLOW DISMEMBERMENT

PART TWO

EFFECTS OF LOW LEGAL LIMITS

My students would jump in here and say, "Okay, okay, we like this thing with the Irishman. We smell sex, we smell intrigue, and these are fragrances we enjoy. That said, is it too much of a convenience? You're bored? He's back in town?"

"Well, truth is often stranger than fiction and therefore—"

"Are you sure you even saw him? We didn't see you seeing him. Is this some sort of plot device?"

"Well, I—"

"Your sister is disappearing from the narrative."

"She's more of a choral figure, a foil, someone to bounce ideas off—"

"What's with your father? He's losing his mind? Are you also supposed to be losing your mind? Is that what's going on?"

"I don't know! I can't say! Maybe whatever is short-circuiting in him is also beginning to short-circuit in me. For instance, on the plane, I ordered vodka and—"

"Plane? What plane? There hasn't been a plane!"

"A hundred and fifty-eight pages from now. It's nine a.m., and I order vodka on the plane and—"

"Time hasn't collapsed," they say. "One universe at a time, please.

A little consistency? There's a difference between a mystery and a complete breakdown of order."

"Fine," I say. "Okay. One universe, one chapter, one time line at a time. Forget the plane. Forget the vodka. We'll come to that eventually."

"How about a vampire?" they ask. "Vampires solve a lot of problems. Vampires are sexy *and* scary. We like sex! We like scary!"

"No vampires," I say. "This is reality."

"Sort of this is reality."

"Yes, yes. Sort of this is reality."

"If not a vampire . . ." There is tittering, murmuring, perhaps it's Willow who pipes up with the idea, perhaps Mateo, perhaps one of the amorphous brunettes whose name begins with *K* or *M* or . . . "Have you considered"—more tittering, then—"a talking kitten? You never let yourself have any fun."

And so . . .

I hear the tabby's mewl before I see it. For several hours, in fact, I hear its call while I'm in the backyard pruning the roses and weeding the flower beds and not thinking about the Irishman, not thinking about my ex or my father or my nephews and their tiny peeing penises across the street.

When Bruce gets home from picking up his daughter from school, I tell him to leave the garage door open because there's a cat trapped in the rafters. This idea delights the eleven-year-old, who wants permission to climb up to the second floor and poke around. Bruce says, "No way." I whisper, "Maybe later."

The entire time they're outside with me—black-capped chickadees chirping, crows cawing, tulip poplars raining down their bloated shuttlecock blossoms—the cat doesn't mewl once, and I worry that it's died and now there's a dead cat in the rafters or, worse, that I've invented it.

Later, while they're biking around (something I don't do since I fell off a bicycle and sprained my ankle at a writers' residency ten years ago), I pull down the attic-style stairs in the garage and crawl up to the second floor.

Blood and shit, like horrible ink splotches, cover the several sheets of plywood that are balanced tenuously atop the rafters. I suck in air and cover my mouth and nose. It's a sauna up here, the smell baked and putrid. I'm about to clamber back down when I hear the mewl again—high, plaintive, scared.

"Cat," I whisper. "Cat, are you there?"

There's a light scrambling, a delicate scratching in a darkened corner of the eaves.

"Cat," I whisper. My hairline is damp, my upper lip slick with sweat. "Cat-cat?" I tap my fingernails lightly on the flooring in front of me. "Are you there?"

I'm here, the cat pules, almost indiscernibly.

My heart pitter-patters with the joy of an animal rescue and the discovery of an intelligible cat.

Later this evening, over dinner, I'll tell Bruce that I want my tombstone in some way to acknowledge my pastime as a savior of animals of all kinds—dogs and cats and turtles and reptiles. His daughter will say, "Turtles *are* reptiles." Bruce will say, "I thought you wanted to be cremated." His daughter will say, perky with curiosity, "What's that? Can I do it, too?" Bruce will say, "And also, I don't like to think of you being dead. It makes me sad. Please, can we stop playing this game?" His daughter will say, "It makes me sad, too." And I will wonder, as I eat fried chicken and drink white wine, *What is wrong with me? Why doesn't it make me sad to consider my death, his death, hers? Why does the contemplation of their deaths and mine register as math equations, while the possible passing of this strange cat turns my insides to jelly?* Even later—after dinner, past midnight, when I am awake and alone with my thoughts—I will wonder why, when I had the chance, I neglected to tell Bruce and his daughter that I located the injured cat, that it's equipped with a provocative vocabulary, and that it's currently sleeping in a Spanish boot box on the far side of the garage where no one who isn't looking would notice.

But to the cat, now, I call out, more loudly than before, "Where are you? Are you hurt?"

I'm here, you idiot, the cat hisses.

A fringe of orange fur comes into view across from me. It's barely detectible against the saffron of the plywood. I catch the glint of an eye. "Can you come to me?" I whisper.

I'm hurt, idiot human. Can you not see the blood and shit, like horrible ink splotches across the plywood?

"I can," I say, feeling rightly reprimanded. "I can see the blood! I'm sorry." Then, tempering my enthusiasm, lowering my voice to a purr, I ask, "What can I do?"

Bring me one of those small blanket thingies.

"A towel?"

A blanket thingy. A clean one. Cats like to be tidy, even injured ones.

"Okay," I purr. "You stay where you are, and I'll go get a towel."

Wait.

"Yes?" I'm already two rungs down, but I climb back up. I am so, so eager to please. "What is it? What more can I do? How may I be of additional service?"

Warm milk. Fresh water. A little kibble. A titch of shrimp if you have it, but only if you've just opened the can. Day-old shrimp is inedible.

I nod in agreement. Day-old shrimp *is* inedible. I say, meekly, "I don't have any kibble. Or shrimp, day old or otherwise."

What about the warm milk and fresh water? And the blanket thingy?

"How about we start with the towel? Milk and water's a lot for one human to carry up a steep ladder. If you climb into the towel, I can bundle you like a baby and carry you down. Then we can talk about sustenance."

The cat laughs darkly, but the laugh turns into something pained and wheezy. It spits out, *Stupid, useless human.*

"Yes," I say. "Yes, I agree. It's a sad state of affairs, this degraded humanity of ours. But hey!"

Quiet down. My ears . . .

In a dulcet tone, having remembered what's in the vegetable drawer—a treat for Bruce this weekend—I say, "I've got salmon. Currently unopened."

Is it . . . smoked salmon?

"Smoked . . . and citrus cured. How about I go get the blanket thingy, and you gingerly scoot your way over to the stairs?"

Go then, stupid human. Go forth and see what you can do for me.

I start to climb down again but stop. "Hey—cat? Are you, like, in heat? Is that what's with the blood?"

No, idiot human, I've been hit by a goddamn car.

Later—one day, maybe two, after the mewling in the garage—a knock on the door: a woman. Cut-offs and a crop top. Two brown teeth, front and center on the bottom. She's skinny, with a tremor across her brow that screams pills. Before I think better of it, I've opened the door.

"I'm looking for my cat," she tells me, and pulls out her phone to show me a picture.

I'm bobbing my head in disagreement before I've even looked.

Her cat got out, she's explaining, brow twitching, tongue darting. Her kid left the front door open, and the cat got out and was hit by a car, and they brought the cat back in and were trying to take care of it themselves, but her kid left the front door open again, and the cat— bleeding, injured—escaped a second time.

"I'm sorry, no. I haven't seen it." I barely glance at the photo in the woman's hand.

The eleven-year-old materializes at my side, reeking of boredom. "Isn't there a cat in the garage?" she asks.

"What? No." I flit away her comment, play dumb. "Nope. I was wrong about that."

"You said it was hurt?" The eleven-year-old looks at the photo of the cat. "Cute," she says. "Aw. I want a cat."

"Your dad's allergic," I say.

The woman takes a step inside, and I step back, angling myself so the eleven-year-old is more behind me than in front of me, a parental instinct that turns me queasy just to register it.

"You've got a cat in your garage?" the woman says, and the left side of her face spasms into a frown. "That's my cat." She holds up her phone again, high, so that it's right across from my face.

Sure enough, there's my injured tabby: same orange fur, same short tail.

I straighten my lips into an apology, still shaking my head no.

"Is that the same cat?" the eleven-year-old asks, bouncing a little, energized by the idea of a mystery solved.

"Listen—" I start to say.

"I've got a tracker," the woman says.

I look again at the screen. She's moved it from the cat to a map with a blinking icon. I peer a little closer.

"Oh!" I say. "But look. That's not our house. That's not even our street." I reach out to touch the phone, but she yanks it away.

I watch as she studies it, all the while worrying that my tabby might have run off from our garage only to be hit by yet another car or, worse, to be found later by this drug-addled woman with a kid who treats front doors like barn doors and who can't afford to—or won't!—give an injured cat the help it needs.

"Anyway," she says, darkening the phone. "Anyway, it was. I saw it. It was on your street and in your backyard. You've got my cat in your garage. The girl said so."

"Ma'am," I say, and my hands open up between us, performing a gorgeous gesture of the sincerity I am so perfectly faking. "Ma'am, I don't have a cat in my garage. There *was* a cat—I mean, I think there was a cat. It could have been anything. It was there, and now it's gone."

"How do you know it's gone?"

"Because it's my garage, and it's not there."

The woman checks her phone again. She's torn: follow the blinking dot or call the homeowner a liar in front of her kid, the kid who is just now giving a little shrug as if to say, *Yeah, everything my grown-up is saying checks out; also I'm bored; also I'm hungry; also who cares?*

The woman takes a step back, out of the house and onto the porch. She says, "How about I leave my number?"

"Sure," I say, grateful I could now slam the door closed if I needed to. "Great idea. You leave me your number. I'll call if anything happens." Then, to the eleven-year-old, I say, "Get a pen, will you?"

The eleven-year-old starts for the kitchen but then stops. "Can't you just plug it into your phone?"

"My phone?"

The woman says, "Yeah. Good idea. Just plug it into your phone. No pen required."

I fumble at my pockets. "Sorry. I don't know where my phone is." I push the eleven-year-old toward the kitchen. "Can you get us a pen, please?"

Mostly I'm being gentle, but the eleven-year-old stays put. "Can't she just plug *your* number into *her* phone?" she asks.

"She doesn't need my number," I explain. "I haven't lost a cat. I need *her* number."

The woman says, "Yeah. Duh. Of course. Give me your number, and I'll text you. Then you'll have it."

I open and close my mouth, stammering, "I—I . . ."

The eleven-year-old says, "I know it! Dad made me memorize it in case of an emergency."

Then, before I can stop her, she's correctly repeated my number twice, and the woman must have correctly recorded it because just as she's finally turning to leave, I feel a tiny—the teensy tiniest—vibration in my back pocket.

The woman stops short. She gives me a long, hard look. Then she looks at the eleven-year-old and smiles—a big pretty smile that unnerves me for how quickly and completely she's changed. "Thanks for your help, you," she says. "What's the name of this street again?"

The eleven-year-old, this sudden wellspring of information, says brightly, "Sycamore!" It's not her fault that she likes to be useful or that she wasn't raised in the eighties by a pack of rabid wolves.

"Sycamore," the woman repeats, pointing her smile in my direction. "I think I can remember that." And then, with a flash of a turn and a few fast bounds down the front stairs of the porch, she's on the sidewalk, jogging briskly out of sight.

I close and lock the door. *Fuuuuuuuuuck*, I think, and also: *Idiot human!*

The eleven-year-old looks up at me. "Do we have a cat in the garage?"

"Nope."

"But you said—"

"There *was* a cat in the garage."

"But you said—"

"The other day, while you and your dad were biking around, which is something I don't do because—"

"—because you sprained your wrist thirty years ago."

"Ten years ago. I'm not that old. Your dad is the old one. And it was my ankle."

"While we were out biking, you . . . ?"

"I found the cat. It was in the rafters just like I thought."

"So there *is* a cat in the garage! Why didn't you tell that woman?"

"The cat's gone," I say.

"It left?"

"Mm-hm."

"I thought it was hurt."

"Nope. Just in heat."

"What's 'in heat'?"

"It wants to have babies."

"Why?"

"That's a really good question," I say, glancing out the side window—no sign of the cat lady—and then walking into the kitchen. "And it's a question we'll have to ask your dad. I'm not being cagey, by the way. I would tell you why animals want to procreate, or even humans for that matter, if I understood, but I don't." I pat my stomach. "Case in point: no babies."

The eleven-year-old, who's followed me into the kitchen, says, "You've got *me*. I'm basically your baby."

"You're not a baby. You're a young girl. An old girl, really. An old girlie. A preteen. A tween! But you're not *mine*. You're mine adjacent."

"Basically, though. But that's not what I meant."

"I'm lost."

"Why didn't you tell her the cat was here? What's the big deal? Why didn't you just tell her it was here and now it's gone?"

I grimace. *Why indeed?* Then I nod. "Because," I say, "it wasn't the cat in the photo."

"It wasn't?"

"Nope."

"Are you sure?"

"Yep."

"How can you be sure?"

"Hers had a short tail. The one in the garage has a long tail."

Her eyes get big. "So it *is* in the garage! Can I see it? Can we keep it?"

"No!" I say, louder than I intend. Then, trying for calm indifference: "No, no, no, it's not in the garage. I just meant . . . Well, you know what I meant."

Her shoulders droop a little in defeat. Just like that: she believes me.

"Two lost cats," she says, more to herself than to me, then shakes her head in genuine wonderment, and my worry—at her capacious belief not just in the truth of the world but in the truth of me—swells so large in that moment I must actually catch my breath when I hear her murmur, almost wistfully, as she leaves the room, "What are the odds of that?"

The text reads, *Hot stuff.* And my very first thought—in its rawest state—is this: *Eat the phone; eat it; eat it now.*

My second thought, or realization, is that my legs are clenched, and my trachea is constricted.

The eleven-year-old is at her mother's for the night, and I am in the basement, sitting on an enormous velvet sectional that I purchased with a grant meant to improve the lives of mid-list and floundering writers. Bruce is upstairs, getting us both scoops of ice cream so we can finish watching the finale of the seventh season of *M*A*S*H.*

The number on my phone is restricted.

I listen to Bruce's movements in the kitchen overhead. The faucet is running. He's heating the scoop.

Who is this? I write.

Three dots appear, disappear, appear again. And then: *You know.*

I text: *this is a bad idea*

He texts: *hot. stuff.*

The water above me stops. He texts: *meet me.*

Somewhat spastically, my hands trembling from the effort, I delete the conversation and silence my phone. My entire body is vibrating.

Bruce, in stocking feet, comes down the basement stairs gingerly, a mug in each hand. Recently, he was forwarded the obituary of a former colleague who, at forty-something years old, was found with a broken neck at the bottom of his basement stairs. He'd been wearing socks. Even more recently, a current colleague of ours, about my age, was found in her entryway, also at the bottom of her stairs, her ribs cracked and her skull fractured. She'd been wearing rubber slippers, but the coroner's office issued a statement speculating she'd been tripped somewhere toward the top by one of her four cats. This is just to say: recently, Bruce is wary of stairs.

"Ready to watch?" he asks.

See me on the couch: cross-legged, breathless, in sweatpants, hair disheveled in a high bun; my T-shirt is worn thin, my stomach distended from dinner, my arm outstretched to receive a coffee cup filled with ice cream. See my ordinary life; see it ticking by one second, one hour, one television episode at a time.

I indicate my keenness to Bruce, hoping to appear composed, relaxed, living contentedly in the present and within the walls of our happy home. Inside, my pint-size shadow self is bounding up the stairs, phone in hand; she's in the bathroom, door locked, water running; she's opening her messages, desperate to know what more there is to read—words of seduction and betrayal. She is bouncing with agitation and confusion, throwing haymakers at the ceiling. *He wants me*, her tiny brain is screaming. *He wants me again after all this time.*

The other me wills my outer self to be still. *Eat the ice cream*, I tell my shell. *Take a bite. Do it now. Eat the fucking ice cream.* I do as I'm told.

"Pistachio," I say. "*Mmm.*"

"Strawberry," says Bruce, giving me side-eye.

I wink. "Duh."

What am I doing up there in that bathroom, alone and unsupervised, the door still locked and the water still running? Am I making smart choices? Can I be trusted? Or have I—the vampire having knocked, the door having been opened, the hostess having said, "Come in"— have I already gone too far?

Later, while Bruce is brushing his teeth—he's closed the door again—I chance a glance at my phone. There are five new messages, all within the last few minutes. Individual words pop out before I can slow down, pace myself, see exactly what he's written:

> *I'm going to get up, flirt with the hostess, and when I get back I expect*
> *you to be sitting in the seat next to me*
> *I'm back she gave me her number*
> *Haha*
> *last chance . . .*
> *Time's up, Hot stuff*

I read the messages twice, three times, try to memorize them. The water stops in the bathroom. There's the sound of Bruce's stream, then a flush. Woozy with nostalgia for something I can't have, I delete everything—*Time's up, Hot stuff*—and block the number. Can you even block a restricted number? I don't know. But I try. And there I am, phone tossed quickly out in front of me, on the bed, legs splayed like a rag doll's, when Bruce finally emerges from the bathroom.

"Leave the light on? Or?"

"On," I say. "I still have to brush."

He turns away and strips down to nothing, which is how he sleeps every night, regardless of the possibility of sex.

"Why did you close the door?"

"Come again?"

"Just now. To brush your teeth. You closed the door."

"Did I?"

"Are you catfishing me?"

"Am I what?" he asks, pulling back the covers and settling under them. He clicks off his bedside light and repositions his pillow to facilitate reading the news on his phone, which is something else he does every night, regardless of the possibility of sex.

He begins to scroll the news. I'm still sitting up, phone still tossed away from me as if it weren't a thing to which I was spiritually tethered, as if it were a meaningless sidekick and not a means to something forbidden, something dark, clandestine, irresistible for its wrongness.

I elbow him. "We were talking?"

His dimples flex but he won't look my way. I cover his screen with my hand.

He turns to me, gives me a look of extreme patience that he usually reserves for his daughter. "Dog-dog," he says, which is a sometime endearment between us, "it's bedtime. Brush your teeth. I'm reading. I have no idea what you're talking about. If I closed the door, it was unintentional." He removes my hand and returns to the news.

His forbearance is maddening. I want to rip the phone from his hands, jump on the bed, demand a bruise-inducing round of Dead Body. I want to shake us out of ourselves—pull his skin, bite his thighs, call each other by made-up names, fuck like strangers . . . Instead, I focus on my own silence, my own secrets. I plug my phone into its charger—deliberately leaving it visible on my side table—slip out of bed, and close the bathroom door behind me.

To the mirror, gritting my teeth, pinching my cheeks between my thumbs and forefingers until tiny red welts appear, I tell myself, *There's a reason people have affairs and that's because they're titillating. And there's a reason people don't have affairs, and that's because they're exhausting.*

Mateo approaches me at the statue outside the building of the English department. I'm waiting for Bruce, so we can walk to his car together. Bruce is late, but I'm not even annoyed, not yet, because I've been staring at my phone, at another text from a restricted number, one that came in while I was teaching. It's another invitation: *Meet me. Now.* Apparently, you can't block a restricted number.

I type the words: *I told you. This is a bad idea* and let my finger loiter above the blue arrow.

When Mateo stops short next to me, his shoulder suddenly against mine, I'm so startled and frightened that I push the message through.

"Hey," he says. "Watcha doing?"

"Excuse me?"

He gestures toward my phone, which I awkwardly pocket.

"You busy?"

"What? No. I'm waiting."

"You should be on TV," he says.

I take a deep breath and shake my head. "No."

From his back pocket, he produces a baggie of tobacco. "I can roll you one," he says.

"It's a smoke-free campus."

"I can just roll it for you."

"I'll pass. Thanks."

"I'm serious about television," he says.

Just then, Jane wafts from our building, an ankle-length raincoat catching like a seventeenth-century poet's in the wind. She flashes me a hang ten. "Rock star," she calls out. "Total rock star." I have no idea what she's talking about.

"What are you doing later?" Mateo asks. It's like he hasn't seen Jane, didn't register her funny remark.

I take a step back and look up at him. "You shouldn't be talking to me like you're my peer."

"You'd be great on TV, reviewing books or something."

Jane disappears down the sidewalk. I look at my watch. Bruce is nearly fifteen minutes late. *Now* I am annoyed.

"You have a physical presence," he says.

"Are you flirting with me, Mateo? Because you should not be flirting with me."

"Are you flirting with *me?*"

I glance quickly over both shoulders. Anyone could be watching this, listening to this—to me, a professor, being spoken to by this . . . this . . . *person*. But the quad is empty.

"Who are you waiting for?" he says.

"None of your business."

"You're divorced but you have a boyfriend, who's also a professor." He's grinning. "I gotcha. Okay. I get it. You have a type."

"What do you want, Mateo?" I tighten my watchband as though doing so will magically conjure Bruce.

Mateo says, "Your husband has a book coming out."

I whip my face in his direction. "How do you know that?"

"I read the newsletters."

"Newsletters?"

"The trades. The weeklies. You know."

"I don't have a husband."

"The synopsis sounded dot dot dot *familiar*."

"What do you do for a living, Mateo? What exactly is your job? At this university?"

"You know the thing about the student who taught his class?"

"How do you know all this? Really?"

"That was me! I was the student. I mean, he flubbed some because he describes me as a twenty-year-old undergrad and not as an employee, but still. That was me. I taught his class." He angles back on his heels, his chest puffed. It's a gesture of triumph? He's bragging? "I had no idea that I was quote-un-quote aiding and abetting."

"You mean he *fibbed*, not *flubbed*."

"If I told you I was an electrician, would you assume I'm good with my hands?"

"I'm not talking about my ex with you."

"Why didn't we workshop my story last semester?"

"Give me a break, Mateo. Please?"

"Just tell me why?"

"Because it wasn't appropriate."

Last fall, Mateo handed in a story about an older woman—"plump, borderline sexy, but not what she once was, and certainly not nearly what she thinks she is currently"—who's a has-been playwright and now a deadbeat teacher at a community college in a nameless but dreary-as-Detroit city. The teacher in Mateo's story is also a known flirt who openly plays favorites and who scribbles cheat sheets on her palm to remember the girls' names in her class but not the boys'.

In Mateo's story, this plump teacher—sitting across from a male student at a bar—masturbates beneath the zinc countertop. This public act is a dare. The teacher and her star student are drunk. Flirting, she tells the student, "One day I'll be asking *you* for a recommendation." The teacher, slurring, goes on: "One day I'll be an anecdote, nothing more. I'll deny it—whatever you tell them about us. You'll get famous writing plays about me. You'll love the rumors. You'll never tell them who it was—this older professor—but they'll all know, and you'll love that they know." In the margin, I wrote, *issues of consistency*. I circled the word "zinc" and wrote, *relevant detail?*

In the story, the teacher professes that what she hates about best practices and equal opportunities and sexual politics in the academy and the hashtag movements of the twenty-teens is that she never got to take proper advantage of the way things used to be. Next to this, I wrote, *not synonymous*. Then I drew a large equal sign and through it made a long slash.

"Men," the teacher says, between sips of her umpteenth gin and tonic, "ruined it for us, for women. And it's unfair. We should have gotten a proper stab at it before they took it fully away." *Provocative*, I wrote, *but unearned*.

In the story, the teacher is married to another teacher and is known to be having an affair with yet another and known additionally to be somewhat of a she-wolf when it comes to her students. Here I checked the page number, then I wrote, *ROR—rate of revelation is off. You're introducing new and unbelievable material with only a few graphs to go.*

On the last page, after a decent but purple description of the teacher in her fourth-floor office looking longingly at the pink-lit snow accumulating delicately atop a gazebo in a private courtyard across the street, I wrote, *Grasping, don't you think?*

On the morning we were supposed to discuss it, I tore up Mateo's story along with all my notes and sent an email to the class informing them that my father was in the ER and we'd need to reschedule. I never did.

"Why wasn't the story appropriate?" Mateo asks. "Because it was about you?"

If I were drinking water—if I were drinking *anything*—I'd have spewed it out my nose when he says this. Instead, I spit out the words: "It wasn't *about* me."

"Sort of."

"You have a rich fantasy life."

"So what's fair?"

"Meaning?"

"What's off-limits? When I'm writing?"

"*I'm* off-limits."

"*You're* off-limits?"

"Yes."

"Why can your ex write about you, but I can't?"

"You weren't writing about me, and neither is my ex. We didn't workshop your story because you can't use fiction as a means of making false accusations about living people. It's unethical. Fiction isn't a platform for revenge."

"Not according to Elizabeth Hardwick," he says.

Overhead, a red-tailed hawk—one of the half dozen that nest on window ledges across campus—circles. Maybe it thinks we're prey. Certainly, I feel like prey.

"Please," I say quietly, as the hawk spirals up and into the clouds and out of view. "Enough. You win. I don't care. But please, please go away before someone sees us standing here talking like we're friends."

"We *are* friends."

"No, we're not."

"What would happen?"

"I wouldn't like it," I say. "Your classmates wouldn't like it." I realize I'm shivering but also sweating.

"Which classmates?" he asks.

"Pardon?"

"Which classmates wouldn't like to see us talking?"

"I didn't mean to say that."

"Just kidding," he says, pinching tobacco into a neat and thin line along the crease of a rolling paper. "I know who you mean."

"You couldn't possibly," I say, "because *I* don't know who I mean. You're my student. It doesn't matter who sees us talking. That's all I mean."

"It's not that they don't like you," he says. "It's that they don't like each other because of me."

I can feel the arrhythmic pulse of my aorta, the quickening pump of my lungs. "Mateo, are you . . ." I begin to ask, looking over his shoulders, scanning for any sign of Bruce, any sign of anyone. "Are you trying to put me in my place? Because I feel . . . I feel like you're both flirting with me and trying to put me in my place, which is absurd." Then, after a beat, I quickly add, "Not to mention unacceptable."

He squints a little, then gives me an amused smile. "If I were trying to put you in your place, I'd say you're too old for me. But you're not, and I appreciate everything you said just now. I appreciate you saying it out loud." Carefully, with dramatic precision, like he's performed this bit a million times before, in front of a million different women, he very deliberately—with the flattened tip of his tongue—licks the length of the paper he's been rolling. When he's finished, he tucks the cigarette behind his ear and says, "You say a lot of things out loud that you probably shouldn't."

"Are you threatening me?"

He laughs. "We should get a drink."

"No."

"The last thing I'm doing is threatening you, Teach."

"Can't you leave me alone now?"

"One drink."

"I don't drink with students."

"Sure you do."

"Never one-on-one," I say.

In the distance, I catch a glimpse of Bruce, finally, heading in our direction.

"Never one-on-one," he repeats. "I can make that happen." And then, as if he's sensed Bruce's approach, he says abruptly, "Catch you later." Then he turns and walks away. Just like that. He's here, and then he isn't.

Bruce gives a big grin when he sees me. I am aware of the skin on my face, a tingling in my ears, a chill across my shoulders . . . I am incredibly embarrassed. I am incredibly turned on. And I am very, very scared of myself.

The tabby is swaddled in a towel in a box in the passenger seat of my car, and it won't shut up. It wants to know why I sent its mother away. It wants to know what the plan is here. It wants to know why the salmon tasted like lemons instead of like fresh dead fish. It wants to know where I'm taking it. It wants to know why its mother's kid kept leaving the front door open in such an alluring fashion. It wants to know about squirrels and hummingbirds and especially those cute little chipmunks. It wants to know if I've ever eaten chipmunk, and it seems annoyed and put out when I say that I haven't. *Have you at least played a chipmunk to death? Swatted it and batted it and broken its bones? Please tell me you've at least known the joys of slow dismemberment and the crunch crunch crunch of thin bones cracking.* I assure the cat I am deficient here as well. The cat tells me it's in pain, real pain. It hurts all over, especially in its belly. "I know, I know," I say, driving my neighborhood in circles as I figure out a plan. *Can't you just keep me?* "No," I say, "I'm sorry." The cat wants to know why, and so I explain my love for animals and how it triumphs my love for humans. "I'm an animal person," I say. "The eleven-year-old and her father aren't. They think they are, but they aren't." *What does that even look like?* "You know, they say 'down, down, down' to a dog that hasn't even nosed them when 'off' is what they really mean." *Fun fact: cats don't pay attention to either of those commands because cats don't care about diddly!* "I worry I'd stop loving them if we ever got a pet. When we moved in, they asked for a puppy. I said no. Then they asked for a young dog. I said no to that as well. They asked for an old dog, a rescue dog, an aged kitten, a foster guinea pig, a parakeet. No, no, no, no, no." The cat doesn't understand the problem. *So don't keep them*, it says. *Keep me. I'm lovable.* "It's not that easy," I say, taking the roundabout on South Hanover for the third time. "I own a house with him. And she thinks of me as a stepmother." *Are you married?* it asks. "Only in our hearts," I say. *Ditch the humans*, it says. *Pick me. Choose me!*

My phone vibrates. I pull over outside a gorgeous stone manor with the kind of slate roof I'm always threatening Bruce I'll put on our house the minute he's dead.

Meet me, says the text.

Who is it? asks the tabby.

"None of your business," I say, my thumbs hovering.

I'm dying. Tell me who you're texting.

"You're not dying. You're hurt. You don't even know what texting is."

I'll scream, the cat says, and then, before I can respond, it lets out a grizzly yowl the likes of which I've never heard before. I cover my ears. "Stop it," I cry. "Stop it!" The yowl gets louder, grizzlier. "It's a man," I yelp, my ears still covered, my eyes clenched shut. The yowling stops.

Thank you, the tabby says. *I thought you already had a man.*

"I do have a man," I say.

The tabby says nothing.

"It's complicated. This one is Irish."

The tabby, self-righteous, purrs.

My phone vibrates: *Tell your boyfriend you're meeting your dad for a drink.*

Not thinking, I text back immediately: *you know my father?*

He writes: *everyone knows your father meet me*

I write: *I have a sick cat*

He writes: *sorry?*

I write: *in the car*

He writes: *bring the cat*

I write: *no*

He writes: *what? You're in this thing with your boyfriend for the long haul?*

I delete the entire string of texts.

I look at the cat, who is licking itself in a visibly performative fashion. "You're not going to ask?"

Does he want to adopt me?

"No."

Then I'm not interested.

I drive back home, a now-silent cat in tow. Before pulling into the drive, I confirm that Bruce's car is still gone.

I scoot my seat as far back as it'll go then pull the box with the cat onto my lap. I lower my face for a forehead bump. Its sea-green eyes and mine are very close. "I like you, cat," I say.

I tolerate you.

"I like talking to you."

Go on.

"New plan. Tomorrow, I'll take you with me to school. I'll take you to my class. I've got a lot of cat ladies in my workshop. Like, really, they write stories about their love for cats."

Tell me more.

"One of them will take you. I guarantee it. And they'll get you help. And give you a forever home. They'll probably let you sleep in bed with them."

What about other cats?

"Do you want another cat?"

Absolutely not.

"I can make that a provision. I'm the teacher. What I say goes."

You're a god?

"No, a teacher."

People do what you tell them to do?

"Not people, students. But, to be honest, which is something I'm trying to do lately, sort of, students don't really listen to me either. They ignore me. Or they ignore my advice. But in this instance, regarding you, a cat, who is in my possession, what I say goes. Feedback they can ignore, but rules regarding animals are not to be fucked with."

What's a workshop?

"Young people sitting around writing stories about themselves in third person."

The cat belches. Then says, *What do you write about?*

"I'm a chronicler of the everyday mundanities of life."

Huh?

"One woman's odyssey through the ordinary."

What's the through line?

"I'm the through line."

Hm.

"My ex has written a book about me. About him and me. But I haven't read it yet."

Ooh! purrs the tabby, licking itself again. *Drama! Drama! Drama!*

"It's fiction. So I can't disagree with it. Because it's not real. But the fake me—the one he invented—doesn't come across well. That's what I've heard. And it's driving me kind of mad, you know? Being someone else's character and having no say in the matter."

How are you?

"In real life?"

In the book?

"Smug. Narcissistic. Vaguely unhinged."

How are you in real life?

"Smug. Narcissistic. Vaguely unhinged."

That's funny. Are you sure you don't just want to keep me for yourself? We could do this forever . . . My phone vibrates again. It's under the cat's box, which is still in my lap.

That feels funny, the cat says. *I like it. Do it again.*

I put the box back on the passenger seat. *Party pooper,* says the cat, then dramatically turns away from me and gazes out the window.

There's a new text, but it's not from him. It's from the woman, the tabby's mom, who I've saved in my phone as Crazy Tabby Mommy. It says, *Have you seen my cat? The tracker stopped tracking.*

Who is it? asks the cat, slowly turning back to face me. *That man again?*

I write, shielding the screen on the off chance it can read: *I haven't. Promise to keep you posted okay? Good luck.*

She writes: *Promise?*

I write: *yes promise geez.* I delete *geez* and push send.

Tell me, snarls the cat.

"Yes," I say. "Yes. It was that man again, but I've gotten rid of him. He won't bother us again."

Good.

"What do you want for dinner? I'm going to set you up in my garden nook behind the garage for the night. If you stay put until morning, I'll find you a nice coed with a soft belly and an even softer mattress who will spoil you to pieces and love you in proportion to the depths of your hatred for her."

I want tuna. And warm milk. And baby shrimp. And leg of chipmunk.

"I can get you the tuna."

Human grade.

"Human grade," I say.

Have you told your friend Jane about me?

"How do you know about Jane?"

She gets great light.

"She already has two cats."

Are they old? Maybe they'll die soon.

"They're practically kittens."

Maybe they'll get hit by a car.

"They're indoor cats."

Losers. Does she know about your extra man?

"I don't have an extra man."

Does she know about the texting?

"She doesn't need to know."

What about that student?

"Have you been spying on me?"

Tuck me in. Tighter. Tighter. I'm sleepy. My butt cheeks feel like they've been tenderized by a hammer.

"Do you—"

No more talking.

My mother shows up at our side door with grapes, a bottle of wine, and a five-page list of everything she still owns. The taxidermy, the Oriental rugs, the jewelry, the antique furniture, the quilts, the mirrors, the paintings, the photographs, the turtle shells, the glass eyes, the ostrich eggs—they're all there.

Bruce pulls out her chair, takes the wine, swaps it with one of ours, and pours us all a glass.

"The Canadian wants to visit," she says. "He wants to spend the night and take me to brunch."

"Is that a good thing or a bad thing?" I ask.

"He wants to take me to *brunch*."

"And?"

"You know how I feel about brunch."

Do I know how my mother feels about brunch? I know how she feels about horses, well-dressed men, hats worn inside, hats worn backward, children who talk too much or require too much attention, salted butter, cream cheese, gin and tonics, margaritas . . .

I say, "I know how you feel about eating more than one meal in a day."

"Your mother hates brunch," Bruce says.

I squint my eyes at him, at this man who lives in my house and sleeps in my bed and to whom, ostensibly, I am married in my heart.

"How do you know about my mother and brunch?" I ask.

He says, "For someone who thinks she pays attention to the smallest details, you really miss a lot."

My mother hands me her life's possessions. She says, "I printed a copy for your sister, too. I want you to go through and put your initials next to everything you might want. We need to talk about what happens when I die."

Bruce says, "What's with this family and its fixation on death?"

I tuck her five-page list into the junk drawer. "We did this last year," I tell my mother. "We've already divvied up your stuff. We don't need to do it again."

"We did? Well, I can't find that list. This is a new one. It's updated. We have to start over."

Bruce shakes his head. In the five years we've been together, my mother has produced no fewer than five lists.

On the other side of the street, my father is parking his orange MINI. My mother notices and says, "Is he coming here? Is that man coming here?"

I shake my head, and the three of us watch as he hobbles his way to my sister's front porch.

"If nothing else," my mother says, "he was at least competent. That's more than I can say for my other husbands."

"He's not dead," I say.

"Right after we were married—have I told you this?—right after we were married he took me to British Columbia. We drove up in the 280SL that we'd imported from Germany. We drove it into a forest. That little sports car. Into a forest . . ."

I get out my phone and, as nonchalantly as I can, turn on the recorder. Bruce sees me, rolls his eyes, but says nothing.

I ask, "Was there at least a path?"

"There was a kind of narrow dirt lane. We had a map. He was an excellent reader of maps. We wanted to explore. So we took the 280 into the woods. We came to a little river. Your father looks at me and gives me this smile and then down into the river we drive. Whoopsy-daisy."

"And?" Bruce asks.

"And the car dies!"

"In the river?"

"I'm thinking to myself, *The engine is flooded. It's this. It's that. Something is broken.* Yes, we're in the water, and he gets out, and he starts improvising, and I'll be damned if a few minutes later he didn't get the car going, and we were able to get someplace farther on in the forest. We parked the car and hiked."

"Was that the plan?" asks Bruce. "There was a plan, right?"

"We stayed the night in this—because he was also able to find it on this really nebulous kind of map, this kind of 'I'll meet you at the airport' map—we got to this cabin, and it was really dark by then, and I was terrified." She laughs. Her glass is already empty.

"This wasn't part of a plan?" Bruce asks.

"We spend the night in this cabin while this thing, this creature is outside going—" My mother thwacks her hands together loudly.

"I'm so confused," says Bruce.

"We went into this empty cabin, and outside this thing was walking around. The cabin had three rooms. Two bedrooms and a main room and—"

"You broke into this place?" I ask.

"It was British Columbia. There were no furnishings. It was the kind of cabin you go into if you're out in the woods alone. It's just shelter."

I say, "Just an empty cabin in the woods."

She says, "A kind of place you go when there's nowhere else to go."

I say, "Just the kind of empty cabin in the woods you go into when there's nowhere else to go."

"Yes," she says. "We got in, and I immediately went into one of the empty rooms—with this thwacking thing outside going all around—and I had the most ferocious diarrhea and nothing to wipe with."

I cut in again: "There's a toilet, though, right?"

Bruce looks disparagingly first at me and then at my phone, still recording.

"There's no toilet," my mother says. "There's a coffee can."

Bruce barks a laugh of surprise.

"You could have gone outside," I say.

"For sure I was *not* going outside because this thing"—she's thwacking again—"this thing is going all around the cabin—*crrr crrr crrr*—and it's scratching at the windows, and I thought, *grizzly bear brown bear wolverine I am not going out there.* So the next day your father—"

"Wait," says Bruce. "So there's something outside, and you two . . . you just decide to go to bed?"

"We go to bed."

"On the floor?"

"On the floor."

"And the coffee can is?"

"Hiding in the other room. And the next day your father walks outside. It's this beautiful sunny day and I say, 'Just do not go in that room. Do not go in that room.' And he says, 'Oh, there's a lake!' So now here's this big lake, and it's a beautiful glacier lake. It's not huge but it's gorgeous. He walks down partway and shouts, 'Come down with me,' and I thought *Lake's here, cabin's here, thing-creature walking around . . . nah-ah, not for me . . .* I shout, 'I'll wait here. You go on.' He keeps going down. There's some sort of raft he goes out on. He catches fish, comes back—"

I ask, "Did you get rid of the diarrhea?"

"No, I didn't get rid of the diarrhea because I would have had to go outside. I was just waiting for him to come back and then we . . ." She trails off. "I mean to say only that he's competent. He is hugely, admirably competent, even useful."

Bruce sings, "*Your mom likes your dad!*"

"I don't!" she says. "I *admire* his ability to— Because, listen, my second husband would look at something and say, 'It doesn't fit; it's not going to work,' and he'd go kick a piece of furniture. My next husband would say, 'I don't know; I can't do it; let's hire someone; I'll call someone in the morning.' Your father had admirable, get-'em-done qualities."

"Compelling," I say.

"Would I want to spend five minutes alone with him in this kitchen?

No." She pushes her empty wineglass toward Bruce. "But if I'm dying on a plane—Of the three? Sure, I choose him. Because if he weren't able to fix the problem, I would be so ready to die just listening to him verbalize his shock at his own uselessness that crashing would be okay."

My phone buzzes. It's a text from my sister: *There's a cat in your garage.*

I text, *don't touch it please. And don't say anything.*

My mother says, "Are you turning on your recorder? Because you won't trick me into repeating anything I just said."

I text, *Why are you in my garage?*

She texts, *I'm loaning Dad your leaf blower.*

I text, *Don't tell Bruce.*

My father texts, *I'm at Sissy's. Come on by if you want champagne I'm opening*

I turn off my recorder and say to my mother, "I'm not recording."

"Who wants the library table?" she asks.

"I get the library table," I say.

"What's a library table?" asks Bruce.

My mother and I stare at him; then she says, as if to a simpleton, "To go in a *library?*"

In bed with Bruce, lights off, fan whirring, somewhere north of 10:00 p.m.—

HANA: You don't delete messages, do you?

BRUCE: What kind of question is that?

HANA: Do you send anybody the types of messages that you'd need to delete?

BRUCE: Do you?

HANA: Would you tell me? If you did?

BRUCE: Of course not.

HANA: 'Of course not' about writing illicit messages or 'of course not' you would tell me?

BRUCE (*deep sigh*): I wouldn't tell you. This isn't a successful line of questioning. I dislike it. But I'd also eventually like to get some sleep tonight, so I'll play along. If I were writing illicit messages and deleting them and you asked me this, I would tell you that I wasn't writing illicit messages—else, why delete them?—but I'd also tell you that of course I'd come clean if I were doing such a thing. But I'm not.

Hana: I don't like this.

Bruce: You started it.

I had a boyfriend when I was in grad school who once asked me about my family's fixation on death. He was a chef, and even though we hadn't been dating long, I let him move in with me. My sister and I were renting a giant white house on East High Street in Charlottesville. We had plenty of room, too much room.

My ex, not yet my husband, not even yet my boyfriend, introduced me to the chef, who was skeletal and covered in tattoos. One time, the chef picked up a photograph of me that had been taken while I was at a writers' seminar in Russia. He said, "You were really thin then. I like how you look." I'd been both bulimic and anorexic when the picture was taken. I said, "I almost died when I got home. That's how skinny I was." He said, "Still. You look good."

When he moved in, my stepfather—the furniture kicker—was in hospice, having turned yellow with cancer just like his father, and my sister was living on the second floor with a boyfriend I didn't like. A few years later, I wrote a novel about our time in that house on High Street. It never sold. In the book, my sister is an eccentric knockout married to a deadbeat, who is also the narrator. I am the wife's awkward and mysterious younger sister who lives with the couple in their big, dilapidated house. At some point, our father dies. A few weeks later, my sister vanishes. A few weeks after that, I vanish, too. The narrator never finds us.

In my real life, the night my stepfather died, I called to tell the chef. A few days earlier, I'd driven home to the Eastern Shore, to a different farmhouse, whose den my mother had turned into a temporary hospital room so that my stepfather might die in comfort, or at least surrounded by the familiar.

Back then, I sometimes liked to walk around my mother's house pretending to have the eyes of a stranger. In her farmhouse, there was a zebra-skin rug with the mane and tail intact, as well as a lion-skin rug with its entire head still attached. There were gazelle antlers, elk antlers, and buffalo horns; there was an accidentally illegal Machynlleth crocodile skull and a largetooth sawfish rostrum whose origin in my mother's life predated its status as endangered. There were several dozen skeletons, a giant tortoise shell, and a Victorian birdcage with taxidermized songbirds that sang when you turned a lever. There were butterflies and beetles and prayer rugs and a few birds of prey in the deep freeze that she'd found on the property and one day hoped to stuff. On top of the fridge, there was a bottle of fingernail polish remover filled with years' worth of dead deer ticks. By the time a stranger made their way to the den, which was many rooms deep into the house, the dying man in the hospital bed might not have seemed so unusual.

Before I could tell the chef my news, he told me he'd totaled his car, gotten a DUI, spent the previous night in jail, and only just gotten back to our place. I hung up the phone.

A few weeks later, he came home from a dinner shift to find me crying in our living room. "What are you crying about?" he asked.

I looked at him dumbly. "My stepfather," I said.

"Oh," he said. "I didn't realize we were still dealing with that." Then he asked, "What's with your family and death? It's like you're fixated."

After Pops died, my sister and I received letters from the state of Maryland informing us we were orphans. With only seven months left to live, he'd adopted us. To make it official, we'd had to ask our father to disinherit us. There was paperwork involved. It was ugly and sad.

According to the state of Maryland, we were orphans, and our mother didn't exist. Cackling with delight, we called to tell her.

The chef and I lasted only a few months. I came home one night from my own dinner shift at a different restaurant and found him passed out and spread-eagle on the floor. In his right hand was a chef's knife. In his left was a torn piece of paper covered in his chicken scrawl. At his side was an empty bottle of bourbon. I closed the door without taking a step inside and walked upstairs to my sister's half of the house. Without saying anything, I communicated that she and her boyfriend should follow me. They did, and together the three of us walked downstairs and into my living room.

For several minutes we watched the chef without comment. Then my sister took the handwritten note, and her boyfriend took the knife, and I confirmed he was still breathing.

Back upstairs, we took turns reading the note aloud, which began, *Dear World.* We regarded the entire scene as hilarious not because we were bad people but because he wasn't truly suicidal and because Pops had just died and because, legally, we were orphans and because nothing just then could compare to our year of watching a man decay into a strip of human jerky no thicker than a blanket.

That winter, late at night, after the chef had been kicked out, my sister would sometimes knock on my door already wearing a pair of full-body camouflage Carhartts. She'd hand me my matching pair, and I'd suit up, and we'd walk four blocks to Fellini's—through the same park where several years later there'd be a riot and a girl would be murdered—and we'd sit at the bar in our hunting suits. Sometimes we'd take the letter from the state and allow unappealing older men to pity us and buy us drinks. We must have looked like lunatics, but we also felt like lunatics, unmoored, unparented, unqualified for our lives as grown-ups, which we were, at least according to age and circumstance. I remember feeling very young then—not youthful, but *young*, naïve, a child suddenly in a woman's body but with barely an adolescent's basic understanding of the world around her.

As I drive the cat to school—having feigned late-afternoon office hours in order to take my own car—it says to me, *This sister of yours, she lives across the street.*

"How do you know that?"

I know things.

"She and her boys and her husband live across the street."

How's that going?

"I like it. I didn't think I would, but I do."

What about your boyfriend-husband?

"How do you know to call him my boyfriend-husband?"

I know things. I told you. You're kind of slow?

"He probably liked it better when it was just us. He probably thinks my sister's influence turns me juvenile."

Does it?

"Probably."

I miss my real mom.

"Cat, listen, that woman told me your story. She's not going to get you help. And her kid's going to keep leaving the front door open, and you're going to keep escaping, and then you'll get hit again, and then you'll die."

I was talking about my cat mom.

"Sorry. I misunderstood."

It's okay. She's dead.

"Sorry."

You didn't kill her.

"I meant in the Yiddish sense—sorry she's dead."

She got hit by a car.

"Oof!"

I come from a long line of cats killed by cars.

"I come from a long line of grifters and con artists and liars."

Have you ever killed a cat?

"No," I say. Then, feeling wistful about my dwindling time with this tabby with whom I've already formed a troubling and deep, though very likely one-sided, bond, I say, "I had a dog . . ."

Tell me about him?

I have a sense the cat's being cruel, that it would like to make me cry, but I don't care. I'm a sucker for any excuse to talk about him. "His name was Elmer," I tell the cat, as we begin circling the university parking structure's upward drain. "He was a Boxer–Bluetick hound mix. He weighed seventy-four pounds and had four white socks. He could catch, roll over, sit, stay, and shake. Road trips turned him calm. Thunderstorms turned him jumpy—as did lightning, heavy rain, hotel rooms, swimming pools, empty houses, other dogs, and strange men. On the rare morning I slept past eight, he'd stand on my side of the bed and stare at me until I woke up. We called him the Creep."

Who called him the Creep?

"My ex and me."

Oh.

I go on: "But he was our creep, and we loved him and treated him like a child. When friends told stories about their children, I'd respond with an anecdote about Elmer. To couples I didn't know well, I often neglected to point out that he was a dog. 'When Elmer can't sleep,' I might say, 'we put him in the car and go for a drive.' 'Oldest trick in the book,' some father might say back. 'We do it all the time.'"

I'm not sleepy, says the cat. *And I'm in a car.*

"You're not a dog. Dogs are more like human babies than cats."

What happened to him?

I confess to the cat—more than I've confessed aloud to another human ever—that I killed Elmer in December, four days before my thirty-ninth birthday. The cat looks over at me, worried about how this story will end, worried now about how its own story might end.

I ignore its fear and tell it that the night before I took my dog to the vet, he and I stayed up late, and I tried to explain it to him—how in Chicago, only a few years earlier, he'd bitten a woman on the arm. She was old, and her skin was like onion paper, and we almost didn't think it had happened. But then we looked down and watched as a long red line appeared on her forearm and blood poured out. The woman let me take her to the emergency room. I begged her not to report him. There was a chance in Illinois that we'd have been required to put him down.

In Kentucky, where my husband and I moved a year later, Elmer's anxiety increased. He finally had his own backyard, but he hadn't grown up with a backyard, he'd grown up on a leash, and he didn't like to be outside alone. This drove my husband crazy—one more way in which our new state had let us down.

"We moved here for him," my husband said. "We moved here to give him space, and he doesn't even want it."

"We didn't move here for him," I said. "We moved here for us."

"Maybe I don't want it," he said.

"Don't want what?"

"Whatever we moved here for," he said.

Elmer was with us for every fight, and in Kentucky there were many. He whimpered constantly through his nose, a high-pitched insistence of discomfort and sadness. He whined to go outside, he whined to come inside, he whined to play, to sleep, to be near us. He didn't especially like to eat.

The tabby interjects, *Did he ever try squirrel?*

"He is the only dog I've ever known who didn't like food—canned, fresh, or otherwise."

Me-wow!

We've come to a stop on the fifth floor of the parking structure in a spot near the exit. "I don't have to finish the story."

Keep going, it says.

A few coeds walk by—none of them my students—and one happens to glance in the car. She sees the tabby and smiles. Then she sees me talking and scowls. She trots to catch up with her girlfriends and whispers something. All of them turn back to look at us, even as they're still moving away, and they break into spastic back-bending laughter. *One day*, I think to myself, but do not say aloud to the cat, *one day those young women will become middle-aged women—they'll have jobs, marriages, affairs, children, bills, houses, pets . . . One day, they will understand the subtleties of the world, the absurdity and sadness and isolation of what it means not just to be alive but to be alive and a middle-aged woman on the brink of invisibility.*

To the cat, I am saying, "Two years after we moved to Kentucky, my husband and I divorced. There were only two things I wanted, and I kept them both—the house and the dog. By then, Elmer had become untrustworthy. He snapped at everything that moved that wasn't me. A friend of my mother's came to visit. When she saw Elmer—a true beauty of a dog, you have to believe me—she opened her arms expansively and cried, quite loudly, 'Who's this gorgeous hound?'"

Uh-oh . . .

"Before she'd finished the sentence, her thigh was in his mouth."

I explain to the cat that my vet agreed he'd become a liability. By this time, we'd tried drugs. We'd tried training. Nothing helped. The day I finally drove him to the clinic, Elmer sat in the back seat with his favorite toy, a monkey with ropes for arms and legs. At the hospital, the tech asked me if I wanted to leave him. "Leave him?" I said, nearly frantic with grief. "Leave him?" She told me it was too painful for some people to witness. I was appalled. "I'll stay with my dog," I said.

I look at the cat, who is shaking its head sadly in disbelief.

"She led us to a room at the back of the building, pulled the blinds, and left. I sat on the floor and Elmer sat in my lap. He and I waited for the vet."

Then what happened?

"That's it. That's the end."

Oh, says the tabby, and then, after a moment, understanding having set in, *I'm sorry.* The cat pauses again before adding, *In the Yiddish sense.*

As I'm walking the cat in the box across campus, it interrogates me about my ex and the book he's written in which I play the part of an embarrassingly successful she-wolf (to borrow Mateo's expression). I explain that, while annoying, it's also a relief to know finally of the book's existence.

"Like a roof taking on water," I say. "Conclusively, you know. And you can begin to make plans for how to fix the problem."

It looks at me, expressionless.

"Are you comfortable in there?" I ask. "I'm trying not to jostle you too much."

It's okay, the cat says. *To be honest, I'm a little bit nervous. I'm feeling uncertain and sad about what's about to happen. Like, I've never been to summer camp, obviously, because I'm a cat, but I've got this feeling in my stomach that's like a Ferris wheel of fireflies.*

"Homesickness," I say.

Or maybe it's just my internal injuries from being hit by a car.

My phone does its Morse code, and I carefully shift the box so that it's clutched between my forearm and my stomach. It's a text from Bruce: *Say hi when you get here? I'm in my office. Some kid was parked outside your door. He's gone now.*

At a bench, I pause and put the box down. The cat has its eyes closed and is purring softly. I position the box so that a little ray of sun hits the cat's face. Eyes still closed, it leans into the light, and I swear I see the flicker of a smile. And that's when I know it's happening. That's when I feel that I am falling for the cat, that I'm a little bit lovesick.

Though it's all I want to do in the world at this moment, I resist the urge to run my fingernails against the grain of its fur and across the line of its jaw.

I text Bruce: *Running a little late. Straight to class. Will stop by after. What did kid look like?*

My phone buzzes. It's still Bruce, but now he's calling.

"Hey," I say.

"Hi."

"What's up?"

"Are you sitting on a bench right now? Next to a large open box with a cat in it?"

I turn around. He's not behind me. I look up and then over at our office building.

"No. I told you. I'm running late to class."

"That's funny. You're funny. But really, babe, what's with the cat?"

"It's not mine."

"I know it's not yours. You look foxy by the way."

"It belongs to a student."

"Which student?"

"What do you mean, which student? Would you know if I told you?"

"Is this— Is this the cat from our garage? You know I'm allergic, right? That's not a joke. Deathly allergic."

"There is no cat in our garage. I was wrong."

"Doesn't that cat have an owner? There are missing signs on our street. I saw them. Is the owner meeting you on campus?"

"This isn't that cat."

"Listen," Bruce says. "Are you okay?"

The cat's mouth is open, the very tip of its pink rough tongue discernible between its teeth.

I say, "Isn't that a little bit like me asking if you're writing messages that need to be deleted?"

"Do you want to talk to someone?"

"About what? The cat?"

"About the crying."

"Who's crying? I'm not crying."

"No one *is* crying. But you have *been* crying. A lot. Tell me you'll at least consider it."

"I haven't been crying."

Bruce is quiet. I think I hear his chair swivel. I look again at our building and this time count up to our floor and his window. I hold up my hand and give a little wave. Maybe he's watching me still. Maybe he's not. Maybe I'm just a woman on a bench with a stolen cat in a box waving up at an empty window. Is this my life? For the rest of my life?

There's a knock on Bruce's end. He says, "I've got to go."

"Who's there?"

"See you at home, okay? If we can't talk about the crying, we're going to at least talk about the cat."

He hangs up without saying goodbye.

Just after we moved in together, a man showed up at our front door. We were upstairs, getting dressed to go out for dinner. I'd been looking out at our street, thinking about how happy I was to own half of such a nice home on such a nice street and feeling worried that my happiness might equal contentment or an acquiescence to normalcy and complacency, which then might lead to boredom. It was while I was looking out the window, contemplating existential ennui and the disadvantages of privilege, that I saw the man. He was on the sidewalk immediately in front of our house, at the bottom of our front porch steps. He took out his phone and held it up as if to take a picture. I stepped back from the window—I wasn't wearing a bra—but continued to watch him. He turned and looked at the house across the street. Then he turned back to our house and walked up the steps.

I said to Bruce, who was in the bathroom, "There's a man on our porch," and Bruce, because he is nothing like my ex and because he takes care of me and tries, when possible, to view the world as I have to view it—as a person who, because of her gender, sometimes feels more vulnerable than he does and sometimes *is* more vulnerable—told me to stay upstairs, he'd see who it was.

Downstairs, I heard Bruce open the door. I heard the man announce himself as a previous owner of the house. "I raised two boys in this house," he said. I heard the brass knocker hit the door several times. "My mother gave me that knocker," the man said, his voice getting thick. "It makes me tear up some, seeing that knocker." He sounded it several more times. I wanted him to leave; instead, Bruce invited him inside. The man said again that he'd raised two boys in this house and Bruce told him he should come back another time but that we were getting ready to go out. The man asked if he could go upstairs, and I instinctively clutched at my bare chest. Bruce said, "My wife is changing," and the man said something I couldn't hear, and there was a laugh, first from the man and then from Bruce. They moved to the back of the house, to the Florida room, and I couldn't hear them any longer. I closed the bedroom door and finished getting dressed. A few minutes later, they were at the front door, and I could hear Bruce again telling the man to come back and I heard the man say, "My wife told me not to knock. She told me not to do what I'm doing." And Bruce assured him he was welcome another time, and the man said maybe next time he could go upstairs, and they both laughed again. On his way out, he repeated that his mother had given him that knocker, that it was a kind of family heirloom, and I knew that the man wanted the knocker, and I knew also that Bruce knew that the man wanted the knocker, and I knew that Bruce would never offer it and that the man would never outright ask. These are things I knew, and I was right.

When he left, I went downstairs, dressed and annoyed.

"That guy used to live here," Bruce told me.

"You know he wanted you to offer him the knocker."

"Yeah," he said, "not going to happen."

"What were you laughing at?"

"When?"

"With the man?" I slipped on my shoes, which made me an inch taller than Bruce, who was still in stocking feet. The stairway deaths of our colleagues hadn't yet occurred. "You told him your wife was upstairs and then he started laughing."

"Did he?"

"You laughed, too," I said.

He gave me a puzzled look. "I don't think that happened, but if it did, I don't remember."

I was enraged in that instant—either by his unwillingness to tell me what they'd been laughing at or, worse, by his genuine inability to recall a precise event that had only just occurred. As someone who spends nearly every minute of every day recalling, analyzing, and translating recent events, I suddenly couldn't stand the idea that I owned a house with a man for whom the daily inconsequential details that make up a life didn't register.

I said, "I'm not your wife. Are you ready yet?"

The cat, awake again, but sluggish in a way that makes me think its condition is worsening, perhaps rapidly, says to me, *To be honest, I fail to grasp the gravity of the Irishman.*

"I haven't suggested any gravity."

You have a specific thought in your mouth.

"Is that a fancy way of accusing me of being obsessed?"

I can't hear what you're saying if you refuse to think out loud.

"It represents a time when I was almost bad but wasn't."

What's the big deal about being almost bad? Isn't that anticlimactic?

"I told Bruce we didn't have sex, but maybe we did."

I get that. I get that. The cat is on its side, its stomach moving up and down rapidly. *But if nothing really happened, then why does it matter? What's at stake?*

"Are you okay? Maybe we should skip class and go straight to the vet."

You promised me a forever home, idiot human. If you take me to the vet now, I know what'll happen. Because you won't be my mom, they'll take the easy way out and send me to animal heaven. I need a human who's going to fight for me. Are you going to fight for me?

I look away, unable to say the truth.

Your story is bogus, is what I'm getting at. You're leaving something out.

"Everybody leaves something out. It's a fact of storytelling. Even if we try to tell the whole truth, we can't. Because we're human, and humans are flawed."

No, says the cat, its tail whipping the box in annoyance—one, two, three times. *Intentionally, deliberately, you are leaving something out. The Irishman matters to you in a way that he doesn't yet to me. Make him matter. Tell me the secret.*

I look around the emptying quad. I should get to class, but I'm not yet ready to give this little guy up. "Can I move you onto my lap?" I ask it. "Will that hurt you? I want you close so I can whisper."

It's okay. I'll be fine. Just keep me horizontal.

Gingerly, I slip my arm under the towel and very slowly lift the cat from the box. Its muzzle twitches, and I worry that I've hurt it, but it says nothing, and so I lower it onto my lap. I can feel the vibration of its breaths in my stomach, and I want nothing more than to close my eyes, lean my head back, and fall asleep with the weight of this creature against me. I resist. I hold the cat, but I do not brush it, do not massage it, do not stroke its scruff or rump or chin.

The cat kneads the towel nearly imperceptibly, and I lower my voice to a whisper and begin: "You might not understand this, but humans come in a variety of appearances, some more attractive or appealing than others—"

It's the same with cats.

"Of course. The same with cats. That makes sense. Well, this human—the Irishman—was exceptionally good-looking, the kind of good-looking that I'd normally avoid. The kind of good-looking that, even if he were mine and I trusted him, I wouldn't have trusted other women. Ever. He was good-looking like that."

I'm more into smells. But sure.

"Right. This man smelled very very good to many many women, which meant that I was flattered by his attention but nothing more. One night, when the bar was crowded, I had to move seats to accommodate a couple on a date, and he had to move seats to accommodate a different couple, and soon we were sitting in the middle of the bar side by side."

They call this a meet-cute.

"That's right. Only he was married. Technically, so was I. And that night, even though we were finally sitting side by side, we didn't speak, and there was a kind of frisson between us—"

Frisson?

"Does the word 'piloerection' help?"

Erection what?

"How about 'horripilation'?"

Horror how?

"Are you familiar with heraldic art?"

Are you?

"My mother likes old things. You know how your hair stands on end when you hunch your back?"

I haven't puffed up in years.

"In heraldic art, there's a word to describe a domestic cat who's simultaneously spitting *and* arching its back with its hair on end."

I'm bored.

"The word is 'herissony.'"

Still bored.

"That's what this frisson felt like between us. A kind of magnetic kinetic energy in our mutual decision not to speak to one another that let each of us know we were cripplingly aware of the other."

How can you be sure it wasn't one-sided?

"Because he touched me."

That sounds skeevy—touching a stranger without their permission.

"But he wasn't a stranger. We'd been seeing each other at the bar, making eye contact, looking away. And, anyway, it wasn't skeevy because I liked it."

Where did he touch you? Or do I not want to know?

"He brushed his forearm against mine. At first, it was so fast and so soft I thought I'd imagined it. But then he did it again and didn't move away. I let my own arm lean into his, and then he leaned more into mine. We stayed that way for another hour, talking to the people on either side of us, never verbally acknowledging each other, looking to everyone else like two strangers at a packed bar."

What happened next?

"I went home alone. A little stunned, a little excited, a little devastated.

The next morning, I had an email from him. He'd looked me up online and signed off with his cell. Later that night, I texted. He texted back. He told me he and his wife had an agreement. I didn't care because my husband was out of town, and whatever I was after wasn't long-term. We texted for several weeks and then one night I made a kind of decision. My husband would be home in a week. I got dressed up. I did my hair. I went to a bar. I got very drunk. Do I need to explain 'drunk'?"

Too much catnip?

"Exactly."

And?

"He put his hand on my leg, which gave me a sensation I hadn't experienced in ten years—a feeling of newness and pure longing."

I see.

"We left together in his car. By then, I was barely coherent, but I knew I was attracted to him, and I knew I wanted to . . . to be with him in the way that humans sometimes are with each other . . ."

The cat says, *I get it. I'm a cat, remember?*

I nod, unsure how familiar a domesticated cat can be with the desires of humans, but I don't bother clarifying or contradicting. "I woke up the next morning in my own bed. I was alone. I was naked. I had no memory of what, if anything, had happened. I was thirty-five years old and deeply ashamed, but also angry at myself for having been so drunk I couldn't remember the pleasure of whatever might have happened. I didn't have it as a memory to return to whenever I wanted. I got out of bed but was immediately sick. When I went downstairs, I remembered—for the first time—my dog, who was in the backyard alone—had I put him there? Had the Irishman?—and that's also when I discovered that my front door was wide open. I felt so . . ."

Afraid?

"Yes," I say. "Afraid and alone and worried for myself, for what I'd let myself do, for how out of control I'd been, and also for what might have happened. I stayed home from school and lavished attention on my dog and drank juice and crunched pain pills until it was night. When it was finally late enough, I locked all the doors, turned off all the lights, and got into bed so that I could wake up the next morning and feel human again—human and healthy and in control. Right before my husband came home, right before he told me about his own affair, I cleaned our house from top to bottom and discovered that the Irishman had left a sock under my husband's side of the bed. I threw it away. Very nearly my husband came home to another man's sock under our bed. Instead, he confessed he'd been sleeping with my dear friend. The sock wouldn't have mattered at all."

My belly hurts, says the cat, who's kneaded itself into a perfect line with my body: its chest against mine, its paws beneath my clavicle. I know I shouldn't, but I tuck my chin and lower my head, and the cat stretches its generous neck and knocks into my forehead with its own.

"Is that better?" I ask.

I see now, the cat says. *My belly really aches, but now I see a little more clearly*.

I shake my head. "But there's more," I say.

Are we late for class?

"Let me tell you. Please? Now that I've started, it feels crucial that I finish. To have said it aloud just once, this feels newly necessary to me."

I've got time. I think. Is that worry in the cat's voice? If it is, I can't detect it, haven't yet discerned it. I'm so wrapped up in my own story, I've forgotten about the injuries, forgotten the day's mission of finding the cat a home. In another few minutes, I'll remember, and it won't be too late—it will not be too late for this cat—but just now, all I am thinking of is myself.

I continue: "He texted one more time to tell me he was sorry. I didn't know what he was sorry for. I wanted to meet him again, to do whatever we'd done again, just once, so that I could remember, so that I could be a participant. I suppose I believed that if he was willing to see me again, then something good must have happened. But if he wasn't willing . . . The open door, after all. Who leaves a door open? Once my divorce was underway, I tried to make a new plan with him, but he demurred. The third time I tried, he ignored me altogether. I pursued him, this man who'd called me 'Hot Stuff' again and again but who was now clearly done with me. I kept going, long after I should, becoming the kind of woman I've always pitied, becoming desperate and deranged. It's a fog now—the desperation—but it's the lowest I've ever let myself go, and it was for a man who, ultimately, didn't want me the way I wanted him. It was for a man who might have . . . I was humiliated. I humiliated myself. One day, I made myself delete his number. And that was that. Now do you see? Now do you see what it means that he's been in touch after all this time?"

The cat's posture has changed. There's a tension in its haunches. It says, weakly, *I see. I do see. But I think we need to go now. I think you need to find me someone. Or take me yourself to the doctor. I think we've been careless with time. I'm not well. Something is happening in my belly that isn't right.*

My cheeks redden with shame. "Oh," I say as I return it to its box. "I've been too cavalier. Oh! Oh! Forgive me."

I arrive to workshop flushed and sweaty and thirty minutes late with a panting cat in extremis. Inside the classroom, the only students still here are Mateo and Willow, who's far too young and inexperienced to be sitting so close to such a man in a room as empty as this one.

I put down the box and push the hair from my face, fully aware of how horribly I've botched the day. The cat says, *We're too late, aren't we?* And I almost respond aloud but remind myself there's an audience.

Willow says, "Is that a cat?"

The cat says, *Not her.*

Mateo says, "Everyone left."

I say, "I can see that."

He says, "You owe me a workshop."

The cat says, *Maybe him.*

I say, "I owe you what?"

Mateo says, "Today's my day. You missed it."

Willow purrs, "Omigodthiscatisthemostbeautifulcatintheworld-canIholditcanIhaveit?"

The cat says, *Maybe her after all.*

Mateo says, "We can do coffee, discuss my story."

"We can push it to next week," I say.

"That's what you said last semester, remember? Your father was in the ER, and you never rescheduled. You owe me."

I ignore him, and to Willow I say, "It's not my cat. It's an injured cat, and it needs a home." I slump into a chair. "You can pet it," I say, then look at the cat, who gives me a nod. "But delicately."

Willow takes the seat next to me and pulls the box toward her. To my surprise, before putting out her hand, she lowers her face to the cat, tucking her chin just as I had. I think, *No way is it gonna head-butt her just like that right off the bat*, but I'm wrong, because the next thing I know, the tabby and Willow have their foreheads locked together and Willow is rubbing its back as it audibly, almost embarrassingly audibly, vibrates in response.

"Get a room," says Mateo, winking at me, but coming over to our side of the seminar table and taking a seat not next to me but to Willow. He says of the cat, "This guy's a sweetie." Then to Willow, "I think he's in love."

"I'm not sure it's a boy," I say, caught off guard by the easy intimacy between Willow and Mateo.

The cat says quickly, shooting me an ugly look, *I'm a man. I go with the girl. The girl is mine. I want this one.* His forehead is still glued to Willow's.

I say, "Willow, do you live in a dorm?"

She says dreamily, not looking at me, "Off campus. I have an apartment with two other girls. We've been talking about getting a cat." Then she says, running a finger along its—*his*—jawline, "Haven't we, boy? Haven't we been talking about a cat?"

The cat says, *Ask her if she's got money. Ask her if she can afford me.*

Before I can think of an appropriate way to pose the question, Mateo has his hand on Willow's lower back and is saying, "I like him, too. I think you should."

"What?" I ask. Things are moving too fast. Mountains are shifting, polar ice caps are liquefying, time is a piece of Camembert draped across an easy chair. I say, "What?"

The cat says, *Give her me. Give her me.*

"Willow," I say. I'm short of breath. My rib cage feels tight. "Is your apartment pet-friendly?"

Mateo rests his sharp chin on Willow's shoulder.

I say, "Wait, are you two together?"

I say, "Never mind, ignore that question."

I say, "Willow, this cat is hurt. It's been hit by a car. It needs to go to a vet. Today. Now. I should have . . . I didn't. If you can't, then I will, but, oh, but maybe this is all a bad idea."

Mateo says, almost whispering in Willow's ear, "I can pay for the vet. Let's take my car. I'm parked on campus today."

It's possible I'm staring—almost certainly I'm staring, so shocked by this turn of events—Willow and Mateo are together?—when Mateo, his face in my direction but his chin still resting on Willow, whose own face is in periphery since she's still head to head with the tabby, suddenly cuts his eyes right at me. He gives me this Cheshire smile that sends a chill across my upper back. I think to the cat, *This is not right, this is not right.* But the cat says nothing. The cat is being picked up by Willow, taken from the towel, enveloped in her arms. He's not resisting. He's practically dissolving into her grasp.

"Prof P," Willow is saying, "can I take him? I know a vet. My friend is an animal technician. I want to take him right now. There's blood on the towel. Is it cool? Can we go? Can I get the cat help?" She glances at Mateo, who stands. They're both standing. I'm still sitting, breathless and unprepared to have it all happen like this and so fast and without a chance privately to say goodbye.

Mateo's got his arm around Willow. He's shepherding them out of the room, like they're some sort of family, some sort of family of three. Willow is looking over her shoulder. "It's cool, Prof P. I'll email you, yeah? Things couldn't be more perfect. I love cats. My next story is about a cat who can ta—"

But now they're out of the classroom and down the hallway, and

Willow is no longer looking over her shoulder at me. She's looking down at the cat, talking to it—to *him*—and Mateo, so tall, so so very tall, has his arm still around her shoulders, and he's talking to her or to them and just as they're about to turn the corner, he faces me, closes one eye, and aims a finger pistol in my direction.

Bruce and I and my father are sitting on my front porch. It's night. A storm has moved in. We're drinking wine and cocktails and watching the lightning. My father has overstayed his welcome, but even Bruce won't ask him to leave in weather like this.

"I'm a complex person," my father is saying, "same as you."

"Of course you are," I say.

"If I could replay your sister's wedding weekend—"

"That was five years ago! Six years ago!"

"If I could replay that weekend—well, maybe when she has a big fiftieth anniversary or something, I'll give it another try. You know the story I'd tell if I could do it over again?"

"You think you'll be around for her fiftieth wedding anniversary?"

"Where the hell else will I be?"

Bruce lets out a loud sigh.

My father says, "I have always been a maniac. I really believe the bull I put forth. For instance, about the petardiers."

My phone buzzes. It's Bruce. He's written: *He can stay as long as he wants but I can't do this particular anecdote again.*

My father says, "A petardier was a guy who worked for a nobleman in the Middle Ages. He was sent to a castle of *this* nobleman to get *that* nobleman's wife or gold. He put charges on the sides of buildings until they blew them apart. It's in the *Oxford English Dictionary*. Look it up."

Bruce writes, *Navel gazers*. Before I can respond, he slaps his knees, pops up, and holds out a hand to my father. He says, "I've got some papers to grade. You two knock yourselves out. I'm beat."

My father clasps Bruce's hand with both of his. "You are an appropriate man," he says. "You are good and right and very appropriate."

"I won't be much longer," I say. Lightning slices the sky. A new torrent of rain drops dramatically down.

Bruce says to me, as he opens the front door, "I know this one, sweetie. It's not short."

When the front door closes, I say, "You're talking about petards. P-E-T-A-R-D."

There's a bottle of wine at my father's feet. He picks it up by its neck, as though it were a bottle of soy sauce or olive oil or swill, and pours the last of it into his glass. "In the old days," he says, "you had to have a walled city because marauding tribes would come to steal your women, dogs, donkeys, gold."

"That's some list," I say.

"You can imagine in those days the quality of gunpowder and fuses." While he talks, his hands twitch this way and that to illustrate. Wine sloshes. "If the petardier rolled a fuse too tight or not tight enough: boom!" My father's hands explode, as does the last of the wine from his glass. "They were . . . hoisted on their own petard!"

"They were blown up by their own weapons."

"Yes." He takes a sip from his now-empty glass then regards me with momentary suspicion.

"And this concept gives you solace?" I ask. "The idea that you—that *we*—come from a long line of men who blew themselves up with their own devices?"

"Sure as there's water on the ground and I'm a Democrat, there's no question but that we come from the petardiers."

"If you're empty, I can get more from inside." The night and storm are fully on us. Thunder and lightning brawl overhead: right hook, left hook, right hook, jab.

My father tucks his blanket under his thighs. "The story I should have told—"

Across the street, my sister's bedroom windows light up. There's my brother-in-law, sorting and folding clothes on the bed. Now there's my sister, dumping a new pile and then walking back out to the hallway. In every house, at any time, is there ever not laundry to wash or change or sort or fold?

"When I was a young man," my father says, "nobody was more nuts than me. One day I found myself in the backyard of the house on Tanglewood, putting up this picket fence with bricks, and my two kids at the time were playing in the backyard." My father is facing the street. His hands are once again in front of him. He can see the crowd he's talking to. He can feel their energy. He's somewhere else entirely. In a ballroom, at a restaurant, on a stage. I'm under a storm on my front porch in Kentucky. But my father isn't.

"We had pea gravel back there and a big oak. I'd pulled the 280 next to the tree along with a hose and was planning to wash it. Sissy and her big brother were under the oak, like something out of a vaudeville routine. It was backlighted and I could see only the silhouettes. It was like looking through a prism. There's Sissy, always her brother's straight man. He was such an arrogant little prick. He's screwing around with the hose's spray gun—you know, like a little boy would do—and he's spraying her foot or her elbow or her shoulder or whatever the hell. Finally, she ran to me. She was crying. She said, 'He won't let me have the goddamn hose. He's such a little jerk. Blah blah blah.' And I said, 'Okay. I got it. Here's what you want to do. Go back out there and tell your brother there's some chewing gum under the seat and he can have it. In a minute, he'll drop the hose, and when he drops that hose, you pick that son of a bitch up in both hands and hit him right in the face.' She looked up at me like, *That'll work*, then ran straight back, and I'm seeing these backlighted subjects. She's going—" His hands indicate chatter. "And he's going—" More hands, more chatter. "And then finally he drops the hose and turns toward the car. Her hands went up, went down, picked up the hose, and when he came out of the 280, she hit him square in the face. She ran back to me just screaming with laughter. It was the most wonderful thing in the world. Probably one of the greatest memories I have from your childhood. That's the story I should have told at her wedding, and then I should have said to myself, 'Shut up, you pompous ass.'"

"It's too much regret," I say. I do not say that his greatest memory of my childhood is from a time before I was born.

"You're much smarter than I am," he says. He's back with me on the porch now. He's walked off the stage. The applause has ended. The crowd has dispersed. "Generationally, you learn. Shit gets passed down. Different people have different regret files, and you stuff shit in there." There's lightning but it's farther away now. Soon, the rain will lighten. Soon, my father can go home. "You wind up pulling the files out in the middle of the night—dreams and stuff. Listen, I made so many mistakes. I'm like a hairshirted monk. I'm always beating myself, but I'm late in the game. My wool is dyed."

I get out my phone. My father doesn't notice. I text Bruce, *In soon*.

He says, "Generally speaking, people like me—people like *you*—they live for their moments. They live for those instances of energy and the passion of something new. They try to remember the energy and the passion, so they can run away with it again and let it pull them down the road again, and they say, 'Wow. Here we are. We're on the road again. It ain't over yet.' That's me. And that's you, too, kid."

I start to fold my blanket. The rain has let up entirely.

My father jerks a thumb in the direction of my house, inside which is Bruce, inside which is his daughter. "Nobody in this world is as important as you are," he says. "Never allow yourself to get brought into a relationship that's all-important or that means the world to you. The world is what matters. If you're not enjoying life where you are, and you're not having fun with the people you're with, take a big step to the right, keep going, don't look back, and smile!"

"It's late," I say, picking up my glass.

My father pulls the blanket from his legs and tosses it onto the floor of the porch, which is slick with rainwater.

"I get the message," he says. "Later, kid." He unfolds himself from the chair, limps down the front steps, and disappears into the night.

I gather his now-soaked blanket from the ground and brush away a few damp leaves.

From somewhere in the darkness, my father bellows back at me, in caps lock and italics, "*SMILE.*"

And I do smile, and it's a mean smile, and now there is another load of laundry.

If I still had the cat, I'd explain that these texts from the Irishman—arriving seven years after I was dismissed, arriving now, as I am, seven years older, less elastic, seven years closer to female invisibility—these texts erase that lingering uncertainty, making me feel alive again, desired, important, powerful, feminine. They make me feel dangerous, and I want to feel dangerous for as long as I can. This is something I know now, something I understand.

If I still had the cat, I'd explain it's for this reason—for the reason of life, of electricity pulsing again through my veins, of being pulled down the road by something new, by the world itself—that the last thing I do before turning off the lights in the kitchen and going up to bed tonight is respond to the Irishman's final text, which—in the melee of the cat being taken by Willow and Mateo—I'd forgotten to delete. I write, simply: *w/w*—the shorthand of adultery: where and when.

After I've pushed send, I power down my phone and plug it into the outlet next to the banquette. I do not take it with me to our bedroom.

Bruce falls asleep almost instantly after a quick scroll of the news, but I wait, my mind a battle zone. I can only imagine responses that might fail to satisfy—*Too late* or *Changed my mind* or *Control yourself haha*—and so I wait, eyes wide and adjusted to the dark. I can hear them, hear my eyeballs in their sockets. Each time I move their focus—from the nightshade on my side to the nightshade on Bruce's to the door handle of the closet to the musical unicorn atop our shared bureau—I swear I can hear them as they shift left, right, up, down, a quiet crackling sound that makes me panic all the more for its isolated intensity.

For more than two hours, I wait, think, listen to my eyeballs. When I can no longer bear it—neither the anticipation, nor the scraping of cornea against lid, optic nerve against retina—I inch out of bed and tiptoe downstairs.

Picture me: it is after midnight. The house is quiet save for the occasional sputter of a pipe shuddering from the day's use, of the foundation settling infinitesimally farther into the firmament beneath us. A middle-aged woman sits at the built-in bench on the far side of a kitchen table. Behind her is a bank of windows, the lower half's shutters closed for the night. But the upper shutters stand wide, and out and up and far away is the moon, a gibbous moon, let's say, and it angles its moonshine into the house, through the windows, onto the hair and shoulders of the woman who sits, dressed in an oversize T-shirt and a pair of worn-in terrycloth track shorts, at the table. In her hands is her phone, its face shining to life with a severe beam of light, mirroring the moon in its tiny numinous way. Her eyes—my eyes, the woman's eyes—are electric. Her pulse is quick, her nacre skin shivery to the touch. She is a vibrating live wire of nerves and anxiety.

The woman opens her messages.

The woman takes a breath, looks momentarily away, and then:

From her one-time would-be lover, there is nothing.

In the woman's eyes: confusion.

In her heart: rage.

In her muscles: endless, unused energy.

In the laundry room, I dump a load of dirty clothes upside down and root through until I find yesterday's running clothes—shorts, socks, jog bra. I dress in the dark and smell of mildew, of damp rags left too long in the sink, of clothes not moved to the dryer in time.

Outside, the moon's light overflows from its edges, its penumbra leaking into the very universe itself. The streetlamps buzz with energy, and the pavement nearly shines from the glow of the sky.

I run so fast, so easily, tonight. I pass my four-mile checkpoint and don't feel the least bit winded. *My god*, I think. *My god, my god.* I keep going. In my mind I replay every interaction with the Irishman I can remember, all his texts, new and old. I make up the memories I was too drunk to remember: his tongue here, his teeth there, his hands everywhere . . . We could feel alive together. We could find a detour from everyday monotony. We could find purpose, lust, desire; remind our bodies what it feels like to be turned on, to get turned on, to want. I imagine his hands on my thighs; imagine him pinning me against a car's door, driving my head back and biting my neck, running a thumb slowly along the length of my clavicle, forcing down my jeans and underwear and shoving his—

The break in the concrete is abrupt. I go down hard, my knee landing then sliding on something jagged before my palms are able to catch me. I might have cried out given the pain and suddenness. It seems as though I must have cried out. I push myself up. My right kneecap is frayed, blood pooling at the skin's surface before pushing through. The pavement, I see now, has been torn up, as has the entire front yard of the house attached to it. A yellow piece of caution tape dangles limply from a boxwood. My palms burn. I turn them over. The skin of both heels is shredded and filled with tiny stones. As gently as I can, I brush the pebbles away, wincing in pain. I yank the caution tape from the hedge and wipe at the blood on my knee. A hoot owl hollers in the distance.

Loser, I think.

I should never have texted him. I should never have put him in control.

I turn around, shaken, and jog slowly and stiffly home.

Oh, cat, what have I done?

Five minutes into class, my hands covered in large, ill-fitting bandages that Bruce insisted upon, I've said nothing. Willow is missing, and I'm worried her absence is somehow connected to the fate of the cat. I'm also worried about my ankle, which swelled overnight. I feel inebriated, muddled, unmoored. Is this what my father feels? Am I twenty years away from standing on a front porch in a sweater in a snowstorm, declaring my love for . . . For whom would I declare my love? The eleven-year-old, now grown? Bruce, who's long ago left me, having discovered what I really am? Which is what? What really am I? Am I so different from every woman out there?

I stare out the window above Mateo, who's leading an informal discussion on the Barthelme story in which a bunch of second graders bear witness to a series of increasingly bizarre and unlikely deaths—trees, salamanders, a puppy. The story ends with dubiously elevated dialogue in which the pupils ask their teacher, a man, to make love to his teaching assistant as an affirmation of life and its meaning.

Mateo and the others are discussing the dialogue. I continue, in my stupor, to gaze out the window.

"You know that feeling," says one of the amorphous brunettes. I glance over. The middle one is also missing. That one is Kenzie. The one whose name I've finally learned isn't here. I look back out the window to where a squirrel is newly peeking his head from the knot of a large oak tree. All over town, thousands of gray squirrel kits are born every spring. They venture from their nests. They live or they die. Again and again. Life or death. Live or die. Blah or bleh. Is that squirrel watching me or am I watching it?

"You know that feeling," the brunette is saying, "when you were little, of not being able to wait until your heart had been broken? Of needing that big devastation?"

In fact, I do know the feeling, and I'm surprised that someone so seemingly unremarkable has posed the question. I look at her again. What am I missing?

Across the table from her, Tiffany, a smart Black girl from California, says, "No. I have no idea what you're talking about." Immediately I feel implicated, privileged for having had a childhood in which heartache could be longed for. *Did* I have such a childhood? But then almost as immediately I feel guilty for assuming Tiffany's wasn't a privileged childhood. For all I know, her parents are lawyers or doctors or professors like me.

"The story is meant to provide a lens," I say, checking on my squirrel, who's disappeared inside his tree. Predation rates on city squirrels are higher than ever. One in four makes it to their first birthday. I know because the eleven-year-old told me. She also told me that, by 2053, earth will have run out of sufficient resources to sustain humanity. I, in turn, told her to google tidal rates and the inevitability of an end-of-century ice age.

"Barthelme is being absurd, right?" I say. "The dialogue is absurd. The situation is absurd. But the lens isn't absurd. He's telling us something about our world, isn't he? What's he telling us? Toward what epiphany is he pushing us? What's the point?"

"Cycle of life," says Mateo.

"Life is sad," says Tiffany.

"And then you die," says Mateo.

"That's pretty good," I say. "Does anyone know where Willow is?" I don't look at Mateo, the person most likely to know. "Or Kenzie?"

The class does that thing where no one makes eye contact with me, as though they're scared of being called on because they haven't done the reading.

"Should we invoke the fifteen-minute rule?" I ask. The clock above the window indicates we're now thirty minutes into class.

"That's real?" asks a kid sitting near Tiffany.

"Don't you wish it were?" I ask. No one answers. There is a dull, low ringing in my ears, and I wonder if I could have a concussion. Maybe I hit my head and don't remember. "You know how some days, as students, you're walking across campus unprepared for class or maybe you're hungover or maybe you're tired or maybe your girlfriend broke up with you and you just don't have the stamina to sit through another ninety minutes of bullshit?" I look around the room. Everyone appears eagerly to be listening. Profanity behooves us.

I look back out at the empty oak knot and continue. "And you're thinking, *Please don't let the teacher be there, please just let her be sick, please, please, please just let me off the hook this one time* . . ." In their silence, I sense agreement. I continue: "Well, sometimes your professors think the same thing about you." Nervous tittering. "They think, *Maybe I'll open the classroom door and the seats will be empty. Maybe there will only be one student. Maybe everyone is sick, and I can just go home.*"

"Is today one of those days for you?" asks Tiffany. She smiles at me. I hope it isn't with pity.

"Yes," I say.

She follows my gaze out the window, possibly hoping to see an explanation out there.

"Then why don't we all just go home?" she asks.

The second hand's glide around the clock is cruelly slow. I regard Tiffany. I can deny it all I want, but the truth is, I envy her—the coolness, the wit, the decades and decades of elasticity and collagen still ahead of her.

"Good idea," I say, knowing that I should use the extra time to give Mateo the workshop he's owed, knowing that by not doing so I will necessarily be indebted to a one-on-one discussion; understanding that, even before it's happened, when the class empties out today, he will still be here, either at his desk or near the door, asking to set a time when we can have our coffee chat. And I know also that, when this coffee/chat/workshop happens, he will be a flirt and I will be a scold, and there will be more subtext and euphemism between us than is appropriate.

Despite all this, I say, "Class dismissed."

The room empties. I stay where I am. The squirrel reemerges, another by his side. They take turns nibbling at each other; it seems a friendly series of gestures—mouth to ear, ear to mouth, neck rubbing neck, chin touching chin. It almost makes me happy.

And then I can feel it, the presence of the naughty nursling who's stayed behind.

He's in the doorway watching me.

"You okay?" Mateo asks.

I offer him a wan smile. "Do you know about the cat?" I ask. "Willow said she'd email but she didn't."

"No offense," he says, "but it looks like you've been hit by a Mack truck."

"That good?"

He nods at my tattered hands. "Those are some serious paws."

"The other guy looks worse."

"Abuse humor," he says. He rocks back onto his heels, a curious but puzzled expression on his brow. "I like it."

I shake away the comment. "Willow? The cat? Any word?"

"I think it's sweet how you're more worried about an animal than a person. That must make things interesting at home."

"Forget I asked," I say. My phone buzzes. "I'll email her myself."

"Willow is fine. She stayed home with the cat. He's pretty banged up. She thought you'd be okay with it since you rescued it and all, but we didn't think I should say anything in front of the others in case there's something kind of, I don't know, irregular about the whole thing."

My phone buzzes again. "There's nothing irregular in a student helping a professor save an animal."

"You want to get that?"

"It's nothing important."

"Might be your boyfriend." He smirks, as if to challenge the existence of Bruce.

"Might be." I glance at the screen; the number is restricted. "Nope," I lie, casually opening the text, "just good old-fashioned junk mail."

I scan what's written and instantly flush: *Let me cum in your mouth.*

"Telemarketers," Mateo says. "The worst."

I lick my lips. My left eye twitches. I try to swallow, but saliva is gone from my mouth. "I should go," I say, my voice nearly cracking.

"Sure," says Mateo, disappointed. "Yeah. Okay." He knocks once on the molding, then reluctantly slinks out the door.

I open my phone again, read the words once more, then let my whole torso slump onto the desk. I am a fool. I have been a fool. To have assumed my fantasy was his. To have believed I could bring this daydream to life in exactly the manner I imagined. His words . . . For me, the truth, the childish prudish truth: this isn't sexy. This doesn't turn me on. It repulses me. I am not open, not liberated, not free. I'm a fake, water from a tree masquerading as rain after a storm. I am as closed-off, sealed-up, buttoned-down as any old housewife. At heart, against every intellectual and theoretical desire, I am committed, monogamous, no better than a penguin or a goose.

The phone awkwardly clutched between my bandages, I jab at the screen: *Do not text this number again.* I feel nothing now—not anger, not sadness, just a blank realization that there will be no reprieve from life's manufactured tedium.

"Oh, and hey."

I startle, sitting up quickly. Mateo is back, but my screen is empty. There is nothing now to hide except my weakness and disgrace.

"You're back," I say flatly.

"Before you go—"

"Yes?"

I'm standing now, my bag slung protectively over my shoulder.

"Can we set a date?"

"A date."

"For coffee?"

"Coffee."

"My story?"

"Your story," I repeat. I feel weak as a kitten, tenderized by a hammer. "Mind emailing me your availability? My brain's a sieve right now."

"You got it," he says, knocking again on the doorframe. "Aces."

Aces. The eleven-year-old would love that.

My phone thrums against the gauze of the bandage. I wait until I've heard Mateo's footsteps move fully down the hallway. Whatever it is, I will not respond. Whatever it is, I am done.

I open my messages. Let this be the end, I think. Enough already. Let this be the totality of my folly. Let me risk my happy home no more.

One word is all that's there, and bile rises in my throat to see it:

haha

A brief interview—

Students: What about the cat? Just like that? No cat? The cat dies
and you're fixated and then . . . ? What? Is there a plot here
or . . . ?

Prof P: The cat isn't dead.

Students: Are you sure?

Prof P: . . .

Students: What about Theo? We were promised a mailman!

Prof P: Be patient.

Students *(hurling their phones toward the front of the classroom)*: We
were raised in the era of the internet! What does patience have to
do with anything?

Prof P: I was raised in the era of decadence and conservatism. What
does upbringing have to do with anything?

Students: You should know that we ourselves are writing something
previously unheard of. Something uninhibited and new. It's

entirely in our minds. It need never be recorded in print. It is our brains abuzz.

Prof P: You're describing stream of consciousness. You do need to write it down. That's what makes it writing.

Students: No. This is new. We've just invented it.

Prof P: Have you read James? Colette? Faulkner? Gass?

Students: Have you read anyone other than dead white people?

Prof P: Do you even know how to read?

Students: That comment is going in our end-of-semester evals.

Prof P: Anonymity will be the death of humanity.

Students: Uh, no. Climate change will be the death of humanity.

Prof P: But first: bodily dismemberment by way of other bodies.

Students: Are you drunk? Are you drinking right now? Have you checked Rate My Professors? Do you know what your previous students have said about you?

Prof P: Last time I looked I had a pepper.

Students: OMG. A pepper. Last time you looked . . . That's basically the twentieth century, which is an era during which we did not exist.

Prof P: An era during which students still knew how to diagram a sentence.

Students: You are so a member of the patriarchy.

Prof P: You should read my fiction.

Students: You basically hate men.

Prof P: So you've read my fiction?

Students: No. We've read your Goodreads reviews. You are—and don't take this the wrong way, which is to say don't be flattered by it—basically a narcissistic self-hating misogynist.

Prof P: Did anyone do the writing assignment for today?

Students: "Tell Your Life Story in Three Incidents Involving Hair"?

Prof P: Yeah.

Students: We think your husband's cheating on you.

Prof P: I don't have a husband.

Students: We think the bald guy is cheating on you.

Prof P: He's not.

Students: What's with the texting and all the closed doors, then?

Prof P: That's me. You're talking about me.

Students: Uh, no. We don't think so. Sheesh.

Prof P: My grandfather used to say sheesh.

Students: We know.

Prof P: Want to hear a story?

Students: Will there be a test?

Prof P: This is creative writing. Of course there won't be a test.

Students: May we look at our phones?

Prof P: No.

Students: Is there any story you can tell us during which we are allowed to look at our phones?

Prof P: No.

Students: Fine. The hair, then. Go ahead.

Try This 8.3—Tell Your Life Story in Three Incidents Involving Hair.
(Burroway, *Imaginative Writing: The Elements of Craft*)

The Author's Life Story in Three Incidents Involving Hair

By Prof P

(AN EXAMPLE)

1.

There are only three dolls I've ever cared about. One was bald, a baby called Emma, given to me by my mother when I too was a baby, when I too was bald. The other dolls came later, part of a famous series, one a blonde, the other a brunette. Both had long straight hair and very even bangs. I cared for the famous girl dolls long past the time when my other friends had given up on toys altogether. I brushed their hair; I washed their faces; I placed them daintily in the windowsill in my bedroom so they could look out at the world when I wasn't home.

Years later, when I was grown and after my two nieces were born—one a brunette, the other a blonde—I began preparing for the day I knew must eventually come: the day I'd give the girl dolls away, one to each niece.

2.

My brother and sister were like twins without being twins. They were older, more adventurous, invested in taking risks regardless of potential punishment. I was the undesired sidekick. When we played hide-and-seek, I was always the one to hide. They'd never come looking. The trick worked for years. Once, my brother cut off all my sister's hair to match his own. They got in trouble, but I didn't gloat. I felt too left out to gloat, an emptiness in my stomach like homesickness or the onset of the flu. They'd been sent to their bedrooms, their playtime indefinitely suspended.

I found the scissors where they'd been left, in the kitchen on the table, next to a pile of my sister's hair. I chopped off my ponytail with a single cut. Immediately, I understood my error. Immediately, I realized the club I'd tried to join—my brother's and sister's and their joint decision to be bad together—would still be closed to me, while my parents' punishment would be wide open. I hid the ponytail in a drawer in my father's bathroom, under magazines I didn't realize were themselves already in hiding.

My mother screamed when she saw me.

"Who told?" I said, already crying, the eternal little sister.

3.

A month after I sent the girl dolls to my nieces—tucking them into a box, facing them upward so they'd be comfortable and able to breathe—I went for a visit.

I saw Samantha's head first—on the mantel above the fireplace, where its scalp sat freshly shorn. Kirsten was in the fireplace beneath. My nieces had left her bangs and one of her arms intact. The rest of the dolls' parts were gone. I was glad then that I'd been selfish about Emma, the hairless baby, keeping her for myself.

"Oops," my brother said, when he saw the sorrow on my face.

That was the day I decided for sure: no kids.

(480 words)

I read aloud my essays, then ask my real students, "What did you like or dislike? And why? What would you change? What questions do you have? Would it matter if I told you that my nieces aren't actually brunette and blond? What if I told you only one is strawberry blond and the other is a redhead? Is this lying? Or is this artistic license? What if I told you I only have one niece? Or that it was my sister-in-law who said 'oops' and not my brother? Does any of this change 'the meat' of the story, which is to say 'the message' or 'the purpose' or 'the fundamental truth'?"

One student raises her hand.

"Yes, McKenzie?"

She scowls at me, the face of someone who's just opened a Tupperware container of boiled eggs without knowing what to expect. I open my hand and look at my palm, where I've delicately drawn a three-pronged arrow across my still-healing skin. Next to each vector I've written the first initial of the brunettes, McKenzie, Brenda, and Kayla.

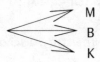

"Brenda," I say. "I mean Brenda."

"Are we going to discuss the Hemingway thing you asked us to read or what?"

I say, "It's called 'A Very Short Story,' and it is, itself, a short story, not a *thing*. It's a classic example of the objective perspective: there is no shading, no subjectivity, no applied judgments or biased language; the reader's only job is to read between the lines."

The nontraditional with graying hair says, "Are we supposed to be impressed by the piece? It's pretty lean."

"It just makes me think that people were really boring in olden times," says Brenda.

"Huh," I say. "That's certainly an opinion. Anyone else have initial thoughts about this story?"

Willow, I notice, is still missing.

I call on Tiffany. "Okay," she says. "Honestly? I don't see how someone realistically contracts an STD in the back of an Uber. I just don't buy these two people having sex in the back of some dude's car during the day with the driver right there watching. It's gross, for one thing, and just not real, for another. Also, that girl at the end comes out of nowhere. He meets her at a mall? And then they go at it in an Uber? Is it supposed to be real life?" As an afterthought, she adds, "And the sentences are clunky."

I say to Tiffany, "You're referring to the line toward the end in which the soldier, freshly jilted by his foreign nurse, returns home to Chicago, where he begins sleeping around, presumably out of heartache, and promptly contracts gonorrhea. Let's stay with that moment but perhaps push our understanding of it."

Mateo smirks. Why is Mateo smirking? Did I forget to write him back? Did I agree to coffee and then forget to go? And where the fuck is Willow? Where the fuck is my cat?

I say, "Look at the sentence before and the sentence just after. What's Hemingway really telling us? What's he saying here? What's the—vocab alert—*subtext*?"

Students look down at the story. I read the sentences aloud. I wait. No one looks up.

"We aren't meant to focus on the realism of the moment. Are we? No. We're not. We're meant to focus on what's not being said, on what's being implied. At this moment, what—anyone can answer—what is being implied?"

The brunette to Brenda's left clears her throat. I surreptitiously glance at my palm. "McKenzie," I say.

"McKayla," she says.

I furrow my eyebrows and look at the girl to the right of Brenda. "But you're Kayla?"

"I'm Kenzie," she says.

"Of course. Apologies." I look back to McKayla. "You were going to say?"

"Well," she says. She's blushing. "I don't know about this thing you're talking about. But I was going to say about wherever the nurse writes in the letter that they had a boy-girl love."

"Yes!" I said. "Let's talk about that line. It's an amazing moment, isn't it? *Theirs had only been a boy and girl affair.* What's the subtext here?"

McKayla's expression is as unresponsive as a wedge of Brie. "I was going to say that it seemed kind of mean? And also, that I don't get it."

"But you do get it," I say. I implore others to join in. "A soldier has fallen in love. Despite the mores of olden times—" I glance at Tiffany. She's wearing a wicked expression. "In spite of these conservative mores, a soldier and a nurse have fallen in love and, while in love, they've spent nights together."

The class is fidgety.

"What does this mean? Anyone. They haven't just spent nights together, have they? It's a euphemism?" I slow my words. "It's a *euph-e-mism*? For? *An-y-one?*"

"Sex," says Mateo.

"Thank you," I say.

Tiffany says, "They're fucking."

I grunt. She's right, of course, but she's broken the cardinal rule. "Let's not say 'fucking,'" I say.

"Why not?" asks Tiffany.

"Because it's the wrong word," I say. "And because it's one thing to encounter that word in a text, and it's another thing to use it in class."

"Why's it the wrong word?" Tiffany asks, and her question—its dogged defiance—along with the glance she's just shared with Mateo, the glance he's shared with me in previous class sessions, spurs in me a minor epiphany: *they've* fucked, Tiffany and Mateo, and fucked recently, and Tiffany wants me to know. She wants me to know because she thinks I care. It's not just Willow; it's Tiffany, too, which isn't a crime but is—

I pause, furrow my brow, suck in hard on the insides of my cheeks, force myself to enjoy a moment of lucidity as I consider Tiffany, Mateo, Willow, Tiffany, Mateo—

My verdict is swift: they *haven't* fucked; he's not her type. But if they *had* fucked, which they haven't, she'd be wrong to think I care.

I say, "These two people, at this time in history, would never have thought of what they were doing in that way. It's anathema to the story. It's incongruous. It's wrong. But this isn't even the point." Tiffany won't look at me. "The point is *boy and girl* love. What does this mean? What's the subtext?"

A brunette raises her hand.

"You don't need to raise your hand."

"My name's McKayla."

"I know your name. You don't need to raise your hand, McKayla."

"Boy and girl love?" she says. "No way. Total ick. And she's being all soft about it. Patronizing him and stuff."

"Thank you, McKayla. Yes. That's right. And why exactly is it an insult?"

"It's like telling your boyfriend he has sex like a boy," she says.

"And?" I ask.

"And she doesn't want to have sex with a boy," McKayla says.

"Why not?" I open the question to the entire room. "Why does the nurse, who not too long ago was madly in love with this soldier, why does she no longer want to have sex with him?"

I scan the room. No one but Mateo is looking at me. His expression says, *This is both funny and sad, yes? Simultaneously exhilarating and disheartening? It is amazing, is it not? What they don't know? And they don't know so much . . .*

"Why," I ask again, "does Luz no longer want to have sex with the soldier? How does she know now that theirs was a boy and girl love?"

Tiffany, exasperated, finally spits out an answer. "Because of the Italian."

"Yes." My armpits are damp. "That's right. Because she's met an Irishman."

"*Italian*," Tiffany says.

"Italian," I repeat, flustered. "But the text says, objectively, that she's never known an Italian before this one. So, the subtext here is . . . ?"

"Because," says Tiffany, giving me nothing more than her profile, "she didn't just *meet* the Italian, she had *sex* with the Italian. They *fucked*, and it rocked her world."

"You got it," I say, hopping up from my chair and shoving the day's notes into my bag. "Class dismissed."

4:06 p.m.

Dear Willow,

I'm writing to check in with you. You've missed quite a few classes. Is everything okay? Your name is still on my roster, so I'm assuming you haven't dropped the course. Perhaps you intend to? I hope not!

4:15 p.m.

Dear Prof P,

All good here. I'll be in class next week. My boyfriend dumped me. I haven't really been getting out of bed.

4:16 p.m.

Dear Willow,

I look forward to seeing you next week, and I'm so sorry to hear you've gone through a rough patch. We have resources on campus designed to help students in times like these. Please let me know if you'd like me to send a link.

Be well. See you soon. Let me know if there's anything more I should know.

4:20 p.m.
Dear Prof P,

Thanks. See ya!

4:21 p.m.
Dear Willow,

As long as we're emailing "in real time," I thought I might ask about the cat?

4:22 p.m.
Dear Prof P,

Did you know there were missing signs? Like, for this cat? I found the owner. All's good.

4:23 p.m.
Dear Willow,

Oh wow. I had no idea. I guess it's a happy ending?

4:26 p.m.
Dear Prof P,

Yeah, there were signs EVERYWHERE. And actually I spent $900 at the vet and worked a bunch of extra shifts to cover the fees and I missed a few classes and my boyfriend, my ex-boyfriend, got mad at me because I couldn't go to some stupid frat party and then he cheated on me and I guess I broke up with him but he was the one to cheat and I'm really sorry to unload all this and I should probably just delete but now that I've written it

4:28 p.m.
Dear Willow,

I wouldn't be able to write you a check for $900, but I would be able to pay the clinic who could perhaps reimburse you? I feel terrible about this series of events. Please let me know how I can help. I had no idea Mateo was in a frat. No judgment! But it's a surprise to me.

4:32 p.m.

Dear Prof P,

Mateo? From class? Ew gross? My boyfriend's name is Arnold. EX-BOYFRIEND. I hated his name anyway. The owner already paid me back. Super-cool lady. Sweet kid. They were SO HAPPY. She actually goes to the same vet where my friend works, which is funny. That's how I found her. Not because of the signs. But she told me there were signs and then it was like omigod I see the signs all over now like even at the grocery store. She said she knew you, btw. Small world! Gotta go. Dinner shift.

Three

#FPOP

Days yawn into weeks, and the seasons flutter. All over town, daffodils bloom, followed by tulips, followed by the tentative scapes of hostas. The Irishman—*haha*—sends me filthy one-line texts that I read and delete. My sister comes over for wine in the evenings. Her boys pee from the ledge of our porch. My mother goes on dates, falls in love, gets bored, breaks up, then repeats the process a few weeks later. I see the dentist, the eye doctor, the allergist. My primary physician informs me that it's time to remove my IUD; it's been ten years. She says she can do it herself right now, or I can schedule an appointment for another time. I tell her we should grab time by the balls. She hands me a paper gown and leaves the room.

When the doctor returns, she's with her PA. I remind them what happened when I had my IUD inserted, which is that I lost consciousness, and the last thing I heard before fainting was a nurse yelling, "Help in Celestial! Help in Celestial!"

My doctor says, "We've changed the names of the rooms since then."

"My point is," I say, "it might get ugly."

She slips on a purple glove and inserts her fingers. She says, "Just to see what we're dealing with here."

I ask, after the glove comes off, what we're dealing with here.

She says, "Secret cervix."

"Secret *service*?"

"You have a heart-shaped uterus," she says.

The procedure takes five minutes. I don't pass out, but I do experience a miniature explosion of pain. I ask her if I should get my tubes tied or consider sterilization.

She says, "Oh, honey, you're too old for those things now."

I bite down on the insides of my cheeks and stare at the BMI chart on the wall. I think of starving children, tied-up dogs, pet turtles flushed down toilets. Before I leave, she schedules my first mammogram and informs me that next year we'll be talking about colonoscopies. I think of Bruce; of the mascaraed man who married us in our hearts. One day, we won't have eighty-year-old neighbors: we'll *be* the eighty-year-old neighbors.

At home, I check my email. There's a fan letter from a guy in Water Mill, New York. I know this because his signature contains his full address and also his full credentials: PhD, LCSW, PC. The subject of his email is *Your Recent Interview with Los Angeles Review of Books*. He writes, "I'm taking an educated guess from reading your work that you know Jim Salter's *Light Years* isn't simply about 'heartbreak and betrayal.' Nor do you mention it in your recent *LARB* interview. But your interviewer, whose email I can't find and/or her editor, states in your interview's introduction that your memoir is in line with that literary tradition. I found that offensive insofar as Jim Salter's *Light Years* and your work have more to do with memory, loss, longevity, and relationships than anything close to 'heartbreak and betrayal.' No?" His sign-off is "A reader."

I find his offense adorable and start to write back but think better of it. I text a screenshot to Bruce, who's in his office in the basement. He texts: *Jim!* Then: *Do not write that looney back.* I respond with a crazy-eyes emoji.

I text Jane, *How would you feel if someone wrote a story about you?*

She writes, *Are we talking about your ex?*

I write, *We're talking about you. Pretend I wanted to use you in my fiction.*

She writes, *Would I, as my students say, advance the plot?*

I write, *Absolutely.*

She writes, *Can I be a little bit wicked? A little nefarious?*

I write, *You're saying you'd want input?*

She writes, *If you're writing about me, yes, I suppose I'd like a little bit of artistic contribution.*

I write, *But ultimately your permission isn't necessary, right? It's more about what kind of person I am, yes? I ask or I don't ask? I take or I don't take?*

She writes, *Why do you write? Why does your ex write? Why do any of us write? To make sense of our own experiences, surely, and your marriage was . . . Want to switch to email?*

I write, *I'm looking at an email from my agent in which she's just delivered the news that my ex's publicity team is using my full name in his press material.*

She writes, *I see.*

I write, *Obviously we're using the same source material. It was his marriage as much as it was mine! But he's calling it "fiction"—which offers him a kind of freedom to do and say what he wants—while also attaching that fiction to me.*

She writes, *There are some who would say we've got two divorced people on our hands who can't quite get over themselves.*

I write, *Ouch.*

She writes, *Did you get a cat? I heard you did.*

I write, *Consider me disemboweled.*

She writes, *You know the kind of man who introduces himself by way of saying that his wife is the smartest person he knows?*

I write, *Does such a man exist?*

She writes, *Appropriate me all you want. Permission granted.*

Unprompted, Bruce offers to go across the street to my sister's. It's a little after 5:00 p.m. and drizzly out. He must feel guilty about something, possibly that tomorrow, a Sunday, he'll set the alarm for 5:00 a.m. so he can drive north of Cincinnati for the eleven-year-old's first fencing tournament. She's already there with her mom; he doesn't have to go but he wants to.

We put on raincoats and walk across the street. My mother greets us at the doorway, ready to leave, but Bruce pulls her back inside the house.

"Jesus," I say, instinctively backing away. The place is swarming with children.

A blond boy in an owl mask (maybe my nephew?) runs in front of us, pauses long enough to slap and pinch my thigh (*definitely* my nephew), then beelines for the back stairs, which lead to the basement, which is a children's wonderland of plastic junk and oversize pillows.

My sister appears in the doorway to her kitchen. She says, "No school today," as though it's not a Saturday. Then a neighbor lady I hadn't even noticed adds, "We needed a pop-up. Lots of energy."

Both the neighbor lady and my sister are drinking white wine. A child screams from another room. Nobody—not even the mothers—acknowledges it. If Bruce was feeling guilty about tomorrow's alarm, he isn't anymore. My mother gives me a look like, *This is why I was trying to leave.*

In the kitchen, I find three clean sake glasses and pour wine for Bruce and my mother and me. There's a little girl in here whom I've never seen before. She's got tissue pluming from her mouth and is re-arranging the magnets (creatures of the sea) on the refrigerator. She pulls the Kleenex from between her lips—it's red with blood—and stares up at me. She smiles so that I can see where her two front teeth should be but aren't. Then she points at the fish on the fridge.

"Here is a scene," she says. "This one is eating that one and that one is eating this other one."

What she's arranged is a barracuda facing a shark facing a squid. Her eye contact is making me nervous. My nephews, because they are accustomed to their aunt who never knocks and always enters, rarely consider me, much less acknowledge me, much less make eye contact.

I say to this little girl, "I was always jealous of the kids who lost both their front teeth at the same time. They got to stand at the head of the class and sing that song about whistling at Christmas."

She says, "Christmas already happened," which is technically true. I nod at her gravely. She nods back at me. This is why I don't like parties.

Bruce walks in and says, "Is that a scene?" Then he engages the little girl in a lengthy conversation about sea creatures and marine adventures. My mother takes her sake glass of wine from me and says, "This is why I was trying to leave."

I feel like I'm tripping because I am. I popped a high-end gummy just before donning my raincoat. I didn't do drugs as a teenager—(overly affected by those *This is your brain on drugs* commercials, wherein a dis-embodied hand cracks an egg into a cast-iron skillet)—and as a result, it takes very few milligrams to get me high.

Tomorrow is Daylight Saving, which means Bruce will set three alarms tonight. Two of them he'll cop to; the third he'll think is secret. What will happen is this: because he won't trust either of our phones to reset, he'll also set the plug-in alarm. When he thinks I'm not looking, *which is never*, he'll also do this totally endearing thing, which is set the timer on his phone for the number of hours he's allotted himself to sleep before he needs to hop out of bed—which he does also literally: he hops out of bed because, for him, there is no in-between: there is wake and there is sleep. Once out of bed, he'll wash his face, pour his coffee, fill his water bottle, and leave in time to arrive north of Cincinnati before his daughter's 8:00 a.m. bout, which would have been yesterday's 7:00 a.m.

Bruce is an anxious traveler, but I won't throw stones because I can't get on an airplane without Valium or Klonopin or Xanax. Last summer, we all flew west together for my brother's fiftieth in Denver. It was the first time my sister had been on a plane with me in years. I hadn't told anyone, but I wanted to try flying without my medication. I wanted to prove to myself I could do it—that I could hold the plane up with my thoughts and without panicking or crying or howling. Before takeoff, as always, I assumed crash-landing position.

Twenty minutes in, my hands a pair of claws digging into my calves, my eyes clenched tight, tears streaming into my jeans, my sister (who was sitting across the aisle, next to my mother, who was sleeping against the window) tapped me delicately on the shoulder. I turned my face in her direction and opened one eye. She, too, had assumed crash-landing position, but her body was loose and her face was bright with both amusement and concern.

She whispered, "Did you not take anything?" I shook my head, which was sideways, but she must have understood, because she held out her hand. At the end of one of her fingers was a little pink pill, which, when I opened my mouth, she placed neatly under my tongue. (*Always* place it under the tongue.) Fifteen minutes later, I was upright and reading the newspaper on my phone.

Sometimes I wonder if it amuses or annoys Bruce that my sister has such free access to my mouth and I to hers. Just last week, we were in our dining room—my sister and me on one side of the table, Bruce and the eleven-year-old on the other—when I noticed a large piece of spinach between my sister's teeth. I told her to hold still and, without her permission, reached over and plucked it from her mouth. She didn't even flinch. The eleven-year-old widened her eyes. I could see she was impressed; that she understood she'd just witnessed some new dimension of heretofore impossible-to-imagine familiarity and derangement between these two adult women. On the other hand, Bruce gasped. Though the gasp might have happened after the plucking, when my sister grabbed my finger and ate the spinach from it.

This past Friday, I ran to the cathedral a mile from our house. There'd been a late snow, and the trucks hadn't plowed. The Catholics always salt, which means their sidewalks have great footing. On my second loop around, there was a little girl on the playground who was standing behind the bars of the fence line, watching me run. She was wearing her uniform, a pair of sweatpants under the plaid skirt. As I passed, she meowed at me. I did another loop—it's a city block, exactly half a mile—and she was still there. She hissed as I passed. I considered hissing back. I looped around again, which, depending on my speed and the weather and the footing, can take anywhere from three and a half minutes to five. This time she hissed at me and held up her mittens as though they were talons. The next time around she was gone, which made me sad, which weirded me out. I crossed the road and ran away from the cathedral, in the direction of the hospital run by the Shriners, who can sometimes be stingy with their salt and lazy with their shoveling.

This is something I know: if I'd ever had a child of my own, I would have wanted it to meow at me. I would have wanted it to hiss and purr and scratch and gnash its teeth with dissatisfaction and disdain. I would have wanted something eerie and a little bit sickly. I would have wanted it to look at me with suspicion and doubt, and in the mornings, I'd have wanted it strangely to be already in the kitchen when I walked in, sitting there alone, eating cereal in the dark, waiting, listening, plotting. I could have loved a child like that, I think. I could have cared for it and groomed it and checked it for fleas and lice.

Instead, there is the bald man, and there is his daughter, who is getting too old too fast, even as she isn't getting old fast enough.

Here is a scene: it is morning, and he is driving away from me in the dark, and she is somewhere already awake, brushing her teeth, doing her funny forward lunges, feeling nervous for the bouts to come. And I am here, in the in-between, in a bed on the second floor of a house in Kentucky. I am in the lost hour, the skipped hour. I am alone, without a child of my own, and it's all happening too quickly, and it couldn't be over too soon.

In the few minutes before my class begins, my students inform me that, in the state of Kentucky, a married woman—a *wife*—needs the permission of her husband to have her tubes tied.

"No," I nearly shriek. "That can't be right!"

It's true, they tell me with great satisfaction.

"What about a single woman?" I ask.

"No dice," says the scholar with graying hair. "They've got us there, too. Single women don't qualify at all."

I am aghast, and I tell them so.

They shrug, as if to say, *Yeah, well, life . . .*

Later, walking across campus, I overhear a man in a parking lot say to a woman, "If I were you, I . . ." And for the rest of the afternoon, all I can think of are sentences that begin, "If I were me . . ."

If I were me, I'd care less about what my colleagues think of me, especially the men. If I were me, I'd show more cleavage while I still have it and wear body-clinging shirts and get over my fear of the dark. If I were me, I'd learn to fly a plane instead of living in dread of walking aboard one. If I were me, I'd drink a Tom Collins for breakfast and never get drunk and never be hungover and not care one bit about its sugar content and what it might do to my love handles. If I were me,

I'd trust more easily and love with abandon. I'd leave my clothes strewn all about the house and the laundry unfolded, and I wouldn't make my bed first thing in the morning. I wouldn't vacuum up the coffee grounds with a hand-size vacuum whose sole purpose is to vacuum up coffee grounds. In fact, if I were me, I wouldn't even own the hand-size vacuum. If I were me, I'd have told my husband to shove off, find his own profession, stop following me around and using me as a stepping stone for his career. I'd have told him my name's not Angela and I wasn't knifed to death by a homeless man, but if I had been knifed to death by a homeless man, and the story had been mine, I'd have first given that man a job, a desire, a name, some titch of humanity as opposed to reducing him to a means to an abrupt and unexpected end. If I were me, I'd have interrupted that man in the parking lot who was telling that woman in the parking lot what he would do differently if he were her, and I would have told him that if I were him, I'd—

My phone pulses: *Let's fuck hard.* I nearly scream; in fact, I do scream, and a robin on the sidewalk just ahead flits quickly away. I delete the message, and then I pause—*She pauses,* I think to myself. *She considers and then decides*—I start running. My feet will be ruined by the time I get home. I don't care.

I keep my eyes on the sidewalk, and I run; I bound; I leap over curbs and puddles and cracks. I dodge cigarette butts, crushed mini bottles of booze, at least one banana peel, what may or may not be the tail feather from a red-tailed hawk. I do anything to avoid looking through the windshields of passing cars. I don't want to see who's seeing me—colleagues, students, strangers, the Irishman. And yet I can't help seeing myself in third person: there she is, hair hanging loose like a madman, backpack bouncing cumbrously, hands pumping awkwardly, the cadence of her footfalls all wrong. Is she running toward something? Away from someone? Does she need help? Is she . . . okay?

I throw open the front door to my home. I'm breathless, sweaty, already calling Bruce's name. I'm panting when I tell him that, for Christmas next year, I want to give Theo a pan of lasagna with homemade pasta and pork Bolognese. He balks. "Too impractical," he says. "Also too bizarre." I tear paper towels from the roll and wipe my face, my neck, my arms, as I point out to him that there's a street not a block and a half away where the houses are twice the size of ours and whose occupants routinely give Theo and Oscar front-row seats to basketball games, hundred-dollar bills, gift certificates to high-end clothing stores.

"No lasagna," Bruce says, and I storm off, backpack still on, face slippery with perspiration, to the rear of the house and gaze out at our tiny lawn where one day, surely, there will be a plunge pool.

Several hours later, the eleven-year-old finds me in the kitchen. I've showered, changed clothes, put colorful bandages where blisters have formed on the outer edges of my little toes.

I'm scooping balls from a melon.

She says, "What are you doing?"

I say, "Scooping balls from a melon."

She says, "Did you know there will be no fish in the sea by 2053?"

I say, "I thought you said there'd be not enough resources to sustain humanity."

She says, "I stayed up late last night thinking."

My stepfather, the furniture-kicker, would have said, "Did it hurt?"

I say, "What did you think about?"

She says, "First I was thinking about *Jaws*."

"That makes sense," I say, "on account of how we just took you to see it."

"Why don't you have children?"

"I have you."

"Why don't you have your own children?"

"There are lots of ways to have a family."

"That's what you and Dad always say."

"I don't have children because by 2053 there will be no fish in the sea."

"That's funny," she says. "Why aren't you and Dad married? Wait. Never mind. I know what you'll say, so never mind."

"What will I say?"

"That there are lots of ways to have a family."

"That's funny."

"What if everyone stayed up at night and had big thoughts?" she asks.

"Are these people staying up past their bedtime?"

"But for real, what if everyone stayed up at night and thought about what was wrong with them and the world and . . . ?"

"Do you think about what's wrong with you?"

"I think about what's wrong with the world, and I think a lot about mushrooms."

"Good. You have your whole life as a grown-up to think about what's wrong with you. Concentrate on the world and mushrooms for now."

"Do you . . . ?" She trails off.

"Do I what?"

"Do you believe in . . . ?"

"Believe in what?"

She whispers, nearly inaudible, "I don't believe in god."

"Me neither."

She lets out an enormous sigh. This kid! This eleven-year-old kid!

"Remember that prayer circle I went to?"

"I remember the volunteering you did at that church. I didn't realize there were prayers and a circle."

"Well, there were. We stood in a circle, and we had to hold hands, and this man told us that it was our job to take care of other people. He said it was our duty. That's why god put us on earth."

"Hm."

"I liked volunteering."

"Good."

"I didn't care about the circle."

"How'd you feel about holding hands?"

"I washed them right after."

"Your dad would have washed his hands, too."

"But what I decided was that if people need to believe in a god as a way to be nice to other people, then I think that's okay. Even though, you know, I don't believe."

"Oh, yeah," I say, "me too. Me too! I only care about religion and other people's beliefs if they get in the way of my freedom."

"Yeah," she says, then, pursing her lips, adds, "Except what do you mean?"

I fork her over a melon ball. She eats it. I fork her a few more, and before I know it—without permission and without help—I am explaining to an eleven-year-old blue laws, the importance and danger of rhetoric, abortion, women's rights, 1972, Title IX, gender equality, honor killings, and Malala.

She responds by asking if she can check her email and google a few things. I say sure. Forty-five minutes later she's back in the kitchen with a handwritten list. She says, "Did you know . . . ?" and then she lists what she deems to be Kentucky's most unusual laws, and they are:

Citizens are required to bathe once a year.
It's illegal to shoot off a policeman's tie.
Women need their husband's permission to buy a hat.
Animals are not allowed to molest cars.
It's illegal to catch certain fish with a bow and arrow.
*Women between ninety and two hundred pounds who wish to walk
    down the side of a highway in a swimsuit must either have the
    escort of at least two officers or be armed with a club.*

She says, "That last one specifically does not apply to female horses."

I say, "Meaning that a female horse of any weight can walk down a highway in a swimsuit without an escort?"

"I guess?" She shrugs. "Funny that two men are the equivalent of one club."

I say, "Funny that you assume the officers are men."

A conversation via text—

    Sɪssʏ: guess what

    Mᴇ: what

    Sɪssʏ: guess

    Mᴇ: you're pregnant

    Sɪssʏ: that's your party joke

    Mᴇ: only on April Fools'

    Sɪssʏ: I'm leaving

    Mᴇ: leaving work?

    Sɪssʏ: guess again

    Mᴇ: leaving your husband?

    Sɪssʏ: guess again

    Mᴇ: Kentucky?????

    Sɪssʏ: I'm going to Chamonix for the month!!!

    Mᴇ: with whom

Sissy: our brother

Me: what about me?

Sissy: u teach

Me: when did this happen????

Sissy: we decided today

Me: who's going?

Sissy: everyone

Me: everyone?

Sissy: mom

Me: mom?????

Sissy: and my family

Me: this is nuts

Sissy: everyone will be there

Me: everyone but me

As promised, I meet Mateo for coffee to discuss his most recent story, which isn't half bad. One of the highlights comes toward the end, when a wife, returning with a fresh round of drinks for her husband and sister, catches sight of the two of them. They're not paying attention to her. They don't know that she's watching them. The bar's crowded and they've assumed it will take her longer to be served than it has. But she's just had her own suggestive encounter with a bartender who's flirtatiously caught her eye. As she heads back to her table, she's feeling youthful, sexy, and she almost misses it—this gesture between them. Her sister's hand is on her husband's thigh. Not his thigh, really, but the high side seam of his pants. First the wife sees the hand; then she sees their faces, their eye contact. Just like that, she sees they're in love. Her discovery is instantaneous, and her world as she knows it is changed forever.

But the real strength of the story is in the decision Mateo makes next. The wife delivers the drinks. She takes her seat. She lets her sister know that she's seen her hand on her husband's leg, and the sister—taking it all in—understands they've been caught. To her brother-in-law she says, "Is that denim?" And the brother-in-law looks down at the fabric of his pants and says, "I think it is." The night moves on, they get a few more rounds, and nobody says anything else about it. The reader feels shattered and sad for the wife, but in this way, it is a surprisingly realistic portrait of the decisions we make every day to move forward in life by way of self-delusions and lies.

The coffee shop Mateo chooses is one I've never been to before. It's dark and close and empty, set up like a shotgun diner with a small front counter and two short rows of booths in the back.

Mateo is at a rear booth, close to a dartboard and the restrooms. His computer is open, his hoodie pulled up. A bare bulb hangs from the ceiling just above him.

I approach, feeling jittery and already caffeinated, and drop my bag onto the opposite bench.

He looks up. "You found me," he says, closing his laptop and pushing it aside. It's corny how excited he is to see me, which calms me.

"Let me get you something." He picks up his mug.

"Thanks." I settle into the booth across from him. "Decaf. No room for cream." I take out my wallet.

"You can pay when you leave," he says. "I come here all the time. They trust me."

There's a mistiness to the air, as though the employees smoke after hours while they count their tips.

I shrug out of my jacket. While I wait, I tally the number and types of animals I've saved this year while out for a run. After a few minutes, Mateo returns. Instead of two cups of coffee, he has two bottles of beer.

"I thought this was a coffee shop," I say.

"It is," he says, sitting down. "But it's also a bar."

"Where's my coffee?"

"Too late in the day for coffee. Don't you think?"

He puts a beer in front of me. "Clink," he says, raising his and drinking.

I push the bottle away and cross my arms.

"You're annoyed?"

"You've misled me."

"I just wanted a drink."

I open my bag, pull out his story, and flip to the final scene, which occurs after the couple takes a cab home from the bar and walks silently into their empty house. "Your instinct here at the end is good. And you've made the empty house first and foremost what it really is—an empty house. In the revision, you could push the symbolism a little more, make sure the reader knows you're being intentional."

"Seriously?"

"You disagree? Have I misread the ending?"

"You won't drink the beer?"

"I owe you comments on this story," I say. "I'm here to give them to you."

"You know I'm legal, right? I'm twenty-seven years old."

I hold up a hand and look away. "Don't tell me your age," I say. "I did not ask how old you are."

"Come on," he says, laughing. "I didn't say you asked. I offered the information. You're not hiring me, are you? This isn't an interview. I get beers with my math instructor all the time. This is me saying thank you for taking time out of your day to talk to me."

"Is your math instructor a woman?"

"Is that a sexist question?"

I scowl, then raise a finger. "Hold on." I send Bruce a text: *Mateo ordered me a beer, not coffee.* I wait.

"What are you doing?" Mateo asks.

I raise my finger again. A few seconds later, Bruce responds: *Are you asking permission?*

I write: *I'm asking for advice.*

He writes: *He's over 21?*

I write: *Yes.*

He writes: *Drink the beer. I'll have one when I get home. We'll be even.*

I put my phone back on the table facedown.

"Who were you texting?" asks Mateo.

"My boyfriend."

"Bullshit."

"The truth."

"Show me." He reaches for my phone.

I grab it and shove it under my leg.

"You win," Mateo says, laughing again. "I don't have a math instructor. I only take your workshop. I get it. I get it. But seriously, you've never had a drink with a student before? You never got drinks with professors when you were in school?"

I had. Countless times.

"One drink won't get you fired, will it?"

Of course it won't get me fired, but it's difficult not to be paranoid; difficult not to consider what it might look like if, say, Willow walked in. Or Tiffany. Or Jane. Even so, I take a sip.

"It's a smart move you made," I say, "making the other woman the sister. How'd you know to do that? It's a cheat. But it works."

"Yeah," he says. "I wondered if you'd catch that. I wanted it to be a friend, right? Someone close—"

"But you didn't want to spend time developing the friendship."

"Right, right," he says. "That's not where I wanted the story's energy."

"You made it the sister, because—"

"Because, *sister*! Sometimes it's okay to borrow the ingrained implications."

"Smart," I say. "Different from saying 'Starbucks' as shorthand for 'coffee shop.'"

"Can I ask you something?"

"Sure." I lean back and take another drink.

"What are your thoughts on infidelity?"

"Nope," I say. I shake my head and wipe my mouth. "Next."

"I bet you've at least thought about it, in some purely theoretical way. Because of your ex and what happened. Especially with his book coming out."

"Moving on." I use two hands to steady my beer.

"With regards to my story, then—"

"I take the viewpoint of the wife," I say. "I buy the sister's actions, but I don't relate. Too messy for my taste. That's okay, though. We don't and shouldn't relate to every character. We just need to believe them."

"But potentially it's worth the mess," Mateo says. "Infidelity."

"An easy opinion to have if you've never been married."

"You'd be good at it, I bet."

"At infidelity?"

"At lying," he says.

I glance behind me. The place is still empty. The only employee is at the front of the shop, behind the counter, his attention aimed at his phone. Another person might leave right now, but I'd argue more of us would stay than not—life being what it is: a series of minutes compiled into hours compiled into days. And that's what I do. I stay.

"You say the damnedest things, Mateo."

"People go into affairs thinking it's about sex," he continues. "They think they'll be riddled with guilt and, after a few horny and satisfying interludes, their affection for their partner will be renewed. But what I see right and left is people getting wrapped up emotionally in their mistress." He pauses, then adds, "Or mister."

"Keen insight," I say. "Spoken like someone who's been married and had an affair. You channel that logic into your fiction with clarity."

"I have been married," he says. "I have had an affair."

My beer bottle doesn't make perfect contact with my lips as he answers, and the tiniest bit of beer lands on my chin. His face brightens noticeably at having caught me off guard. I wipe my chin with my sleeve before he can reach across the booth and do it for me.

"I was able to stay detached," he says, "but she wasn't. She told my wife. The marriage didn't last the year."

"Heavy," I say. I run my thumb around the lip of the bottle.

"How did you find out?" he asks. "Did she tell you? Or did he slip up?"

I think of my ex-husband and the first time we saw each other after he'd started his affair and we both knew the marriage was over. I think of the way he slumped through the front door of a home he'd never spend another night in. He was crying. I was crying, too. We held on to each other for a long time. It wasn't a hug; it was something much sadder, much worse than a hug. Call it a cling. Our dog crazy-eighted around us, and we clung.

"We're not here to talk about me."

"I'm trying to make you blush," Mateo says. "It's working."

I try conjuring images of Sarah McLachlan's starving animals—

neglected kittens with flea-infested ears, inbred dogs with skin diseases and missing limbs—anything to keep from thinking about the zhuzh of embarrassment reddening my cheeks.

"You think I'd get attached," he says.

"Attached to what?"

"To you."

I cough a little and push the beer away for a second time, but the gesture is meaningless: the bottle is empty. Somehow, I've finished it. "We're here to discuss storytelling and fiction writing."

"You think I'd fall in love."

"I have no idea what you're talking about."

The sole employee appears at our booth and picks up our empties. "Another?" he asks.

I shake my head. Mateo signals for one more round. Ignoring me, the waiter nods and walks away, reminding me that a boys' club can pop up anywhere, at any time, between any two men.

"Let me ask you something else," Mateo says.

"Are you really twenty-seven?"

He grimaces. "I'm thirty-two. The kids freak out less if they think I'm still in my twenties. Can I ask you one more thing?"

I flit through the pages of the story.

"This one's easy. Everyone has an answer. It's not personal." He's holding back a smile. "Two questions, really."

"I'm listening."

"First question," he says. "Mechanical bull—have you ever been on one?"

"Do they really exist? Outside movies filmed in Texas?"

"I'll take that as a no." He's bouncing a little, no doubt charmed by his own pluck. "But you're familiar. Good."

"Next question."

"Do you think you'd be good at it?"

"At riding a mechanical bull?" Naively, I take his question literally and imagine myself on a bull. "You know what?" I say. "Yes. As a matter of fact, I think I'd be all right."

"Not surprising."

"No?"

"No," he says. "People who think they'd be good on a mechanical bull also think they're good at sex."

"You said this wasn't personal," I whisper crossly.

"Which gets back to your assertion that any man who had an affair with you would get attached."

"I didn't say that. I didn't say any of that."

The waiter brings our beers. I don't look up at him; I don't thank him. Across from me, Mateo is gloating. I want to slap him.

"What I don't like about your findings," I say, "is what I often don't like about the dialogue in your stories."

"Woof," he says. "Low blow."

Frowning, I continue: "You've manufactured this entire conversation. You've steered us toward the bull. In fact, you didn't just steer us here, you introduced it apropos of nothing. We didn't come to it organically."

"And this is what I don't like about you as a teacher."

"You're changing the subject," I say.

"You refuse to acknowledge the artifice at the heart of storytelling— of writing it down in the first place."

"On the contrary," I say, "I'm the first to acknowledge the ridiculousness of the whole endeavor."

"Anyway," he says, "why not take a larger, perhaps more generous look at the situation of our story?"

"We don't have a story," I say.

"The story of the teacher and the student at a bar in the middle of the day."

"A *coffee shop*," I seethe. "I don't have time anymore, Mateo. We've talked too long."

"No, you don't," he says, reaching across the booth and taking hold of my wrist. "You can't go making excuses to leave just yet. You promised we'd talk about my story."

Where his hand touches my wrist, where his fingers fall from the face of my watch onto the back of my hand, my skin tingles. It feels as though my entire arm has taken a giant gasp of cold air—a star implodes; a hurricane makes landfall; an ecosystem sprouts to life—and I know it for what it is: chemistry: old-fashioned, animalistic chemistry.

"Jesus," I say, yanking my arm away and, doing so, knocking over my new beer. Immediately I'm drenched. "Shit. Shit." I move quickly out of the booth, bumping the table as I do. Mateo's bottle wobbles, but he grabs it in time.

Before I know it, the waiter is upon me with a dishrag, and the two of them are suddenly in front of me, both standing and dabbing at my shirt, my sweater, my jeans.

"It's fine," I say, pushing them off me. "I'm fine. It's fine. Most of it's on the ground." I take the rag from the waiter and bend over to wipe up the floor. And as I do—as I bend over to wipe up this preposterous mess in front of these two preposterous men—everything catches up with me all at once: my ex, his betrayal, the Irishman, the injured tabby, my family's trip to Chamonix without me, my sister across the street with her entire family for the rest of my life, Bruce and his daughter, and all of our shit, my shit, everything. And I realize I'm not just mad, but riotously mad, mad not at life, but at the world. On a scale of one to five, I am magnificently beyond a million.

I drop the rag. "I'm leaving," I say. "Move back. Get out of my way."

"It's on me," says Mateo.

"Are you kidding?" I'm on the brink of hysteria. "Not in a hundred years." I take two twenties from my wallet and shove them in the waiter's hand. "Keep the change." I barrel toward the exit, pushing open the door and all but tumbling onto the sidewalk.

Outside, the sky is too bright, the sunshine too strong. A breeze has picked up. I feel drunker than I am; there's an uneven throbbing in my thighs, my palms, my eyelids. And suddenly, with a ferocious kind of vibrancy, I remember forest walks as a little girl when my sister would ask me to play blind, and, my eyes closed, she'd guide me by voice and by hand through the woods, stumbling, the sun coming through my eyelids hot and red. The trick of the trees overhead—the move from sun to shade—always made me fearful of a low branch, fearful she might not warn me in time to duck. I'd shoot my hand up to feel for the tree, its leaves, the foliage I felt certain was nearby, only to find air, clean and shaded air. I never cheated. I never opened my eyes. I played blind best of all.

A hand from behind touches my shoulder. I lurch forward. "You need to stop that," I say, swatting at Mateo.

He holds out my backpack. "You forgot this." He's sheepish, and his expression—the hangdog dumbness of it—unsettles me, and I realize just how careless I've been. Here is someone who gets off on making up stories.

Oh, curse this gormless, gutless girl I have become!

No. Not girl. I am decades done with girlhood.

Mateo begins to reach for me—his hand toward my cheek. It seems he intends to caress my face, bring his . . . bring his lips to mine . . . *here* . . . on a sidewalk near campus in the middle of the afternoon. I feel dizzy, out of control; my breath is shallow, erratic. I stand still as a statue.

And then, just then, like some sort of mirage, like a squiggle in the desert, like a pack mule on the beach at high tide, I see him, my father, a few blocks down on the other side of the street, his cowboy hat utterly unmissable.

This doesn't go where I thought it might.

W alk with me," my father says, and I do.

"I'm doing remarkably okay," he says. "Hanging in there. Getting ready to travel. Good-looking kid you were talking to just now."

"Travel? Where are you going?"

"I've started, in my own fashion, learning French. I met this guy; he knows more shit about more things. He's a really good resource. I got something on my phone because of him. This thing called Duolingo."

"*You're* going to Chamonix, too?"

"I'm doing Duolingo. I tried to find a coach online but it's all bullshit. Then someone said call the damn university, and I did and, boy, a guy calls me back. This graduate student, Gus. He's happy to make twenty bucks an hour, and he's fabulous. I went to Black Swan, that bookstore with the old books, and there was a Berlitz book from forty years ago, with the CD still in it. It's all the same stuff. French is French is French. So I bought that. And then Gus got me a grammar book. Also, he had a terrific idea. He said, 'Man, I'd never have gone to grad school if I hadn't started listening to music in French and having words to read.' So now I've got the sheet music in French and in English. Because French, you know, the pronunciations are so foreign. To me, Spanish—*efe, ese, ay ay ay*—these make logic. But French is *a-whole-nother* world. You've got these words with *cees* and little apostrophes, and they're *this* long. But they're only *one* word." He chuckles. "Getting that concept is wonderful. Gus thought of ten songs, and I got 'em. Including the infamous Edith Piaf. 'La vie en rose.' Gus didn't know Jacques Brel. That was my idea. I told him, 'Look, I'll give you another twenty. Go get me some Jacques Brel and also some ballads or some slow songs.' I want *slow-er* songs because it'll make it easier to learn. So now I go to the coffee shop, and I've got my Bose headset, and I just eat it up. I can do this for hours. I leave for Paris tomorrow, not Chamonix."

"Tomorrow?"

"Not tomorrow. Monday. Tomorrow, I go to New York. I leave from Lexington, from Louisville, I mean."

"And then Paris on Monday?"

"No. Not on Monday. Paris a week from Monday."

"You'll be in New York for a week?"

"I'll be in New York for two nights."

"Where will you be before Paris?"

"It's a lost week. It's private information." He pauses, as if to consider. "It's a place I'm mesmerized by. It's part of Portugal. It's Madeira. It's a marlin-fishing place. They've got twenty-five boats out there. They catch huge marlin. It's reasonably cheap. Temperature seventy. It stays wonderful. Portugal has always intrigued me because you never hear shit about Portugal. Nobody shoots anybody in Portugal. There's never any earthquakes in Portugal. People get along. And the temperature is my kind of temperature. Temperature seventy. A guy told me about a place on the west coast. He said he could've spent his life sitting outside watching the sun go down, and I found an old hotel there. Super reasonable. None of these nine-hundred-dollar rooms and shit. After, I'll go to Paris, where I found a two-hundred-dollar-a-night thing. Balcony and air conditioning. But the temperature—What do you think the weather is in Paris today?"

"In Paris? This time of year? Wouldn't it be somewhat hot?"

"No. I don't think it'll be much over seventy. Wait a minute." He retrieves his phone from his jacket pocket. "I'll say it's gonna be sixty-eight. Let's see." Into his phone he says, "Paris temperature Fahrenheit."

He consults the results on the screen. "Seventy-four! And look, for the week, sixty-eight, sixty-nine, seventy-two, seventy-three, sixty-nine . . . It's not hot in Paris now. Not anymore."

"That's the hourly forecast. Look. See? It'll be eighty next week."

"Really? Well"—his voice is full of disappointment—"that's hogwash. I guess it's getting warmer. That's not what I had in mind at all."

"No, no," I say quickly. "Ignore me. What do I know about weather? What does anyone know about weather anymore? And you dress the same no matter what. You won't have to repack or anything. It'll be beautiful. It's going to be beautiful. Paris this time of year sounds ideal."

"I'm healthy. I've got drugs for the month. I got a cheap flight with a business seat on this airline that's marginal, but they haven't crashed. Here, get a drink with me. Let's dip in right here. Martinis always make me feel more intelligent."

We dip into a neighborhood bistro. The place is empty. They've only just opened. We're still an hour shy of the workday's official end.

To a skinny guy behind the bar, my father says, "You got basil? Great. Beat the blazes out of some basil. Then Ketel, a tiny bit of sugar, no juice of any kind. People put in lemon, grapefruit. I don't want that." To me he says, "What are you drinking?"

I ask the bartender if they have Boodles.

"What did Travis McGee drink?" my father asks me. "Was it Boodles?"

The bartender, who is indeed beating the blazes out of some basil, tells me they're out.

My father says, "Standard Bombay I always thought was great. Just the regular stuff. Not the Sapphire. Take a sample of it. Just do a little shot. He'll pour it for you. They like to pour it for you."

"Beefeaters, please," I say. "On the rocks. With bitters and a slice of lemon."

"Beefeaters is classic," my father says. "Let's hang a little bit."

He pulls out a chair for me. Maybe right this very second, wondering where I am, if I'm still having a beer with Mateo, Bruce is pulling out a chair for my mother—broad-shouldered Bruce, the bald man, whose love for me is anything but boy-girl.

"I look back on these last few years, and I think I've wasted a lot of time being blue. But it's a path. Here's to your generosity and for-giveness. Hey, cheers. I'll get to the airport at two for the eight o'clock flight, and I'll hang. I've got my French; I've got my songs. I've got Spotify now! Your mother said something about Spotify once."

"She gets logged out a lot."

"You can actually store songs! I've got ten, and tomorrow I'll meet Gus and get twenty more. It's so exciting." He grabs my upper arm. "It's so exciting to learn something new. And to know—*ume, ume, ume.* Gus is a perfect guy. He's open. Open to life. I love the idea of being able to . . . I'm not there yet but I'm getting there. We meet at the coffee shop. The sound and the music . . . I love going there. I've got friends. They like me. I can leave my stuff for an hour. No one's gonna touch it. It puts me in contact with people. I'm a connector, you know. I was talking to my doctor. Yeah, that doctor. I haven't talked to him in months. I love that son of a bitch. If he wanted to make money . . . He is so deep. I mean, the guy is so deep and funny, too." He laughs to himself. "He's just embraced the idea that—He knows you're not gonna be here forever. He celebrates living and this idea: *I want to be awake the day I die.* I mean, he's just got this . . . He says, 'When I walk down the street now, it's not like I used to when I walked down the street, and when I sit in the backyard . . .' He's one of those *who's here.* He's present. He's aware of everything he comes into contact with. He said to me, 'One thing—'"

"What's that mean? He 'walks down the street'? Is that a metaphor?"

"He walks down the street. It's not a metaphor. It's life. He's watch-ing the birds, hearing the wind blow, seeing the leaves flutter. He is *at that kind of level.* He was talking about these middle-aged women, you know, how they sometimes get drinking and carrying on in public, and it's true for the most part, they're always messing with each other, touchin' and talkin', and I love that. I want that. To touch and talk and mess with someone. So free with life, so connected. Saturday night I—Actually, I had a date."

"Someone local?"

"No, not local. I know this saxophone player who is out of this world. The guy is cool. He does the Sinatra-type stuff, of course, but he can *play. the. sax.* like you cannot believe. He's extraterrestrial. The thing is, Small Fry, I don't have any extra time. Not anymore. There's no meanness to it. I'm not trying to get even with anything. I just want to be here, too. I want to have fun. I want to be with people who are alive."

"Sure. That makes sense."

"I want to be as alive as I can for as long as I can and be as attractive as I can"—he smiles, but it's more of a growl, his teeth barred, his lips wide—"so I can have people who want to be with me."

"In Portugal, you'll be with a woman? Am I right to think that?"

"Sure."

"Not someone local?"

"The truth is, she's a friend. Someone I've known a long time. It's not going anywhere. It's like *Same Time, Next Year* with Alan Alda."

"The woman from New Orleans."

"Maybe I'm having misgivings. Maybe not."

"Are you divorced yet? Or still married? My question isn't a judgment."

"I'm on the other side of lost love. I'm over it. The papers are down there. She procrastinates."

"Do you have your will in order?"

"No."

"You should."

"I plan to return alive from my travels."

"That's not what I meant."

"I'm working toward trying to get things straightened, straighter. I should have done that already. I'm kicking myself. But I will. Look, even my lists have lists. Look." He pulls out an envelope, on the back of which is a long list in his handwriting.

"This is today," he says. "And I've got"—he reads from the list—"Hana, Hana's book, deposit, drugs, send book to friend, call Arnold in Edinburgh, corroded switch—" He looks up from the list. "In the islands, there's a big switch under these bushes. That's a grand I have to cough up." He goes back to the list. "Jeanie's groceries for guests next week, leather samples, belts." He folds the list up and puts it back into his pocket.

"Kid, I got a good carry-on." He presses his hands together as though he's praying. "I finally bought 'the Pilot's Carry On.' I'm sick of these doodads that rip and tear. This one will last forever. I plan to buy two copies of *The Little Prince* in New York. One in French and one in English. There's a bookstore near the park. Gus told me about it. A little place that specializes in French. I'll be there tomorrow, Saturday, one o'clock."

"Tomorrow in New York."

"Flight was a grand. I leave from Lexington. No, Louisville. To New York. Then Portugal. Then Paris, then Edinburgh. Did I tell you I learned to preorder an Uber? I put it in my phone." He holds up his phone. "I've never done it before. I want to learn *to do* things. I want to learn *how* to do *more* things. I want to be younger again. I'm functional now. I can walk and talk. I can sleep. I have vivid, incredible dreams. I'm still like a teenager about some things, but what the hell? I think, in a way, because I had no real discipline, and I've sort of run everywhere and from everything, I've found, finally, a few nuggets. I found an art form I do, which is my leatherwork—the belts, the wallets. And I'm having connections."

"You're a connector."

"I'm a connector! Yes! I've been absentmindedly selfish about so many things. I'm much more sensitive now. I can listen, and I can share. I'm happier. Coming to grips with 'I've found the enemy, and he is me.' I have a blazer. I like to wear a blazer to the airport, because when I get there, I take all the crap, cram it into my pockets, put it back on, on the other side of security, and I've got all my stuff. Bam . . . But this new bag I got. It's a carry-on, and it's just so nice to have a good carry-on. Military grade. All the old-time pilots have them for sure. They cost an arm and a leg. The latch, the handle—down there at the base—there are these two little things and you do it like this, and you cram it down or you pull it back up, and it catches. Ta-da! There's no funky contraption at the top. I don't like that. I like it down at the bottom."

A waitress, a tatted-up beauty, comes into the bar with a plate of food. "Hey, y'all," she says, "I want to show you something. It's our fish feature tonight, which is pompano and—"

"Pompano!" exclaims my father.

"Yeah!" the waitress begins. "Florida p—"

"I don't know where in the hell you get it," my father interrupts, "but pompano is the best fish in the ocean."

"It is," she says. "It's *so* sweet, and it's got this *lovely* text—"

"You take a pompano," he says, "you put butter on it, and put it in the oven—you don't need anything else."

"Well," she says, "that's the thing I was going to say: it's just salt and pepper on the fish itself because it tastes so good, and then there's a brown butter emulsion—"

My father burps.

"—on the plate underneath, and then a mix of baby squash and—"

"Best fish in the ocean," he says. "But you never find pompano in a market."

"Chef just recently started getting it," she says. "I can't think of the name of his supplier. He gets them really, *really* fresh and—"

"They're such a great fish."

"It's my favorite that we serve here."

The bartender asks how we're doing on drinks, and the waitress exits with the food.

"I'm developing a little faith," my father says. "The direction I want to go can lead me to what I want to find. That's kind of basic, right? Kind of like Chauncey the Gardener?"

I say, "'Study finds people who smile more are happier.'"

"No question. It's obvious. I never thought about it before this very instant, but the title of that movie *Being There* . . ."

My father raises his hands before him as if genuinely astonished by something he can see, something impossible, something right there on the bar top in front of us, something he could touch if he'd only reach out.

"*Being there,*" he says in italics. "Being *connected* to mindfulness and being *present.* That's the way he was. He was without any pretense about anything. He was just . . . Put him in front of a television and he likes to watch TV. He talks about the trees when they move in the wind . . . It's a play on this concept of mindfulness. I still love to see those outtakes. Do I sound okay?"

"You sound enlivened."

"I've let go. It's okay. Did you know some of the best shotguns in the world are in Edinburgh? The best shotgun in the world is a McKay Brown that sells for eighty thousand bucks, and this woman carves by hand every mark. Imagine. You've got an eighty-thousand-dollar work of art. Amazing."

"You're in the market?"

"Are you kidding? I'll never buy another gun. I like to cook those game birds, and I like to show off, but I don't believe I'll ever shoot another gun again. Did you know that your father is a philanthropist? That's who I am. That's what I do. It's true."

"Okay."

"I'm glad I'm this way. I could be one of those guys who lives in Idaho and makes bombs and sends them to people. Couldn't communicate with a human being. Remember that? I like connecting with the right people. When people are nuts, I try to avoid them."

"Sounds right. Avoid the nutjobs."

He pulls out his phone and stops talking.

"Everything all right?"

He laughs dully. "Just seeing if I connected. A year ago, by accident, I met somebody. I didn't think it was going anywhere. I still don't. She's a lady. I was sitting here. I was sitting outside. I'm not sure you see people exactly the way I do. Do you understand? You see somebody go by, and a lot of people, they're just dead eyes, they're dead faces"—he makes a face like a zombie; he slackens his jaw, turns his eyes expressionless—"but you see someone who's smiling"—he growls again to show his teeth—"their eyes are open. This woman walked by, and I said something to her, and eventually she sat down, and we had dinner . . . She's from Arizona."

"You told me about her once. Different from the New Orleans gal."

"We had a good time. We had dinner two nights in a row, and that's all. Nothing else. She loves to fish. I texted her once after she left. Got no response. Texted her twice. Nada. But then the other day, out of the blue, I get a text, says, *Mister, I'm here. I'm back again.* I said, *You wanna go eat?* She said, *Yeah.* We made a date. We had dinner. She's—I'm like a twelve-year-old about this right now. I think she likes me. She's a remarkably attractive human being. She's got a wonderful face, and she's sharp as a tack. She finds me fascinating, I think. We saw some music Saturday night. She had a thing Sunday morning, so we didn't stay out late. There's no carnal action. But at least the door is open for me to say I think I'm acceptable in one respect to someone I could love, which is exciting for me."

"But she's not who's going to Portugal?"

"She's fifty-five. Relationships are okay if you can give all you have, until you can't. She's on LinkedIn. I swore I wasn't going to say anything about her."

"You said something last year."

"I can't keep my mouth shut." He pulls up a photo on his phone and flashes it in my direction.

"She's got a great face."

"She's got a *wonderful* face. She's a nice person. She's not a lunatic. I just like looking at her. We'll see what happens. It's like being a teenager. It's silly. It's nice to meet somebody nice."

"I'm happy for you."

"The Old Man."

"Time passes for everyone."

"I guess it does. I'll have one more drink, and then I'm going home. There's a famous fly shop in Paris called Lords of Rivers. I can't wait to meet them. It can be fun connecting with people. My doctor makes Dr. Phil look like an idiot. He's so knowledgeable. He's done all these different things that make you think he's got tattoos on his nose and bones and stuff—"

"He has tattoos on his nose?"

"No. He has *no. strange. marks.* But he's done ayahuasca and all that stuff. He's my spiritual brother."

"And this is his job? When you microdose? This is what he does for a living?"

"He does therapy. Constructs doorways directing people to the right places. He has this elaborate website with so much information about the experiences . . . Complete antithesis of the Timothy Leary thing. People who are real, not trying to make money. That's gonna be a huge part of the mental health world in the next thirty, forty years. You're going to see incredibly dramatic changes."

"Have you started packing yet?

"I got my carry-on where I can put all the major shit."

"To think," I say, genuinely wistful. "This time tomorrow you'll be in New York. And two days after that you'll be in Paris. Then Portugal, then Edinburgh. I'm envious."

"Listen, Sticks. I leave for Massachusetts in the morning. I'm checking myself into the funny farm. But a man can dream, can't he? When I was a young man, I sold dreams. That's what I did. Now I'm buying dreams. You're selling; I'm buying. Or maybe it's the other way around still. Don't be cross. I wanted you to know. You'll get a call. I put you down, you know, I gave them your number. Emergency contact and shit. Just in case. Have I startled you? I'll be fine. I know what I'm doing. I just need time. I need to relax, put my feet up, get horizontal. Listen, I've got to go. I need to pack. It'll be beautiful up there. Leaves turning colors. Sun setting. Sun setting. Sun setting. I just need time. Don't look at me like that, goddamn it. You look like your mother. You look good, kid. I'm remembering, is all. I'm remembering. I'm not sad. I gotta go."

I get a summons the next day from my dean asking me to come for an informal meeting with Legal. Bruce doesn't ask if I've gotten a summons from our dean, and I don't tell him. I do take a Xanax and then, thinking better of it, pop a second one right under my tongue. I pull my hair into a prim and unflattering bun and put on a too-large pencil skirt and an ill-fitting dress shirt. I'm trying to look like a woman who wouldn't have beers with a male student in the middle of the afternoon, a woman who would never give a stolen and injured cat to a female one, a woman who's never heard of Dead Body, much less invented the game.

In short, I am trying to look like a woman who is not me.

In the room when I arrive are my dean and a person I've never met. The dean motions me to a chair, then says of the person: "This is Legal."

The person, a woman, winces. "Office of Inclusivity," she corrects.

"Let's cut to the chase," the dean says.

"Please," I say, realizing as I take a seat that I'm nauseous from the pills.

"We've had a complaint," the dean says.

The woman—I'll call her Legal—corrects him again. "Let's not say 'complaint.' Nothing is official. But let's also say we've had more than one. But, again, nothing official. Nothing in writing and therefore nothing actionable."

The dean picks at his cuticles. Behind him, along the far wall, the window shades are at half-mast, and low, full clouds puff across the sky. In my brain, while a sad song plays in the background, Sarah McLachlan is pleading for donations, pleading for an end to animal neglect.

The dean pushes a wastebasket toward me with his foot. "You look a little green," he says.

"That's what my mother keeps telling me."

He smiles. "I've always liked you."

"I've always liked you," I say.

"I know how I'm talked about."

"Leadership's not kind to anyone," I say. "First rule is never to take it seriously."

"First rule is never to take it *personally*."

"It's wonderful to be among such collegiality," says Legal, "but I'm wondering if we could, as you said, cut to the chase."

The dean slurps from a can of diet soda, evidently his signal that she should continue.

"Did you—" The lawyer woman consults a yellow pad resting on her lap. "Did you tell a student she couldn't use the word 'fucking'?"

I nearly guffaw in disbelief. "That's what this is about?"

The dean squeezes his soda can until the aluminum pops, startling us both. He says, "Did you tell the only Black girl in your class that she couldn't use the word 'fucking' while you were teaching a story that was, literally, about fucking?"

"Whoa," I say, sitting up straight.

The dean says, "Are you that reckless? In this climate?"

Legal says, "All right, all right, let's let her speak."

"Tiffany complained?" I ask. "About that?"

The dean says, "Her classmates complained."

Legal says, "Technically, he shouldn't have told you that. Students have the right to anonymity."

I say, looking only at the dean, "Tiffany's white classmates complained?"

He says, "They did. They weren't sure if she knew how to defend herself; they weren't sure she felt safe."

"That's completely infanti—"

"I'm reporting the facts," he says. "This is a learning moment. Nothing official is happening."

Legal clicks and unclicks her pen, studying me, and then, after again consulting her pad, says, "Do you teach a story in which a group of first graders ask their teacher to have sex in front of them?"

"They're second graders," I say. "That story is anthologized."

"That's a yes?"

"It's a classic."

"Do you also teach a story in which a young man contracts a sexually transmitted disease in the back seat of a taxicab?"

"Gonorrhea," I clarify. "And that's Hemingway. Another classic. It's in a textbook. That's actually the story in question."

"Do you consider your classroom a hostile place for learning?"

"Are you kidding?"

"She's not kidding," says the dean limply. He chews at a hangnail. A trickle of blood sprouts where he's gnawed. I imagine one of McLachlan's rabid rescues biting off his hand, the blood spurting everywhere. *Grrrr*, says the dog, tossing about the hand like a plaything. *Grrrr*.

I say, "Did any of the students who came in—We're talking more than one, yes? Two? You can't say. You won't say. Okay. Did any of them actually *say* they feel unsafe? Or is 'hostile' your word and not theirs? Because I greatly admire Tiffany, in fact, and it's because of my respect for her that I felt comfortable telling her that the word she was using wasn't appropriate to the text we were discussing. This is my classroom, remember, my place of work. I have a right to feel safe, too."

The dean sucks blood from his cuticle. The lawyer woman clears her throat. A rash rises along the surface of my skin at my neckline. It's very possible I'm going to be sick.

Legal says, "Since you've broached the topic of respect and admiration, we've got something on the list here about that as well." She checks her pad.

"What could possibly be wrong with saying I admire a student?"

Grrrr, says the rabid dog. *Grrr.*

"It's not that you admire a particular student," she says.

"Okay."

"It's that you don't admire all of them equally."

"Give me a break," I say.

"It's been brought to our attention that at least three female students feel as though they receive less respect from you than the other students in your class."

My jaw clenches. The gray-haired nontraditional. She's probably a mother; likely she's a grandmother. In some sort of misguided maternal way, maybe she tried to give Tiffany a voice. But one or two others in addition? It's all I can do not to snarl.

The dean says, "Do you write your students' names on your palm?"

"No."

"No?" he asks. "Can I see your hand?"

Reflexively, my left-hand clenches into a fist.

"This isn't an investigation," the woman says. She's got her hands in the air now, and the legal pad on her lap slips a little in my direction, and at the top, in all caps, I see, *DON'T FORGET ABOUT CAT.*

"What is it, then?" I say. I can really hear it now, the dog's insistent growling; it's no longer a deliberate fantasy, but something real that's humming in my sinuses, grumbling and groaning and threatening to fill my head up with its sound. There's moisture under my arms. I can smell the rank muskiness of silk meeting perspiration. It's increasingly difficult to swallow. "Why is Legal here?" I ask. "If it's not permanent and there's no action being taken, why is she here?"

The dean tries to say something ("Let's just—"), but I cut him off: "Fuck," I cry. The growling is so loud, too loud; my frontal lobe is pulsing with the pressure of its mounting roar. "Just ask me about the cat already!" I gesture somewhat maniacally toward the lawyer woman's pad. "Get it over with already," I say, nearly shouting above the racket. "Ask me. Just ask me!"

Abruptly, the growling stops. I slump back into my chair.

The dean frowns and looks to Legal for an answer. She consults her notes, sees what's written at the top, and says, almost shyly, "Oh, ah, that's, that's my reminder to buy cat food before I go home. I keep forgetting. We've been feeding her lox, but . . . Is there something we should know about a cat?"

I drop my face into my hands and shake my head slowly. To my palms, I say, "What's the plan here? What do you want? Do I apologize or . . . ?"

The dean lets out an avuncular sigh; I uncover my face and look up.

He says, "I was talking to your father the other day and . . ."

And the school is giving me two weeks of family medical leave, which gets us conveniently to the end of the semester. Officially, I'll be taking immediate time off to be "available" to my father, who the dean happens to know is about to check himself into a mental health facility in Massachusetts. But off the record, they're anxious to get me out of the classroom with this particular mix of students. No Prof P equals no new chances for an actionable complaint. Everyone gets an A.

"Hell of a guy," says the dean, standing to shake my hand after it's all been sorted. "Hell of a fisherman. Salt-of-the-earth type. Once-in-a-lifetime kind of gentleman." He pats me on the back as I'm leaving and calls after me, "Two weeks. Take a break. You'll be fine."

What makes it an odyssey?" my students—if I still had them—might ask. So maybe now it's my therapist or my long-dead dog who's asking, or maybe it's just me, my flaky shadow self, the lurking loser cowering in the corner.

"It's a metaphor," I say, my voice a hoarse whimper.

"But a metaphor is a comparison between two unlike objects," comes the answer from the cavernous dark of oblivion.

"You're being too literal," I say.

"We demand a wandering! A voyage! A blah blah change of fortune!"

"I . . . I guess . . ."

"No more excuses!"

"You insist?"

"We insist!"

I think, *Grizzly bears brown bears wolverines . . .*

I think, *A cabin is a place you go when there's nowhere else to go . . .*

I think, *Fine, then, since you insist . . .*

I tell Bruce I'm leaving. I tell him I need two weeks to howl at the moon. (Obviously, he knows by now about my mandatory make-believe medical leave.)

"FOMO," he says.

I say, "No. Not FOMO."

"Your mother and sister and brother are going to Chamonix. Your father is going to Massachusetts. They're leaving, and now you're leaving, too. Ergo: FOMO."

"It can't be FOMO because I'm not going to the same place. I'm going to New Hampshire."

He says, "You're a family of cripples. You're a bunch of big babies."

I say, "Yeah, well, I'm not going with them. So there."

He says, "But you're leaving. You're all leaving. You all do everything the same all the time. Even when you're alone, you're together in your aloneness."

"I have boundaries."

He scoffs and nods at my hands. I'm holding a bottle of white wine and two glasses. My sister is just outside our front door, on our front porch. Through the window, we watch as her six-year-old turns toward the street and moves his hands in front of him. Two seconds later, a clear stream of pee hits the hydrangea plant below.

"Boundaries," he says. "Sure."

"I take your point."

"You're leaving. I get it."

"I can trust you," I say.

"I know you can."

"And?"

"And what?"

"You can trust me," I say.

"Your sister's waiting."

Several hours later, my sister and her boys back on their side of the street, Bruce finds me in the kitchen.

He says, "I know what it is. You don't want to be here without them. You don't know how to exist without them anymore. Five years ago, it was you and me. Now it's you and me and them." He slices an apple into eight perfect sections.

I say, "It's called an emergency residency."

"What's so special about New Hampshire?"

"There's a cabin."

"You hate cabins."

"I love cabins."

"You're scared of the dark."

"I'm scared of the dark when I'm in the woods alone."

"Is this cabin in the woods? Will you be alone?"

"Yes and yes. Also, they'll feed me. Three square meals a day."

He says, "You hate three square meals a day."

I shrug.

He eats an apple slice and studies me. What does he see? This bald man who may or may not have a private life as rich and demented as mine, who may or may not live as much of his life unseen and in his fantasies as I do, who may or may not have secrets he'll never share just as I have . . .

"Not to be too much of a pragmatist," he says, "but how much is this going to cost? This cabin in the woods? And how long will you be gone?"

I outline the situation, which is: it's an artists' residency program, one I've been to before, and one that occasionally accommodates last-minute requests from alumni in need. "In other words," I tell him, "it's free."

"You're an alum in need?"

I nod again.

He eats the last of his apple and wipes his mouth. Then he walks to the sink, washes the cutting board and paring knife, sets them in the drying rack, and dries off his hands. For several minutes, he stands at the sink looking out the window, which has an unremarkable view of our driveway. The window in the house across the way is open. Its frilly white curtains are fluttering in the breeze. I wonder if the math-ematician's wife is over there, washing her own cutting board, having her own thoughts and fantasies, considering something unexpected her husband has just told her about himself or their future or his own hopes and dreams.

A stink bug kamikazes into the screen, buzzes, then flies away.

At last, Bruce faces me.

"You've made your emergency request?"

"I have."

"I have to ask." He crosses his arms and leans back against the sink, which will leave a line of wetness across the rear pockets of his chinos. I know this because he never wipes the sink after he's done the dishes, and there is always a line on his chinos after he leans this way against the sink. As I always do, I will wonder about the line, whether or not he can feel it, whether or not he cares. As I always do, I will say nothing. I will carry the curiosity with me for the rest of the day, for the rest of my life. One of the millions of mosquito-size curiosities that flit and dart about inside me. Where do they flit and dart? Only in my head cavity? Or do they flit and dart all over, in my shins and knees and neck and stomach?

"Where is your soul?" asked a philosophy professor my freshman year of college. "Where do you feel it? How do you know it's there?" The class was mute. "Where is your *soul*?" he demanded a second time, louder, angry almost. I wanted to answer. I wanted to scream, to shout. I wanted to be correct. I had no clue what to say. He held up his hand high above his head. "Is it here?" We all looked at his hand, its trigger finger missing. There were gasps, there were chuckles. One kid whispered, "Yikes . . ." I shook my head. It wasn't an answer. It was a response to everyone and everything. I was thinking of that finger—the missing one—wondering what it meant, worried already about my tendency to imbue meaning where meaning might not exist. I wasn't thinking in sentences. I was thinking in discrete words: *War? Gun? Soul? Finger?* I was thinking of my father, who once introduced me to a man who was missing a toe. He'd lost it to a lawn mower. Correction: he'd lost it intentionally to a lawn mower on the day his number had been called. At that moment, in that seminar room, shaking my head, thinking in one-off, disconnected words, looking at the hand of my wizened professor with whom, during that single class period, I'd fallen temporarily in love, I was also thinking: *Lawn mower?*

Bruce says, "My question is, does this emergency in the woods have anything to do with you and me, with the probability of our future?" The sink water has surely seeped in by now, having been absorbed first by the layer of chino and then, possibly, almost certainly, by his briefs, inching infinitesimally closer to the tiny white hairs and epidermis of his ass. I try not to stare at his crotch. I try not to look like I'm thinking about anything other than what he is saying. What is he saying? He is saying, "There is only so much I can tolerate. There is only so much I can take. I am real. I am a human. I'm not a character. You understand? I have dignity and pride, and even for you, even considering the vastness of my love for you, there is only so much. I am not your ex-husband. You understand?"

My nose is tingling, my eyes burning. I swallow and take a stethoscope-size breath. "I do," I say.

"And?"

"I'll be gone two weeks, and then I'll be home."

He says, "What's that mean? You want to have sex with strangers?"

"I want to get away from this place—"

"From me."

"From this place and—"

"From my daughter."

"I want to write. I want to write, and I want there not to be laundry to fold and dinner to cook."

"We can get takeout. No one asks you to cook."

"I love cooking dinner. But to keep loving it, I need to be away and to feel like this isn't my life. I need two weeks to not chop vegetables or fold clothes or bake bread or pay bills. I don't know. I—"

"Are you about to leave me?" He stands up straighter, his palms suddenly on the island between us. He seems prepared to become a stranger, an enemy, a person looking out only for himself if the right words—the right *wrong* words—are spoken.

I try to touch his hand, but he brushes mine away.

"Say it," he says.

"I'm not leaving you. I just want two weeks of writing. Two weeks of pretending I'm not—"

"Say it."

"—a family of three."

I tell Jane about my mandatory vacation from campus and that I'm going to New Hampshire alone. She oohs and ahhs at the possibility. We've been walking the street of our neighborhood with my imaginary dog, marveling at all the lost-cat signs, which haven't been taken down. They're laminated, which I hadn't noticed before and, at the bottom, read, *Last Seen on Sycamore*, which Jane suggests might make a good title for a thriller.

"I hope the cat's okay. I love cats," she says. "More than most people."

"You love cats more than most people love cats?" I ask. "Or you love cats more than you love most people?"

She wiggles her nose at me and says, "There are certain patterns of your mind that are distinctive and persistent, my friend."

I tell her, then, about the reasons for my mandatory vacation—the cat, Tiffany, Mateo.

She sighs wistfully. "We've all had our Mateos," she says.

Have we all had our Mateos? I wonder, but to Jane I say, "Once, when I was at boarding school, I had a teacher, he was Irish. I was madly in love with him but not in any physical way. I wanted him to adore me. I wanted him to admire me. I never fantasized about him sexually. Then one night I dreamed he was on top of me. We were both clothed. But he was straddling me. He kept saying, 'You're mine, you're mine.' The next day, I retreated from him. Any overture he made—to take me to lunch in town, to drive me to the used bookstore—I suddenly rejected."

"You never explained it to him?" Jane asks.

"I was fifteen years old. He was thirty, maybe forty. He might have been fifty! What would I have said? 'I dreamed you were a creep'?"

"What happened to him?"

"He was only there one year. He was a poet forced to teach fiction to a bunch of privileged brats. After I published my first book, he wrote me a letter."

"What did the letter say?"

"He congratulated me. Then he told me I'd gone too far with a certain scene, a scene in which a group of teenage boys at a boarding school masturbate off the balcony onto a group of teenage girls. He told me that a good editor would have saved me from such gratuitousness."

"Did that really happen? The jerking off?"

I nod. We pause at a corner. In my mind, my dead dog is sniffing a lilac bush, debating whether or not to lift his leg or wait for better shrubbery. We continue.

Jane says, "What else happened at boarding school?"

I tell her about the time my father sent me a gingerbread house, five feet by five feet, made of real gingerbread. It arrived in a crate and had to be opened in the mailroom. I tell her about a different time, for my fourteenth birthday, when he reserved a table for me at the only fancy restaurant in our small New England town and told me I could take four friends to celebrate. He'd pick up the tab. When we arrived, the five of us, we saw that the table was set for six. I was confused. My friends—who were from New England and were accustomed to over-the-top surprises—insisted my dad was going to pop out from some corner, balloons and flowers in hand, having shown up to celebrate my birthday in person.

Instead, when we sat down, we saw that a life-size cutout of my father awaited us at the table. From the waist up, there he was. He wore a bow tie and a huge grin. My friends swooned, but also, I think, they looked at me differently after that. By the time he sent me six dozen long-stem roses for my sixteenth birthday, two years later, I'd learned how to avoid a scene. In the mailroom, the employees, especially the ladies, fawned over the roses. I accepted them—unsurprised yet also horrified—walked them one flight of stairs up to the main floor of the administration building, ducked into the women's visitor's restroom, and left them on the counter.

To Jane I say, "Perhaps you've seen what six dozen long-stem roses look like taken together in a single bouquet. If you have, you understand the unwieldiness of it, and perhaps if you understand this, you can also see that such an image—such a gift—has nothing to do with the recipient and everything to do with the giver."

Jane smiles sweetly at me as I talk about my father. When I finish, she says, "I was hoping for more stories about sex or, you know, inappropriate relationships between students and teachers."

Jane's got a theory that my ex's book might ultimately triumph a woman, just not me. She's studied the novel's synopsis as many times as I have, maybe more. She keeps coming back to the line about my dear friend's past as a once-talented writer. She says, "Women buy books, and I think women will have very little interest in reading a story about a man who's pouting because of his wife's success. Unless, of course, the man doesn't win in the end, but the woman does, the *other* woman, your former pal. She's the hero. Not you, not your ex. *Her.* That might sell books."

I say, "My theory is that he wrote what he thought was a Very Important, Very Serious, Very Big Book, and he sent it off to an agent who read it and was like, 'This is funny as . . .' And the agent sent it to an editor who was like, 'Oh, it's a satire!' And the agent and the editor went back to my ex and were like, 'At first we thought you were being serious and then we saw the humor and now we understand it's been a satire the whole time!'"

Jane laughs. "'Springtime for Hitler,'" she says.

"Exactly." I stop under a giant ginkgo and imagine my dog sniffing, always sniffing, his ears nearly brushing the grass blades, they're so long. "I never finished telling you about the Irishman."

"After you saw him at the stop sign?"

I shake my head. "Not then. Before."

She says, "You know I've been unfaithful."

"I know that."

"Not unfaithful to Teddy."

"No, I know. Unfaithful *with* Teddy."

"Yes."

"You don't judge me?"

"The truth is . . ." I close my eyes. I search the darkness for flashes of clarity. The green vest. The flicker of tea candles. Fingers pressing into the seam of my jeans. "The truth is, I don't know what happened that night with the Irishman. I've never known. I've always been a little frightened that I was . . . that my body was used in a way that, conscious, I'd have wanted, *did* want, but that, unconscious, wasn't his to . . ."

She puts her fingers to her lips, and I swear I can see the word as she says it, see the shape of its letters—small, cloudlike, white—as they trip from her mouth, slip between her lips, and bounce their way through her lightly draped fingers into an airy freedom:

oh

"When I saw him at the stop sign—"

"Yes?"

"He got in touch a few weeks later. After all this time, I thought it meant something. I thought it meant nothing bad could have happened."

"Oh, sweetheart."

"Maybe I led him on a little. Or maybe he led me on. But the back-and-forth wasn't what I expected."

"Has something more happened since?"

"What's funny," I say, letting myself breathe again, "is that if my family had lived here back then, it never would have happened. It's too small a town. I'd never have dared." I almost laugh at the stupidness of the thought. "Imagine all the trouble they're keeping me from now. Trouble I have no idea I'm avoiding." Am I thinking of Mateo? Of his hand moving toward my cheek? Of my father's cowboy hat suddenly in view on the other side of the street? If I am, I'll never tell.

"Maybe it's less about your family and more about who you are," Jane says, adding, "Who you are *now*."

A chipmunk tumbles from a mottled white branch overhead, nearly falls to the ground, recovers, then shimmies back into the foliage, invisible now but noisily clucking its relief.

"All you fiction writers," Jane says, walking again, "playing at being people you're not."

I gently pull at my dead dog's leash to catch him up. "I'd be mortified if Bruce ever found out," I say.

"Bruce adores you," Jane says to the trees overhead. "You're his life."

"Are you Teddy's life?"

She laughs. It's a breezy, friendly, purely female laugh. "Of course," she says.

"And is he yours?"

She stops laughing. "Dear heart," she says, holding my hand for only a moment before letting it fall. "I'm a woman, same as you."

Four
EASY, DARLING

DAY ONE

Upon arrival in New Hampshire, I'm assigned a sweet-talking tour guide called Sam. There's another newbie, a poet from Croatia, who takes the tour with me.

The guide shows us the kitchen, the lunch baskets, the laundry room. He shows us how to use the honor system should we need to buy paper, postcards, sweatshirts featuring the residency's logo. He walks us to a bike rack behind the dining hall and explains the process by which an artist can rent one while on campus. I tell him that the last time I was here I fell off a bike, sprained my ankle, and didn't get back on for several years. By then it was too late—fear had set in. "No bikes," I tell him.

The Croatian also indicates an aversion to bicycles.

What I don't tell these men is that I'd borrowed a bike to grab something last-minute from my studio before dinner. On the downhill, I realized there were no hand brakes. I couldn't slow myself. I kept gaining speed. I didn't know what to do. Finally, taking it all in, just before the grade steepened, I steered myself into the grass, knowing it would at least soften my fall. I wrecked myself intentionally, tearing wide open both my palms. By morning, the entire left side of my body had turned purple. My ankle had doubled in size. I told anyone who asked that the brakes were faulty. For the remainder of my time in residence, nobody used the green bike with the faulty brakes. But what I realized years and years later, watching Bruce teach his daughter how to ride, was that there must have been brakes on the pedals. All I'd needed to do was cycle backward. I hadn't known. No one had ever given me lessons or taught me how a bicycle worked.

"Well," the guide says to us both, "if you change your minds, there's a new checkout system now."

At dinner, a friend from my old days, who's also in residence, says, "We didn't like your husband. Is that okay to say? He was a bad loser. He pouted."

My friend from the old days used to play poker with my ex back in Chicago, back when we were still married.

"He wasn't likable," I say.

"No," he corrects me. "He *was* likable. We just didn't like him. He was a bad loser and he pouted."

"He was bad at poker," I say.

"No," he corrects me again. "He was fine. But he was a bad loser. He was likable. *We* just didn't like him."

"He was charming," I say.

"No," he corrects me yet again. "Well, sure, yeah, maybe. But he pouted when he lost and then one day he stopped showing up to the game."

"We moved to Kentucky."

"Oh . . ." he says.

There is a table full of strangers watching us, listening to us.

A woman says, "Do you two know each other?"

Later, unpacking alone in my dorm with its one twin bed, one rocking chair, one bureau, and one sink, I call Bruce.

"I want to come home," I say.

"You made me promise not to let you."

"I've changed my mind."

"Too bad, sweetie."

"I hate it when you call me 'sweetie.'"

"'Hurt me,' said the masochist, and the sadist said, 'No . . .'"

I tell him that the last time I was here, I was eight months from being married, four months from being proposed to. I was here to finish a book that never got published. In my tiny dorm, feeling isolated and blue, I unbosom my doubts to Bruce.

He says, "These are interesting realizations to be making now, at this moment, while you're there, in New Hampshire, and not, say, here, in Kentucky, for example."

He speaks so that I am aware of every comma. I say, "You're starting to talk like me."

He says, "I must miss you."

I say, "Hm."

After we hang up, he sends me a heart and a kiss. I send him a punch and a brain.

I'm desperate for a drink. I eye the mini bottles at the top of my backpack. On my second flight, the one out of Atlanta at 9:00 a.m., anticipating the residency's scarcity of alcohol, I asked the flight attendant for two miniature bottles of vodka. I'd been proud of myself for feeling not an ounce of shame when the flight attendant raised an eyebrow and my seatmate checked her watch.

My phone vibrates. And in quick succession, a series of messages arrive from Crazy Tabby Mommy—

FYI found my cat
Cute girl told me you had something to do with it
Been meaning to write and thank you
Not sure why you didn't contact me yourself
Grateful anyway

I move the mini bottles from my backpack to the bureau.

The messages continue—

I was going to say thanks but then forgot
Sad news today though
My boy didn't make it
And I thought of you
Two surgeries nothing the doc could do at the end
That's all
I wanted you to know
Loved him like a person

My cheeks spasm, and I put a hand to my face to steady them. I brush my teeth, check the dead bolt, turn off the lights, and get into bed.

DAY TWO

The Croatian poet is late to our mandatory library tour the next morning. He's already made friends, he tells the librarian and me when he finally arrives. "I was caught up in wonderful dialogue at breakfast."

We're shown how to check out books, watch movies, borrow equipment. The librarian tells us we have access to anything at all while we're here. Anything in the library is available to be checked out. She says it like a boast, like she's yet to disappoint a single artist's request.

In the reading room, I spy a portable soft-sided desk, perfect for writing in bed. I say, "Can I check out that husband?"

The librarian is flummoxed. I hold up the portable soft-sided desk.

"I've never heard it called a husband before," she says. "Here in this library, we call it a laptop pillow."

I say, "Can I check out this laptop pillow, which is not at all a husband?"

Later, I'll google "husband + pillow" and be greeted by images of giant sofa cushions with overstuffed arms. Looking at these pictures alone in my dorm, I will say aloud, "Ah-ha," and then I will say, with the nerves of a person who is alone in a tiny room in an isolated lodge with dozens of other tiny rooms, most of them empty, at the edge of a sprawling property, "Who said that?"

The librarian scans my laptop pillow for a barcode. There isn't one. She shows me how to fill out the honor sheet on the clipboard next to the checkout. The Croatian is bemused by the situation. As I'm leaving, he asks if I'd like to get coffee later in the afternoon. I tell him maybe, depending.

At dinner, I sit with two European beauties. One's from Belgium, the other from Poland. They go to exquisite efforts pretending not to understand each other. Their mouths are gorgeous as they play this funny game, each of them in possession of a highly stylized, perfectly understandable version of the English language.

I ask the Belgian, a filmmaker, how long she's been here. She says, "What month even is it?"

The Polish beauty, a painter, says, "All the days are the same."

"What?" asks the Belgian. "What's that? All the days are a *shame*?"

The painter says, "The food here is too spicy." She pronounces "food" as "feud." "I can barely touch this fish."

"How can you stand it?" asks the Belgian.

"It's not just food for me, you know. It's emotions."

"*Eee*-mages?"

"E-*motions*," says the Polish painter. "But, yes, also images. Images and emotions. I feel them all very extremely. Spicy fish, too."

The Belgian turns to face me with great deliberateness. She says, "You've been here before."

"Yes," I say.

"I can tell."

"Because I'm old."

"You have an energy."

"A middle-aged energy."

"Yes, an energy."

The painter says, "Emergency?"

I return to my blackened catfish, which isn't remotely spicy. The beauties return to their game.

The Croatian poet joins us. "I missed you for coffee," he says. Then: "This thing in the library you said. This 'husband.' What is this?" The Europeans ignore us.

I say, "A husband is a pillow that holds you."

His face brightens. He repeats, wonderment in his voice, "A husband is a pillow that holds you," and I know he means to steal the line for his poetry. He has no intention of asking my permission.

The Croatian shifts his body toward the women, who've moved on to the merits and defects of the dessert.

"It's too sweet."

"Is it sweet? Maybe it's not at all sweet for me."

"It's simply too much for me," says the Polish painter, who, when she departs this place tomorrow, will take her images and emotions and overly sensitive palate with her.

I leave dinner early, before it gets too dark to walk the half mile back to my room without a flashlight.

DAY THREE

Having not slept last night due to some intense avian activity outside my windows and my need to check the bolt on my bedroom door every hour on the hour, I stare at my legal pads, my handwriting, my notes. The sky is low and gray, and thunder rumbles balefully. By 2:00 p.m., I still haven't written anything. I leave my studio and walk the mile back to my private bedroom. On my way up the final hill, a woman with a walking stick stops me. She's old, with long scraggly hair. She beckons me toward her.

"Are you with the residency?"

I tell her I am.

We're stopped now in the middle of a rural two-lane blacktop. She says, "I saw another young woman with a picnic basket two days ago and she was also with the residency."

I hold my lunch basket up. "We're highly identifiable."

She says, "I saw the bear here two days ago . . ."

I say, "The bear? Here? There's a bear?"

She points to a hole in a stone wall, on the other side of which is my lodge, inside which is my dorm. "There," she says. "Just a skinny little thing." She raises her hand so that it's a full foot above my head. "Just a little bit of a thing."

"What did you do?" I ask. "Did you make noise? Did you run?"

She rests her walking stick in the crook of her elbow and reaches for her back pocket. She says, "I talked to it. I said, 'Hello how are you doing this is some fine weather for you and me both,' and it just stood there, and so I took a picture of it." She's got her phone out now, and she's swiping.

"You weren't scared? You didn't run?"

She holds the phone out for me to see.

"Hell no, I didn't run," she says. "I wanted a picture. I moved closer."

At 3:00 p.m., I take my vodka to the dining hall. Someone's left out an unopened personal-size bottle of orange juice. I take it, dump half the juice out, pour my vodka in, and walk to the library.

At the library, I find an alcove, set up my computer and my legal pads, drink my warm cocktail, and fall almost immediately asleep. When I wake up, it's pouring rain, and the sky is ablaze with lightning. Dinner for me is still two hours away.

I call Bruce, crying. "I want to come home," I tell him. I don't tell him that I drank two mini bottles of vodka on an empty stomach in the middle of the afternoon and that I'm not homesick, I'm just sick of myself and depressed that I haven't written.

"Babe," he says, "I love you but I'm grilling."

"Did you know," I ask him, knowing that he couldn't possibly know because it's a realization I've only today made, "that the last time I was here I left early?"

"I didn't know that."

"Do you want to know why?"

"Listen," he says, "I've got the grill on. The meat's on a timer. I can play along later but I can't do any more now."

I hang up on him and wait for an emoji, but he doesn't send one. The rain outside is coming down even harder now. I'm drunk, tired, and trapped.

The last time I was here, to finish a novel that would never be published, I left a week early because my boyfriend, not yet my husband, called to tell me that our dear friends from New York were coming for a pop-up visit to Chicago. He'd said, "You're going to miss them, but we'll try to have fun without you."

I'd gotten off the phone, feeling trapped then, too, and gone immediately to the library and looked up flights and change fees and, before the hour was out, had booked a flight home for the very next day. Even then, even before I'd married him, I hadn't trusted them to be together without a chaperone. If only I'd let them be themselves then, if only I'd let the inevitable unfold earlier, how many years of a different life, with a different version of myself, might I have had?

On my way to dinner, I cross paths with a resident I've not seen before. She says, "You could be a mermaid!"

A half hour later, the same woman sits down next to me and says, "Hi, I'm new. Do you need any cedar oil? Ticks hate cedar oil."

She's bubbly, and it unnerves me, and I say, "Were you on the Zoom orientation meeting last week?"

She says, "Were you?"

I say, "Did you ask the question about access to low-level lighting?"

She says, "Are you the one who's been here before?"

I say, "You don't really like to answer questions, do you?"

She says, "You don't really like to answer questions either," and then, after having taken a bite of her hamburger and wiped her mouth, she asks me if I've seen the bear.

"No," I say. "Have you?"

She nods and takes another bite. I ache with jealousy to see this skinny harmless bear.

I leave dinner early again, before it can get dark. Two baby deer follow me from the dining hall down the dirt path. It's dusk, and I call Bruce. He's drunk and with my mother, who's supposed to be leaving for Chamonix in the morning.

I tell them I made a friend at dinner. My mother says, "Is this friend real?"

I say, "Of course she's real."

My mother says, "'Of course,' she says, 'of course,' as if it's so obvious with this one!" She's talking to Bruce, who, in the background, I can hear doing the dishes.

My mother says, "Are you in a bear's belly? Are you calling from the belly of a bear?" She's had a glass, maybe three, of wine.

Bruce calls out, "There in a sec."

"He's doing the dishes," my mother says.

I tell her about the baby deer that are still trailing behind me. She asks if they're male or female.

"They're babies; I can't tell."

She tells me that the males can be aggressive.

I explain their size. "Like puppies," I say, "with really long legs."

Then, from up ahead in the path, I hear a quick whisper, a shushing, a tsking. Around the bend, where the dirt road forks, is the woman from dinner. She's motioning for me to join her. She's pointing toward something around yet another bend, in a clearing or meadow that I can't yet see.

My mother is still talking, but I interrupt her. I tell her quickly, quietly that I'll call her back. There's something ahead, someone ahead. She's laughing still, making off-color comments about aggressive male deer and the bellies of bears. I hang up.

I call out to my new friend, "Is it the bear? Is it the bear?" I am desperate with anticipation.

Her arm is outstretched, her finger gleefully pointing. "Look," she says.

I look; it's a prairie dog.

She says, "It's a porcupine."

I say, "My book is practically writing itself all of a sudden."

She giggles and says, "The porcupine's name is Darling."

Thirty minutes later, when I remember to call my mother and Bruce back, they want to know if I've been eaten by a bear.

"No," I tell them, my bedroom door bolted behind me, my windows shut and locked. "I'm calling safely from inside the murder lodge."

"IS THAT WHAT IT'S CALLED?" my mother screams into the receiver.

DAY FOUR

At hot breakfast, which ends at 8:30 a.m., the talk is of a giant bear turd in the middle of the path between the library and the dining hall.

"We're basically dogs," says one of the twentysomethings, picking at the edges of her buckwheat pancake. I envy everything about this young person. "Someone puts food in front of us, we eat, time passes, we don't really know where the time goes, sometimes we sleep, sometimes we're moving about, more time passes, then someone puts food in front of us again, and then, occasionally, especially after the evening feeding, a few of the puppies will stay up and play with the others before it's time for bed. Then we start the whole thing over again in the morning."

I tell this twentysomething I'd like desperately to see the bear. She's seen it every day, she tells me. She also claims to have seen a mountain lion. I'm skeptical, but she shows me her bear videos—she has a lot of them—and I fall a little bit in love with her when she says, full of admiration, "Just look at this little feller," and I can see she wants to tickle the bear's belly.

Later, alone in my studio, I rummage through the half-dozen manila envelopes I brought from home. They're stuffed with notes and letters and report cards from my past, pieces of paper and marginalia I haven't looked at in years. In one, I discover sixty pages of a partial novel I don't remember writing. The narrator is mid-twenties, married with a stepdaughter. Her only desire is to be a young widow. I sit on the floor, the sun landing hot on the rug and my shoulders, and I read several chapters without interruption. I'm charmed by the narrator's affection for the little girl in her life, as well as for the woman's wicked desire to be alone in the world. When I come to the end, which is to say, when I turn the page and there is no more to read, I'm confused, then frustrated. I have no memory of the narrative—of writing it or of where I imagined the plot might go. But there are enough autobiographical details to be certain of its authorship. In the narrator's past, as in mine, there is a monthlong Christian camp in which the girls sing and stomp while standing on picnic tables. There's a night toward the end of camp when the counselors sneak the girls to the docks and give everyone permission to "let loose." The narrator is confused, just as I was, and turns embarrassed, just as I did, when she sees all the other girls, in the blue glow of the moonlight, unsnap their bras, wiggle their shoulders, then pull an assortment of lacy fabrics from the armholes of their T-shirts. She alone didn't have a bra. She alone didn't have breasts to necessitate one. The narrator of my half-finished novel is mad with the desire to be a widow. She fantasizes constantly about ways in which she might murder her husband, who is the father of her stepdaughter. It seems impossible to me that I would have written this *before* I moved in with Bruce and the eleven-year-old, and yet it seems even more impossible that I wouldn't be able to remember something I'd written so recently. The tone is all over the place. At times it is a dark and brooding meditation on girlhood interrupted; in other places it's pure comedy: one time, the husband slips at the top of the stairs, and just as he's about to go tumbling down, an accident that could surely break his neck, the narrator, standing behind him, instinctively grabs him by the collar, thereby saving him. She's cross with herself for days. In another section, the husband chokes on a piece of steak he's grilled himself. The narrator knows she won't be blamed if he dies, but they aren't alone. Her stepdaughter is at the table with them. The wide-eyed baby raccoon expression on the poor girl's face is too much, and our narrator saves him once again. The story is mine, but it is also not mine because I've lost the imagination to finish it.

In the main building, an hour before dinner, I find my new friend with the cedar oil and pet porcupine. She's playing pool against herself. "You're a walking metaphor," I say.

"Yeah, but for what?"

She takes a shot, misses, then says, "I was just having a conversation with you," and then confesses that she'd arrived here initially feeling fresh, free, no loose ends, ready to write, but, having been away from her wife for only three days, is already reeling from a past crush, one that's resurfaced deliberately or accidentally as she embarks on six weeks away from home. I'm jealous, but not as I was last week or last month or last year. Not in any desirous way. I'm jealous because angst, because living between two worlds and being pulled by two or three or four appetites, is, as far as I'm concerned, the very stuff of life. One state away, my father is thinking, *Here we are. We're on the road again. It ain't over yet.*

I listen to this woman whom I've only recently met tell me all about her crush, her wife, listen as she lists the pros and cons of each. "I like a good story, a good ending," she says, "and this thing with my crush, if we made it work, after all this time, it would be a good story, a good ending." I do not contradict her, though her assumption that their reunion would be an ending for either of them is unlikely. I listen as she tells me all the things she isn't telling her wife, would never tell her wife, and I, a complete stranger—perhaps worse than a stranger? a cannibal of other people's lives?—I listen and I think, *We are all of us—all the time—aboard the same sinking ship.*

Now she says, having moved on from her love life, "I read the residency's pamphlet front to back before I came here. According to the handbook, there's only one rule: you can't visit someone else's studio without permission. In actuality, there are lots of rules. Forty-eight hours' notice if you want to start a fire. Mugs with lids only in the library. No phone calls in the library. No food in the library. Dinner at six-thirty p.m. sharp. Do not be late. Finish eating by seven-thirty p.m. Return picnic baskets no later than six p.m. Be generous with your car. Sign up for a presentation. Hug the chickens."

"I think those last few are more suggestions than they are rules."

"You take my point."

At about 4:00 a.m., in bed, I make the discovery that the birds outside the windows above my bed—birds that seem to come to life at midnight with their twits and tweets and trills—are hummingbirds: noisy little fuckers staging wars and launching attacks on one another's nests all night long. I get out of bed, check the bolt on my bedroom door, put a pillow over my head, and sleep for an hour.

DAY FIVE

I wake early. By noon, I've run eight miles and written fifteen thousand words. During a break at the library, my friend from Chicago catches me at the communal sink and asks about my word count. He's peeling mandarins. I tell him my number. He whistles, and I think of my students, the way one of them had done just the same when I corrected my number of books.

By 4:00 p.m., I've written another ten thousand, and I force myself to stop for the day.

I take a walk and look for the bear. I locate two different gangs of wild turkeys and several deer. No bear. No mountain lion. No porcupine.

At 6:00 p.m., I'm at the pool table with my friend with the wife and the crush. She says, "Play with me," and I do. Between shots I show her the cover of my ex's debut, which just this afternoon my agent emailed to me under the subject line: *Have you seen this?*

My new friend says, "Is that a little man standing in a big shadow?"
"Yes."

"Are you the shadow?"
"Yes."

She says, pointing to a spot on the cover where the shadow doesn't reach, "Why doesn't that little man just step over here, out of the shadow?"

We laugh. We play pool. She wins.

After dinner, a different woman, a musician and the oldest among us here at the residency, asks me if I need a flashlight. Apparently, I've been talking more than I realize about my fear of the dark. I tell her I've got three flashlights, which seems to alarm her. "So many," she says, "and only two hands. Is it really called the murder lodge?"

"It's a joke," I tell her. "I guess with myself."

"But you *are* scared of the dark?"

"It's kind of a schtick," I say. "But also, yes. I am."

"Bears," she says. "I'd be terrified, too. I drive everywhere."

"I'm not scared of bears," I say. "I'm scared of ax murderers, serial killers, psychopaths."

This too seems to alarm her.

The musician wants to know about my flashlight situation because there's a presentation tonight, which will be followed by a bonfire, which will be followed by roasting marshmallows, which will be followed by karaoke. My friend with the crush bails. But I want to celebrate a good day of writing.

I party. Hard.

DAY SIX

I wake up at 5:00 a.m., mouth dry, hips creaky. I check my phone. There's a text from myself time-stamped 12:34 a.m.: *sleep shorts?* I drink water from my tiny private sink and then use the common bathroom. On my way back to bed, I see that my keys are there, in the lock, on the outside of my bedroom door. *Good job*, I think to myself. I take three Advil and go back to sleep.

I miss hot breakfast. At noon, my friend with the crush sends me a close-up video of the porcupine. She's right. It's not a prairie dog. I text myself a reminder to make a vision appointment when I'm home. At the end of the video, the porcupine slips under her cabin.

I hear my friend exclaim in a whisper nearly inaudible, "It's your home!"

Why, when I text myself a reminder, am I always surprised when the text comes through?

I give a presentation and then go to bed early. In bed, I text Bruce. He sends me a list of the ways he's changed in the almost-week that I've been gone. His list is—

Turns out I like margaritas
I can make really good arrabbiata too
I ate a FROZEN pizza DELIBERATELY
(did not enjoy)
I went to the pool WITH YOUR MOTHER (old news, forgot to tell
* you)*
I drank a Bloody Mary BEFORE NOON
I GOT IN THE WATER

I pull the blinds, turn off the lights, resist the urge to check the dead bolt, and, within minutes, I am dreaming of wild turkeys and hummingbirds and open-air biplanes plunging into bright blue swimming pools.

DAY SEVEN

I run seven miles and call Bruce before my shower. I tell him I don't miss him and ask if this is a problem.

"It's because you can depend on me," he says.

"But I'm homesick for Chamonix."

"You can't be homesick for a place you've never been. You're homesick for your family."

"Does that worry you?" I ask.

"Theo says hi."

"Did you tell him I was cooking something good?"

"I told him you were out of state."

"And what did he say?"

"If you couldn't depend on me, then you'd miss me, like you miss your family."

"You're saying I can't depend on my family?"

"First, I am your family. You have a family with me and my daughter. Second, and I ask this as sincerely and delicately as I can, have you ever listened when you tell stories about your childhood?"

"Point taken."

* * *

At dinner, I sit with the Belgian filmmaker, my friend with the crush, and a German architect who, it turns out, was in residence with me ten years ago. We don't remember each other. Tonight, we sit outside, the four of us, and my friend wants to talk about autofiction. But the Belgian says, "Does everyone in America talk about their exes all the time?" She's referring to the presentation I gave last night after dinner, when I read pages from my work in progress, which is itself a work of auto-fiction. She says, "Because, I would hate that. I would be driven completely mad. All the talk talk talking about one's ex."

My new friend says, "At least in my community, which is queer and largely female, there's an emphasis on the community as opposed to the couple qua couple, which is almost peripheral."

The Belgian says, "And is that your personal experience or just your understanding of the preferred ethos?"

My new friend says, "In my own life, I prioritize the couple. But there are a few exes who fall back into orbit from time to time, and they present a problem."

The German, the only man among us, says, "I'm friends with every ex who treated me well. They know me better than anyone, yes? Because when you're with someone, you open up."

"Yes, yes," says the Belgian, "you remove the walls. You are your very self."

I've never had an ex I didn't walk away from completely. I say, "I think I've never been my very self with any of my exes."

The Belgian says, "Mm."

I say, "I told my boyfriend today that I didn't miss him. He told me it's because I can depend on him."

The Belgian says, "Mm."

The German says, "I wouldn't like to hear that."

My new friend says, "But your boyfriend is right. I bet you'd never have dared to say a thing like that to your ex, especially if it was true."

"Yeah," I say. "And now, having said it, I think I kind of miss him."

The Belgian says, "I haven't gotten a single piece of mail since I've been here. Every day I look. Every day there is nothing."

After dinner, a new guy with a Pulitzer catches me while I'm scraping my leftover food into the trash. He says, "Last night, your presentation, that was good. I was surprised. People think autofiction is easy. They think you sit down and write about yourself. But it's actually quite hard. There's distillation. Like Salter—brief, lucid, and mercilessly clear."

"Speaking of Salter," I say, and then I tell him about the email from the guy who'd been offended by the framing of my work.

He says, "I loved someone once who came from Water Mill."

While we're talking, a woman on the other side of the food dump says to another resident we can't see, "You know that thing the girl read last night? It makes me want to try my hand at it. I'm a painter, but maybe I'm also a writer. Who knows?"

I look at the guy with the Pulitzer. He says, "See? Take it as the compliment it is."

My new friend and I walk home together in the dark. For a little while, we keep our flashlights trained on the path in front of us. As we near the fork in the road—she'll go right, I'll go left—she throws an arm in front of me like my mother used to do when I was little and we were driving and we'd come too quickly to a stop. She says, "Easy, darling," and shines her light just ahead, where my foot is about to land. It's a frog. It, like me, has paused. She kills her light, and we watch the frog hop away. Then we spot another and another. For three or four frogs' worth, we play pause with our flashlights, spotlighting the frogs and then releasing them into the darkness.

Easy, darling, I tell myself as I fall easily, deeply asleep tonight.

DAY EIGHT

Dawn, a dream—

It is my long-dead dog. He's just spent the night at the foot of my bed. He wakes up and says, talking to me for the first time ever and in a high-pitched voice I never would have chosen for him, "Hana, why did you stay the night with me? You know you can leave me alone. I'll be okay." I tell him, "I wanted to stay with you." Then he curls himself into my arm—in my dream he is not the seventy-pound dog of life; he's black and small and wiggly, but it's him—and nuzzles his head against my forehead the way a cat might.

I wake before I can start crying and sit up abruptly in bed. I know, even before the phone call telling me, that it's time to go home.

If this were fiction, I'd get eaten by the bear. But it's not fiction, which means I don't even get to see the bear. In my real life, I do what I did ten years ago: I leave early. But this time it's because I get a phone call from a guy called Caleb whom I've saved in my phone as *Dad in Crisis in Massachusetts*.

"Has he escaped?" I asked when I answered the phone earlier this morning.

"Oh," he said. "Uh, well, that's not how we here would refer to it technically, but—"

"Wait. Is my dad missing? Has something happened?"

"Your father would like to go home."

"So let him go."

"Unfortunately, it's not that simple . . ."

I knock on the studio of my friend with the wife and the crush, which is against the rules. She says, "I was just talking to you."

I say, "God, I'm going to miss you."

She laughs like I'm the funniest person on the planet. She tells me about the conversation we were having in which we broke down the pros and cons of the other residents. She says, "Then we had an argument over Deborah Eisenberg. That was a hoot."

I listen, thrilled to have made such an impression in so short a time. I tell her I'm leaving, that my dad is in crisis in Massachusetts, and he needs a ride home. "He bought himself a first-class ticket to get there and he voluntarily committed himself, but they won't let him leave without a guardian."

She says, "You can't make this shit up."

I say, "You can't. That's the truth. You really can't."

She says, "Who will I talk to when you're gone?"

I say, "Me, I hope. Also, the Belgian, and the German, and the Pulitzer guy."

She says, "Pulitzer has a car. I'm going to wait until I've gotten some good work done and then ask him for a ride to a pond. I'll invoke one of the non-rules: Be generous with your car."

Packing up, I find a slip of paper in the top drawer of my bureau. It says, *From a séance / automatic writing / visitation from a spirit 31 October / present:* And then there is a list of names. There's also a giant swirl of pencil circles on the back, along with this appeal:

troubled,

beautiful

spirit,

rest.

When I was little, my sister gave me a diary with a lock. I hoped that, if I left it lying around locked but with the key in sight, she'd open it and read. I covered the first page of the diary with Wite-Out; then in purple ink I wrote, in wavy letters, *Help! I've just seen a ghost!* It was my only entry.

The only entry in my baby book is this: *Jet-black hair. Big cheeks. Not the world's prettiest baby.*

Second on the list of those at the Halloween séance is the name of my dear friend, the one who's now married to my ex. The sheet is dated two years after our divorce. I use the residency's artist search engine to find her. The internet's slow today; there's been another storm. As I wait, I'm wondering which photo she'll have used. Something recent? Something from the past? Will her hair be short? Will she be utterly stunning? Was I the troubled spirit who visited on Halloween, having been unceremoniously knifed to death by her husband's homeless man?

When the page finally loads, I'm greeted by an unsmiling picture of a purple-haired playwright from Los Angeles. It's not my dear friend. It's someone else's.

Just to mess with myself, I add the slip of paper to my hoard of loose notes and letters that I've returned to manila envelopes. I get a little tingle of glee knowing that one day, ten or twenty years from now, I'll find this note, read it, flip it over, see the circles, look for clues, and have no idea what it once meant to me—a lot or a little, or if I was there, at this Halloween séance, and simply never got around to recording my name. Just imagining my future irritation and confusion is pure delight.

The last thing I do before I get into the shuttle that will drive me to the rental car company is send myself a text, nudging me when I'm finally home to write a little note to the Belgian, who I now understand is so much more than the thing I'd flattened her into at our first meal together. I put my phone away. A second later, it buzzes. I take it back out, annoyed. There's my name on the screen, there's my text, and there in my heart is a lozenge of momentary surprise.

To myself I think, *There she is again, nagging at me, always prompting: remember remember remember.*

Five

GOAT SHOW

I rent a Sprinter van and drive to Massachusetts. My father is wait-ing for me outside. He's sitting in a leather armchair, one he's likely pulled himself from the inside of the facility to the porch. His legs are stretched out in front of him. His head is leaned back, his eyes closed, his face fully lit up by a ray of sunshine. His cowboy hat is resting on his stomach. When he hears the gravel crunching beneath my tires, he opens his eyes, makes a visor of his hand, squints, smiles, then puts on his hat, grabs his bags, and lumbers down the stairs toward me.

When he gets to me, he seizes my arms. I let him. He shakes my entire body, a little roughly, but I don't stop him. "I knew it would be you," he says, as though I'm here because of some oracle and not because he filled me in as his emergency contact.

"Do we need to check you out?" I ask.

"I'm checked out."

"Do we need to let anyone know?"

"Everyone knows."

"Are you okay?"

While we talk, I wrestle his copious luggage—gorgeous stuff, tweed with leather piping, pieces from a collection he once shared with my mother, and the brand-new carry-on—into the back of the van.

"They're frauds," he says. "Charlatans. Half the people in there are hooked on drugs. My feet were cold. I hate cold feet. I didn't sleep the entire time I was here."

"It's a rehab center."

He waves away my comment.

As I'm pulling on my seat belt, I say, as lightly as I can, "Maybe you're an addict?"

"Goddamn it," he says. "Goddamn it. I do drugs with a doctor. These people up here are criminals."

"I'm sorry. Okay. Buckle up."

"I just wanted someone to talk to," he says.

"I know."

"And no one would talk to me."

"The woman who rented me this van told me she kept her dead cat in the deep freeze all winter just so she could bury it when the ground was soft in the spring."

"That's the sort of thing your mother would do."

"I was thinking the same thing."

As I'm waiting to turn onto the two-lane blacktop that will ultimately take us to the expressway that will ultimately take us to Logan International, my dad says, "What are the chances we stop somewhere on the harbor for some oysters and a bottle of champagne? I'm craving oysters."

I check my watch, though I have zero intention of letting either of us out of this car before we get to the rental return. "Too tight, I'm afraid. How about next time?"

He makes this noise I've been hearing my whole life. It's not a laugh, not a scoff. It's a low-pitch wheeze of understanding, disappointment, and bitterness, lined with the faintest rasp of amusement. He says, "Next time. I like that. Next time I escape from the funny farm in Massachusetts, and you happen to be at writing camp in New Hampshire, you'll take me for oysters and champagne. It's a date, then."

"It's a date."

*   *   *

It's the first time we've been on a plane together since I was a little girl and he was the one piloting it. My therapist once asked me about my fear of flying. I told her about my father, who, after his divorce from my mother, took up the saxophone, motorcycles, twenty-year-olds, and then, finally, settled on getting his pilot's license. I used to follow him around his first single-engine with a clipboard and the preflight checklist as he performed the best-practices visual inspection. I'd write what he'd tell me, which didn't always correspond to what I'd seen. He didn't always confirm the fuel quantity, for instance, and when he did, he didn't always tell me the right amount. He often skipped draining the wings' fuel sump or making sure the engine air inlets were clear. He could be especially lazy with the fuel cap and the luggage door. One time, midflight, my sister swiveled around in the copilot seat to tell me to turn down my air vent only to discover that the luggage door, immediately behind my seat, was wide open. Our altitude was somewhere between five and ten thousand feet. My father told me to crawl back into the luggage compartment. He wanted me to reach out and grab the door and pull it shut from the inside. Instead, I doubled over, shut my eyes, grabbed my shins, and tried to weigh myself down, to become a piece of the airplane itself. After that, he stopped letting me help with the checklist.

"Your father took shortcuts," my therapist said.

"He didn't follow the rules."

"You didn't feel safe."

"I didn't trust everyone not to be as careless as he was."

But right now, where there'd once been terror, I feel calm, a little bit safer, knowing there's a pilot sitting next to me. Knowing that, if something were to happen, I'm at least sitting next to someone who knows more than I do about what to do next. For the first time in my life, I understand what my mother meant. Also for the first time in my life, and without any medication, I don't spend the entire flight gripping the armrests in extreme concentration, as though my willpower alone is keeping the plane aloft.

At cruising altitude, my father leans against the window and dozes. I take his hat, which he'd not wanted to place in an overhead bin, and set it in an empty seat across the aisle. About a half hour in, we hit a rough bit of turbulence. He wakes, sits up, rubs his eyes.

"Here," I say. I hand him a plastic cup with vodka, a few cubes, a splash of cranberry, and another splash of soda. Then I hold out my own little plastic cup, and we cheers. "It's not champagne, but . . ."

We face forward, staring at the seat backs in front of us, and we drink our perfectly imperfect drinks in silence. For the life of me, I can't, at this minute, imagine being any other place but here.

When we land, I order us a cab. We go to his apartment. I help with the bags. It's the first time I've been inside. In the entryway, there are a dozen plants of varying sizes and shapes. There's a painted lady and a monstera, a jade plant and a spider plant. They're all thriving. He notices me noticing, and he says, "I wanted there to be life around me. I can get lonely, you know. I like to see something pretty on my way in and on my way out. My landlady's kind to me. I got her to water while I was away."

I nod and swear to myself I will not show him the disrespect of pity. I will not cry. I will not cry.

We carry the bags up the narrow stairs, and I'm relieved to see that the apartment is quite large, quite nice; the light across the floors is bright and inviting. Even Jane would be envious.

"Give me a minute before you leave, will you?" He goes into the kitchen, and I wait at the top of the stairs, where a large gilt mirror is hanging. It's a mirror I know from my childhood, a mirror that once hung in the entryway of the horse farm where we all once lived—my brother, my sister, my mother, my father, and me—as a family of five. But the mirror now is changed. It's covered in sticky notes—yellow ones, pink ones, green ones, big ones, small ones. All of them are in my father's distinctive scrawl. I take a step closer to the mirror, lean in, and my heart—my heart erupts in tiny detonations, little cherry bombs of gravel and silver fulminate popping against my chest. The notes are aphorisms of encouragement—

what you are enduring is exactly what you need and what is supposed
*   to happen*
you have a lot to live for
buy a magnolia
you have a choice OPTIMIST
this moment is not so bad
should I write a book
Robert Frost 12 poems
Spondee! bounce house / pill box / goat show
life may surprise you
breathe
get a dog, don't tell anyone
being alive means being present

"It's stupid," my father says, appearing in the mirror over my shoulder, "but some days it helps me."

"If it helps you, then it's not stupid."

He hands me a piece of paper folded in half. I start to open it; he says, "Later, kid. Later."

"It's not a suicide note, is it?" I'm aiming for dark humor, but even I can hear the wobble in my voice.

"Give me a break. What does the mirror say? I've got a lot to live for."

"What's a goat show?" I ask.

"Look around, Small Fry."

"Are you getting a dog?"

"Would I tell you if I were?"

Before I go, I ask him if he's got any clean sheets, and together we strip the old ones and make up his bed. I do hospital edges on the corners and fluff the pillows.

"Fit for a goddamn king," he says, when he sees the finished product. "But you should get out of here now. You've got people waiting on you."

"It's okay," I say. "The eleven-year-old's at her mom's tonight, and I've got a whole life's worth of time to spend with Bruce."

"Listen, Sticks, I need to get horizontal. I'm telling you I'm tired. I'm an old guy, yeah?"

"Oh, right." I laugh. When was the last time my father was the one trying to get rid of me? "Maybe a drink this week?" I ask. "When you're rested."

"A porch drink. Sure."

"Or out in the world. We could take a walk. Whatever you want."

"I'll have my people reach out."

"I'm going to order you some food for later," I say.

"Sure," he says. He's pulling back the comforter, kicking his shoes off, lowering himself slowly onto the bed. "I'm easy. Order me anything. But can you make it Thai? Something noodle-y, no peanuts, extra sauce?"

On my way out, I steal one more glance at the mirror. On a white piece of scrap paper he's taped toward the top is a giant green smiley face. Above it, he's written: *You will make it thru this.* Beneath it: *Lots of folks need you!*

Back outside, I'm surprised to see the cab driver still here, idling on the side street. I apologize, pay him, and then, instead of letting him drop me at my house, I grab my roller bag and backpack from the trunk and walk the half mile home. This is something I can do—walk home, take my time, pay attention to the birds and the wind, to the forsythia and hydrangea and crepe myrtles—because my father lives here now, just a short distance away from me.

When I get home, I drop my bags in the front hallway and hold on to Bruce for a very long time. He asks if I want to do laundry, settle in, get organized. I tell him I'm taking a break from organization for a while. "The bags'll be fine where they are. I'll unpack in a couple days." I can't guess what he's thinking as he watches me walk past the luggage up the stairs to our bedroom. I'm trying hard *not* to guess what he's thinking.

He stands behind me where I've stopped at the foot of our bed.

"I'm sorry," he says. "I really did try to make the bed the way you like it." The pillows are misaligned, the comforter is folded back into a trapezoid, the sheets have the wrinkles of a Shar-Pei. "It's okay," he says, "you're not going to hurt my feelings when you remake it."

I shake my head. "It's perfect," I say. "Can we go to bed now?"

We don't have sex. We will soon, as soon as tomorrow morning before the sun comes up, but for now, I want only to be in bed, horizontal between cold sheets.

While Bruce is brushing his teeth, I text my mother: *I admire that you're putting yourself out there, that you're looking for connections. That you believe in the possibility of love.* I text my father: *I'm proud of you. I appreciate that you haven't given up on life. That you go go go.* I text my sister, who is with my mother: *Come home already.* I text Jane: *Women dogs donkeys gold.* I do not text my ex: *Take a big step to the right and smile.*

If this were a tragedy, it would end like this: Bruce in stocking feet going down the stairs on a night when I'm out with my sister and mother. He's alone, with a fractured neck, three broken ribs, one fully collapsed lung and another that's collapsing slowly as I'm drinking martinis at a bistro known for its tofu burgers.

If this were a comedy, it would go like this: I take Bruce for a sham errand at the courthouse, where I propose, and he accepts. It's just the two of us, which is how I want it. I've got the paperwork all filled out. For our vows, we make one promise each as requested by the other: I promise to keep only the least important secrets; he promises never to tell anyone we're married.

If this were a tragicomedy, it would end with Bruce accidentally going down the stairs while I'm home, during a game of Dead Body that's gone horribly awry. There's a storm outside, a big one, that ultimately takes down hundreds of trees across town.

A second before he slips on the stairs, there's a crash of lightning, a crack of thunder, and the singular sound of a branch breaking free from one of the tulip poplars out front. The power goes out; Bruce loses his footing; he topples down, pulling me with him. The eleven-year-old is at her mother's, which means Bruce and I are alone; there's no one to call for help, and we die, tangled in each other's broken limbs—his lungs collapsed, my neck snapped.

At the funerals (joint, which I would hate and Bruce would love), my mother speaks first, followed by my father. The publicity of their mutual sadness softens them toward each other. Afterward, they hold hands. When it's time to go home, my mother offers my father a ride. He accepts, but instead of driving to his house she accidentally drives to hers. They're married before the month is out, dividing their time between their two houses just like their children did nearly four decades earlier.

A week after the funerals, Theo is delivering the mail when Bruce's sister, who's driven down from Illinois to collect a few dusty photo albums, intercepts him on our front porch and tells him of our untimely demises. He starts to leave but then—"It was just a wild hare," he'll say, grinning, at their tenth wedding anniversary. "I'll never be able to artic-ulate what got into me that day"—he turns back and asks, "Any chance you're a barbecue kind of lady?"

On another afternoon, not long after, my father is at his place alone. He's in the attic looking for old photographs—all the ones he swore he'd thrown away after their divorce, but hadn't, because he never stopped loving my mother—when he takes a bad step and misses the rafter. He catches himself halfway down. His legs go through the ceiling. He's got a rafter under each armpit, the splinters are digging in, his shirt is torn and bloody, his lower half dangles below. He bel-lows for help, but he's winded from the suddenness of the fall and the exertion of dangling, and he hangs there like that for several hours before finally—crying from the pain and knowledge he's about to do so—slipping through the ceiling, like a swimmer at sea giving up on the surface.

His fall is broken by the washing machine, atop which are multiple loads of dirty laundry, the one thing about which my mother has continued to give him a hard time. He goes down softly with his ass on the top of the machine, then onto his knees as his body hits the floor, then finally onto his side, where he passes out for another several hours before waking up dazed but with enough sense to crawl to his phone in the kitchen and call my mother, who arrives at about the same time as the ambulance.

My mother sits with him for three days, refusing to leave the hospital after he drifts, on day two, into a coma. She continues to hold his hand even after the monitor makes its hideous monotone, even after my brother and sister come to her side, put their hands on her shoulders. She stays like this, her hand in his, her cheek against his chest, until the nurse, who's been so kind, bringing her water, bringing him Vaseline and ice, lifts my mother up, moves her away, says, "Honey."

As only a few months have passed since the last ones, the family, shrunken as it is, decides that they've had enough funerals for the year, and they charter a Cessna to Abaco, where my father always threatened he'd walk one day into the woods with a shotgun if he got too old and life ceased to be worth living. They bring my father's ashes and mine, and those of my last dog, Elmer, because my will dictated that I be cremated with his cremains, but not Bruce's. His daughter, now twelve, has asked to keep them, and my family, not complete monsters, has acquiesced to her request.

As it turns out, the Cessna's right fuel pump is faulty and stops working just before they see land. The pilot attempts to glide the plane into a water landing like that guy on the Hudson, but the nose doesn't cooperate, and, the right propeller having given out, the left one gives, too—not sixty seconds after—and the plane disintegrates on impact with the ocean, killing everyone aboard.

My sister, my brother, my mother, the pilot, and the ashes of two humans and one canine explode, dissipate in the tide, sink, spread, become flotsam on the water.

A marlin, of all things, not known for their taste for human flesh, eats my mother's arm, but a deep-sea fisherman catches the marlin, and Rolex features my mother's watch—which she was wearing in the Cessna, it having been one of the first gifts my father ever gave her, and which was still ticking when the fisherman gutted the marlin—in an ad campaign sanctioned by Bruce's daughter, who splits the proceeds with my sister's boys but keeps the watch for herself because she has the faintest—the very *faintest*—recollection of her one-time almost-stepmother saying something about the Rolex being the only thing she ever coveted in her own life.

The eleven-year-old, now nineteen, loses the Rolex sophomore year of college—well, she's been mugged and the watch is the only thing the woman takes (because the mugger is a woman)—which makes the now-nineteen-year-old sad for approximately thirty minutes before she remembers she's got an exam to study for, and anyway, her father's ashes, which she still has, are the stuff that truly matter.

The mugger, it happens, is a fortysomething woman who once, nearly a decade earlier, lost a tabby cat—a cat she loved like I loved Elmer. She's got a tattoo of the cat—not its name but a colorized photograph of the actual cat, the photograph in fact that she'd used for the missing signs—stamped across her heart and in cursive just below: *Last Seen on Sycamore.*

The woman sells the watch within the hour—for $5,000, which is a startlingly gross underestimation, but it is cash on demand after all—and she uses $3,000 to cover room and board and food for the next four months and the rest to buy a new computer because her old one has lost several of its letters and doesn't hold a charge and because—in her spare time, not waiting tables or mugging coeds—she's been working on this idea for a novel. She thinks it might be good, this woman who once lost a cat on Sycamore. It's a book about privilege, American dreams, narcissism and regret, familial obligation, connections and disconnections, butterfly wings, intelligence property, bounce houses, animal shelters, appropriation, adverse possessions, and shared and lost memories . . . A sweeping book, really, spanning generations, that, at its heart—as reviewers will say when they review it, which they will, because it's an instant *New York Times* bestseller—at its heart is a book about the kindness of strangers . . .

Of course, *this* book is none of those things: neither a comedy nor a tragedy but something much worse: real life, in which the days crawl and the years fly. My ex's debut is released. It's a huge success, everything either of us has ever dreamed of. He's on morning shows, on the airwaves, at festivals across the country. There are a few negative reviews—there must be—along the lines of "A white guy cheats on his wife and then writes a book about it and we're supposed to care? Read the winds, man . . ." But mostly, readers don't mind that he's a white guy, because the book is quite good. I give up nonfiction because, at the end of the day, I'm preternaturally too much of a liar, not suited to the restraints of truth-telling or accuracy and honest observation. I tell people, when they ask, that I'm working on a thriller or maybe it's a cookbook. I can't be certain.

Mateo quits taking my classes, declaring his love, instead, for Shakespeare. He follows Jane around and, for a semester or two when I see him, I'm like an early morning weather report: mostly relieved, but with a chance of scattered wistfulness and bouts of anodyne jealousy.

The Irishman stops texting, and it doesn't occur to me to remember what the final text said because it doesn't occur to me that it's final until weeks, then months, have passed. I never see him again, which isn't the same as never thinking about him again. Some things remain a mystery because that's how it goes in real life. Time passes. Past uncertainties lose their significance. Lurking concerns become more easily swept into the dark, untended corners of a remote hallway in the back of the brain.

One afternoon toward the end of summer, I see Crazy Tabby Mommy taking down the missing sign at the far end of Sycamore. I approach, reintroduce myself, ask her real name.

"Lucy," she says. "My name's Lucy."

I tell her I can help with sign removal if she wants, I've got the afternoon. She says, "Sure, yeah, why not?"

I tell her that once, a million years ago, when I was a little girl, my family had a dog that went missing and we searched for years and years, until one day my mother simply decided he'd gone through the ice off the end of our dock and drowned in the frosty water. It was a hard end she gave him, but a believable one, and it let us say goodbye and start learning to love the new puppy we'd recently allowed ourselves to adopt.

Lucy says, "Okay, but I found my cat, just like I told you. He's dead. But these signs are real hard on my daughter."

We walk all over town taking down signs—there are *hundreds*—and maybe we make a connection and maybe we don't. But for a little while, I am admirably competent, even useful.

I tell Bruce, in real life, though he's long stopped asking, that if he promises never to tell anyone, not even his daughter, I'll marry him. He can pick the day and time; he can give me warning or let it be a surprise—as long as it's just the two of us and a court employee, I'll marry him whenever. He nods when I say this, squints his eyes like he's trying to read me, then asks if I want to watch *Seinfeld* or read on the front porch before bed.

It's chilly out; the leaves are fluttering; I can hear my nephews' high-pitched giggling all the way from their backyard; I opt for the porch.

A few months later, the eleven-year-old turns twelve. As a surprise, I make a beef *Twelvington*, which I haven't done since she turned ten (beef *Tennington*), and probably won't do again before I die.

After dinner—after Bruce has done the dishes and I've put away the food and the now-twelve-year-old has swept the floor—just as we're about to go upstairs, get ready for bed, brush our teeth, etcetera, I call an impromptu meeting, which is still not a thing in our family.

I can see they're both worried, each for their own private reasons: Am I sick? Am I leaving? Am I hoping for a late-night group walk in the sleet and snow to peer into the brightly lit windows of our neighbors?

I tell them, instead, that I'm not here; that, in fact, I haven't been here for a very long time, because I'm dead, lying alone on a sidewalk somewhere, years ago having been murdered by my ex-husband.

"I'm dead and gone," I say to them.

Bruce turns to his daughter, to whom he is duty bound for life, and the eleven-year-old, now twelve, looks up at me with her watery brown eyes and says, "You were *married*?"

If I were me, this is when I'd admit that I am forty-five, exactly half the number of years my mother's mother endured, which, in fiction, would be cosmically meaningful—half a life; a half-life . . . This is when I'd realize that life is short, and this is it: this is my life, for the rest of my life.

Instead, living on this page and in the present, without artifice, hiding behind no guise of fiction—*gauze of fiction*, I would probably say to Jane—right this second, I am thinking about my new friend with the wife and the crush and the cedar oil and the porcupine. I'm wondering how she's doing, if she's still in New Hampshire, if she's left early or gotten an extension, or if she's been eaten by the bear, which is my rightful ending, not hers. I wonder what sort of conversations I am having with her in her head at this exact moment, what I am saying, and if I am right to be saying it; I hope I'm not giving her bad advice; I hope I'm being pithy and charming and a little bit coy (*buy a magnolia, write a book, this moment is not so bad*). Perhaps I am even making her laugh (*get a dog, don't tell anyone*), and it hits me—*splash!*—in the sudden way, the way thoughts occur in real life but shouldn't in fiction. And yet, it *is* sudden; it's sit-up-in-bed, stop-in-your-tracks, frog-in-a-flashlight sudden: to have become a character in someone else's life: it's a gift, really: *Such a gift.*

ACKNOWLEDGMENTS

There are some friends, family, and colleagues who've supported this book specifically or my entire writing career or something strange and wonderful in between. They are Ben Warner, Stephen Eichinger, Eleanor Ringel Cater, Ann Beattie, Adam Ross, Ada Limón, Michael Trask, Stephen Trask, Fred Bengtsson, Maggie Smith, Maria Massie, Caroline Zancan, Leela Gebo, and Nicole Dewey.

I also want thank Kate Tighe-Pigott for writing a wild and unforgettable story in which mermaids are edible delicacies, best enjoyed hot off the spit; Janet Burroway for encouraging me several years ago to continue tackling many of the themes in this book; Amy Sodha Harsch for giving me a place to read and write at a moment when I needed it most; Emily Shortslef for, among other unalloyed absurdities, workshopping a single sentence via text exchange for more than an hour; and Lucy Corin for being the inimitable Lucy Corin and for providing me with a friendship that eventually led to an ending.

My family knows I am a difficult person—stubborn, overly sensitive, demanding, critical—and yet they show me kindness and generosity daily. They've allowed me to coopt and distort their lives for my art, and for that I will never be able to thank them or apologize enough. A few made this book in particular a possibility. They are Greta Wright,

Noah Pittard, Marlo Clymer, and Jeff Clymer. If Jeff hadn't laughed when I read aloud early passages and if Marlo didn't hourly astonish me with her wit and wonder, this book wouldn't exist; if Greta and Noah hadn't long ago given me carte blanche—not to mention their unrivalled support—who knows what might have happened?

My parents—separately and in vastly different ways—taught me how to tell a good story. My father, Jack Pittard, lives such a full and maniacal life that I've spent a lot of this career trying to capture that life, only to deliberately corrupt it on the page. The title belongs to him. My mother, Stacy Schultz, taught me to write; to care about punctuation and precise meaning and the bon mot. She also taught me to read, really *read*. I owe so much to my mother, not least my inclination to make sense of the world through writing.

ABOUT THE AUTHOR

Hannah Pittard is the author of the novels *Visible Empire*, *Listen to Me*, and *The Fates Will Find Their Way*. She is a winner of the Amanda Davis Highwire Fiction Award, a MacDowell fellow, and the Guy M. Davenport Professor in English at the University of Kentucky. She lives with her boyfriend and stepdaughter in Lexington. Much of her family lives nearby.